SINFUL

WITHDRAWN
FROM
STOCK

First published in 2019

ISBN the3percenters Edition 9781916425316

Cover design by Tom Taheny Graphics, Galway

SINFUL

New Irish Crime Stories

the3percenters

Edited by Ferdia Mac Anna

About the Authors

the3percenters is an authors' collective and publishing partnership formed to promote emerging writers. The group were originally associated with the annual Dalkey Creates Writing Festival.

About the Editor

Ferdia Mac Anna is a novelist, film director, screenwriter and lecturer. He has written three novels, *The Last of the High Kings* (made into a Hollywood movie starring Jared Leto, Gabriel Byrne and Christina Ricci), *The Ship Inspector* and *Cartoon City*. His films include *All About Eva* (2016), and *Danny Boy* (2019).

CONTENTS

Sessions With Elena

Caroline Bale

'You have to put your pride aside, Maeve. Today has to be Elena's last session.'

I took the last sip of the flat white I had queued to buy in Insomnia, feeling calmed by the caffeine hitting my bloodstream. It was a ritual I had observed for the last ten years. I liked to have a cup of good coffee in my hand as I discussed my clients at my monthly meeting with my supervisor, Derek.

'I know, I know,' I said, aware of the irritation in my voice. I was not used to finding myself in this position, floundering in my work with a client. My new book—*Your Cheating Heart*, a self-help book on how to survive an unfaithful partner—had topped the non-fiction charts in Ireland. My practice was busier than ever with all the publicity the book had generated. It didn't sit well, giving up on a client in trouble, but this afternoon I was going to do just that.

'Believe me, I know I can't go on with her, and, yes, I admit there's a bit of pride there, not wanting to admit defeat but, to be honest, given all that's happened with her, I think I'm actually scared of what she might do.'

Derek took off his glasses and looked intently at me.

'Do to you or to herself?'

I paused for just a moment.

'To me ...' I answered, and then added, '... and to herself. Both.' The last bit sounded like an afterthought, and it was. The truth was I was scared of Elena, full stop.

I had given her plenty of notice. Three months in which to wean herself off her dependence on me. However, the feeling deep in the pit of my stomach told

1

me it was not enough. Forever would not be enough for Elena, a stunningly attractive thirty-year-old drama teacher from California who had been coming to my office in Booterstown at least once a week for the last four years.

'That's why you have to end with her today. We've discussed this over and over. At the moment, all of her transference, all of her fears, her rage at the world, is focused on you. She needs the help of a multi-disciplinary team so the intensity can be distributed. It's too much for one person.'

I sighed and looked out the window of Derek's cramped office which looked out onto Blackrock DART station and the sea beyond. Waves were crashing over the wall onto the promenade. The sky was an ominous grey. It looked like it was going to lash anytime soon. After my discussion with Derek, I was heading straight back to my office for my last session with Elena Martinez.

'The reality is she won't go without a fight. Every relationship she has ever had has ended with her pursuing the person who left her for revenge. Remember the voicemails she sent to the Swedish guy's wife? Her rage is terrifying.'

Derek paused and looked at me thoughtfully.

'You know how this works, Maeve. She is terrified of abandonment, and now she has you feeling terrified to leave her. It's classic projective identification. Her life is one endless crisis, and she has manipulated you into buying into the drama.'

I knew he was right. I nodded as he continued.

'It has gone beyond what any therapist could cope with. You didn't know the depth of her illness when you started seeing her, but there can be no doubt now she needs more help than you can give her.'

I remembered the point I had realised that was true. It was several months before, when Elena had shown up at my home at midnight, banging on the door until my husband, Tom, answered. She drove an old VW camper van which she had driven right up to the front door knocking over and smashing a bay tree in a terracotta pot. Like most people with her form of personality disorder, Elena lurched from one relationship crisis to the next. She had a longstanding habit of cutting herself—a way of easing the unbearable rage she felt inside at the remotest possibility of abandonment—and that night her arms were covered with knife marks. She was hysterical. Her latest lover had dumped her, and she was demanding that I see her despite the late hour. That was the point when I realised I had to refer Elena on to a psychiatric team, and three months later the last session had finally come.

'Do you actually think she poses any real risk to you?'

A few months ago, if Derek had asked me the same question, I would have shrugged and said, 'Of course not.' But with the events of the last few weeks, I was not so sure. On several occasions recently I had spotted Elena on the street near my home in Monkstown, where I lived in a terraced period house overlooking the sea with my husband Tom and thirteen-year-old twins, Alex and Hannah. Twice I had seen her orange camper van parked near the twins' school in Booterstown.

'Maeve?'

Derek's voice jolted me back to the present moment. I met his gaze, and he smiled and pointed to the clock on the wall—ten to five. The hour had gone so fast. Derek's next supervisee was due in a few minutes. I foraged in my bag, found my purse and handed Derek the payment for the session. He stood up and walked me to the door, pausing before opening it.

'She is meeting the psychiatrist tomorrow, so just stick to the plan. Don't give in to whatever emergency she throws at you today, and there will be one. Just stay firm. Tell her that Dr Nolan and the team will be there for her.

Then say goodbye.'

I inhaled a long, reviving breath. Derek was right. I valued his counsel so much. I consoled myself by thinking that in only an hour and a half I would be driving back home to my family and Elena would no longer be my responsibility.

Back in my office, 5.15 p.m. came and went with no sign of Elena. At 5.30 p.m. I phoned her, but the call went to voicemail. At 5.50 p.m. I was just leaving a text saying how unfortunate it was that we would not be having a last session when Elena burst into the room without knocking and hung her coat as usual on the coat hook. As was her habit, she moved the brown chair to the window, and I moved mine to face her. This moving of the chairs had been agreed upon several years before. It made Elena feel cared for to be allowed this concession. She looked like she had been crying. Her face was covered in angry blotches and her eyes were red. She sat down heavily; her breath was coming in short bursts. I looked at the clock. There was only twenty minutes of the session remaining.

'I was a fool to trust him. He's finished with me. James. An hour ago, by text.'

She reached over and grabbed a tissue from the box on the windowsill and wiped at the tears which were streaming down her face. She had only started seeing James six weeks before, but, as usual, it has been an intense and stormy six weeks.

'In his text he said we both knew this day would come.'

I tried to look sympathetic, but I was aware there wasn't time to explore the ins and outs of this latest heartbreak.

She stared intently at me, her expression one of disbelief tinged with anger.

'That's what the text said. "*We both knew this day would come.*" What does that mean? That it was obvious he

4

was going to end it because he is so much better than me? That I'm some sort of ... *loser?*'

Elena flinched visibly. The word 'loser' had huge significance for her, as I was well aware. It was a word that had come up many times in her therapy over the years—a word her father had used consistently about her to put her in her place. In fact, the word had such significance for Elena that she couldn't bear to utter it and had deleted the word from her vocabulary. Her using it today was hugely significant, but I couldn't focus on that now. I needed to end with her today, as agreed. She was expecting a reaction from me, but I was not going to get pulled down that particular rabbit hole. I tried to focus on keeping calm.

'Did you hear what I said?' Elena shouted. 'It's like he thinks I am a *loser.*'

Her voice was so loud, I wondered if the therapists and clients on either side of me could hear her today. There had been complaints before.

'Remember to keep the volume down a bit, Elena,' I said in a calm voice. I was feeling anything but calm.

'I can't help it, I'm so upset. Tell me, please. Is that what you think he meant?'

I took a few deep breaths and focused on steadying my breathing. I would not allow myself to be sucked into this latest piece of theatrics. I had to stick to what had been agreed.

'I can see how upsetting this is for you, and I'm aware too that this is our last session, so that it's really hard that we only have fifteen minutes left to go.'

Elena's jaw tightened visibly, and her eyes met mine. For just a millisecond, before she looked away, there was pure hatred behind those narrowed eyes. I wondered had she made up the whole James breakup story to derail our ending? With Elena Martinez, anything was possible. The room went very quiet, and it was several moments before she looked up again. When she did, the fury was gone, replaced with a plaintive expression. She sounded like a little girl now.

'Why me, Maeve? Why does everyone leave me? I thought he loved me; I really believed this time it was going to be different.'

She was sobbing quietly. The ticking of the clock could be heard against the backdrop of an ambulance siren in the distance. I felt curiously unmoved. Watching Elena was like watching a great actor on the stage. The emotion felt intense but not quite real.

I sighed. How many times had I heard Elena say 'I just know this time it's going to be different'? It never was. James, twenty years her senior, was a solicitor, married with two teenage children. He had been drawn in by Elena's incredible sexual magnetism. Even with eyes red from crying Elena was stunning. Born in Los Angeles to Nicaraguan parents, she was a young Bianca Jagger with flashing black lashes, light brown skin and dark tumbling hair. I thought of her as a beautiful spider sitting at the centre of a web, waiting for an unwitting fly to land and be trapped in the lies and deceit she spun.

'You've been here before, Elena. I know it's very painful for you.'

I watched as the colour crept up from Elena's chest into her throat and finally up to her face. Her breathing was sharp and shallow now, her skin was flushing red.

And ... Three. Two. One. Here comes the rage, I thought.

'Painful? This is beyond painful; it is excruciating!'

She was shouting again.

'I despise him, and I won't let him get away with treating me like this. Does he think I'm some piece of garbage he can throw away?'—Elena snapped her fingers—'just like that?'

Poor James! I thought. He probably had no idea

about the trouble coming his way. Elena's rage, once unleashed, was incredibly destructive. I had seen it many times over the last four years. Each relationship played itself out the same way. She met some guy in a bar or in the gym. In James's case, she had met him in a doctor's waiting room. In those first days, even weeks, Elena went through her 'chameleon' phase where she became everything the guy had ever wanted in a girlfriend. If his wife or previous girlfriend had been too clingy, Elena would insist that he take Friday night with his friends. She would be out with her (fictitious) pals. If, on the other hand, the guy's previous partner annoyed him by seeing too much of her friends, then Elena only wanted to spend all her time with him. James was a Friday-night-with-the-wife-and-kids kind of guy. This was apparently not his first, or even his second affair.

Her sexual preferences morphed according to her new guy's taste. If he was into straight, vanilla sex, then so was she. If he was into experimentation, like James, then she was a most enthusiastic participant despite the fact that sex brought her almost no pleasure. Sex for Elena was much more to do with power than enjoyment.

After the initial 'chameleon' period, Elena moved into the 'control' phase, where she slowly insinuated herself into every aspect of her new man's life. This played out over weeks or months. She became best friends with his sister, mother, friends—whomever she could latch onto. She found out everything about his life, his past relationships and partners, who he was working with.

Eventually, the sexual excitement of being with Elena would wane under the pressure of the increasing demands for attention. James, like those who came before him, had become painfully aware of the web Elena was spinning around him. He had ended the relationship earlier than most, and good for him. However, unbeknownst to him, he was now entering the 'seek and destroy' phase. The one thing Elena could not bear was to be ignored and, of course, that was exactly what James would now do. If her past relationships were anything to go by, then within a few hours of him not responding to her, the 'Elena volcano' would erupt and emails detailing James's sexual exploits and accompanying photos would arrive in his wife's inbox. There would be threats to post the photos on Facebook.

I looked at the clock. There was only ten minutes left in the session. I had to wrap up. I had to bring the sessions with Elena to an end.

'I'm wondering if you might feel the same way about me, Elena?' I asked, determined to bring the attention back to the pre-agreed ending. 'In a sense, I am finishing with you, handing you over to Dr Nolan and her team. Is some of the anger you are feeling to do with feeling let down by me?'

Her narrowed eyes flashed once again, and then, seconds later, Elena was out of her seat. She pulled the money for the session out of her purse and waved it in my face before tossing it on the table.

'What was it you told Ryan on the *Late Late Show*? "Relationships shouldn't just be thrown aside when things get tough?"'

The irony wasn't lost on me. I had talked for fifteen minutes, lamenting on how people didn't stick with problems in their relationships long enough to work through them. Wasn't that just what I was doing now with the relationship I had with Elena—throwing her aside now things had become too difficult?

'There's a word for people like you,' she said. 'You're a *hypocrite*.'

My heart was beating fast now. I had to stand my ground.

'Elena, I'm really sorry about James, but we have to end today, as we agreed.'

Elena tugged on her coat and slung her bag over

her shoulder before striding towards the door. She turned and looked at her watch.

'I've paid you for an hour; you owe me forty-five minutes.'

I followed Elena out into the waiting room to protest. There were five or six clients waiting for other therapists in the common area who looked up at the commotion.

'Elena, stop. I can't reschedule,' I said, realising before finishing my sentence that I shouldn't be having this conversation in front of clients. 'You arrived late.'

Elena turned around and mouthed: 'I'll text you tomorrow'.

The door slammed shut, and she was gone.

* * *

Two hours later I was sitting at a bar off Grafton Street with my oldest friend, Amanda. Our twenty-year school reunion was on in the Shelbourne Hotel. It was the last place I wanted to be, especially after the session with Elena. Amanda had strong-armed me into going with her—left to my own devices I would quite happily have stayed away. Amanda's divorce had recently come through, and, as her oldest friend, I felt I owed it to her to make the effort. Besides, with the way things had been going lately with Tom, my husband of fifteen years, I was happy to have a night away from him. Tom and I had spent a year in therapy working on our relationship, and it felt like we were right back to square one. Since being made redundant three months ago, his controlling tendencies and angry moods had re-emerged. I had arrived back from work to find the house a mess and no food in the fridge, so I had spent the time I needed to get ready shopping and throwing a meal together for the kids.

'I'd swear he did it deliberately; he was livid when I told him partners weren't invited,' I complained.

Amanda grimaced. 'You know he did. It's so

typical of him. I'm sorry, Maeve, but the guy is a selfish controlling arsehole. End of.'

A text pinged into my phone. Tom.

'Speak of the devil,' Amanda said. 'Tell him for once you are out with your oldest friend, who you won't be seeing for three weeks at least.'

Amanda was flying off the following day to Puerto Rico in the Caribbean for three weeks on a work junket.

'He knows,' I said, not mentioning the victory dance Tom had done on hearing the news.

'Well, tell him to leave off the constant texting for one night, please.'

Amanda waved her hand at the barman and pointed at our two drinks to indicate we wanted the same again.

'I suppose he'll be offering to give you a lift home on his way out of town? Like at ten thirty?'

I looked at the text from Tom and frowned. She knew Tom so well. He was indeed offering to swing by and pick me up. He hated me being out late. I texted him back to say I'd make my own way home. He would be annoyed and moody all day tomorrow, but I didn't care. I was entitled to one night off. I had had enough. I turned off my phone and threw it into my handbag.

'Goodnight, Tom!' I said.

'Thank God for that. We have more important things to talk about—like what are the chances Luke Fitzpatrick has flown in for tonight?'

Amanda was something else. I had some recollection of a lanky nerdy guy who sat at the front in chemistry class. Amanda had no memory of him back then at all, but she was all interest in him now. He had been named as Plastic Surgeon of the Year in some award ceremony in the US. She was busy googling him on her phone as I paid for two more gin and tonics.

'San Francisco to Dublin is a long way to come for

a reunion, even if he is a famous surgeon,' I said, looking at the few coins change out of the twenty I had handed to the barman.

'He's not just a surgeon,' Amanda said. 'He's a *plastic* surgeon. Think about it, Maeve. Any procedure you ever wanted. For *free*.' She looked at her watch. 'Get that down your throat now, young lady, the party is about to begin.'

We tottered up Grafton Street toward Stephen's Green. I couldn't remember the last time I had come into town at night. My shoes were pinching horribly. Amanda clung to my arm, and we laughed, both giddy and buzzing with nervous anticipation. We hadn't seen most of the people from boarding school in over twenty years. Would we even recognise anyone? Would anyone recognise us?

The uniformed doorman at the Shelbourne recognised Amanda: she was a regular in the Horseshoe Bar. He ushered us into the lobby. The function was in a suite on the first floor, so we picked our way through the Friday-evening crowd, past the magnificent floral display in the marble-floored lobby and headed for the lifts. As we waited, we straightened our skirts in the mirrored doors facing us.

'You can thank me for forcing you out of that potato sack you were going to wear,' Amanda said in her usual direct manner. 'That dress looks stunning on you. Too bloody stunning, in fact.'

I had only worn the dress once before, the night I was being interviewed on the *Late Late Show* for *Your Cheating Heart*. I had been terrified at the prospect of appearing on TV, but Amanda, who worked as a stylist, had helped me every step of the way. She had dragged me into Brown Thomas and had forced me to part with a ridiculous amount of money for the dress and a pair of designer heels. I felt uncomfortable as hell, but she was right, the dress looked great on. She had spoken to her hair stylist, and he had managed to transform my long-neglected hair so that I barely recognised the glamorous woman looking back at me in the salon mirror. I had done the interview and had looked the part but being in the limelight was not for me. It should have been Amanda—she would have loved it.

Tonight, Amanda was wearing a completely over-the-top gold lamé backless dress and looked stunning as she always did. Men always stared openly at Amanda, whatever she was dressed in, but I was happy for her to take centre stage and always had been.

The lift was taking ages, and my eyes drifted over the lobby which was milling with people. That's when I spotted her. Elena Martinez. She was standing to the right of the display of huge blue delphiniums, and she had seen me. For a millisecond, our eyes locked. Her face broke into a determined expression, and she started to push her way through the crowd in our direction. There was no way I was going to talk to her—not here, not half-cut with gin. I pressed at the button for the lift several times, and as the door to the lift finally opened, I pushed Amanda forward into it.

I could hear Elena shouting my name across the lobby. 'Maeve ... Maeve Danagher?'

'Don't look round. Angry client headed this way,' I said to Amanda, as I kept my head down and pressed at the button for the first floor.

'Jesus, calm down!' she snapped, as I now stabbed at the Close Doors button, willing the doors to shut which, thankfully, they did before Elena was upon us. I wondered what the hell she was doing in the Shelbourne. She had never mentioned going into town in our sessions. An image of her following me and Amanda on the DART from Monkstown sprang into my mind, but I banished it as gin paranoia. Not that I'd have put it past her. The lift doors opened onto the first floor, and I tried to push all thoughts of Elena from my mind. I wasn't going to let work spoil this night.

We found the function room. Amanda spotted Luke immediately. He was standing surrounded by a group of guys, most of whom were now bald with pot bellies and double chins. Luke, in contrast, looked great. Life in California had been good to him: he was tall, lean and tanned. As usual, all eyes turned towards Amanda, and she strutted across the room like a film star towards Luke who she recognised from photos online. She hadn't known Luke at school and hadn't spoken a word to him since, but that was no problem to her. Amanda was a force to be reckoned with. I shook my head and smiled at her brazenness. We were so different to each other on so many levels, and yet we were really close. Amanda was probably the one person in the world that I could be 100 per cent honest with; I trusted her completely to have my back, and I knew she felt the same about me.

I didn't see her again for a while as I caught up with other old friends. There were so many faces, so many old stories to share. I could see Amanda hard at work. She had Luke pinned in a corner and was working her magic: tits out, head thrown back laughing at his jokes, her long, manicured fingers reaching out to pull a piece of fluff off his shoulder. I left her to it. An hour or so later, when it was time to sit down for the meal, I hesitated to sit with them, not wanting to be a gooseberry, but she shouted across at me to come join them. She didn't look happy.

Luke sat between me and Amanda and, although he was being a perfect gentleman, I could tell immediately that the chemistry between them was not good. He wasn't susceptible to my friend's charms, and she didn't like it one little bit. Luke was not how I remembered him to be at all, or maybe he had changed over the years. At school he was very academic but also painfully shy. If he had a personality, then it hadn't been on view. This Luke was confident and charming with a dry sense of humour. He was passionate about his work which involved treating burn victims and took him all over the world. In response to a question from Amanda, he was vitriolic about the cosmetic surgery industry and the kinds of people who paid fortunes to be turned into 'plastic monsters'. I saw Amanda's expression change. She was not impressed. Over the last number of years, she had had several procedures done herself: Botox, fillers and an eye lift which had left just the tiniest of scars. After a while, she turned her back on Luke and started talking to the guy on the other side of her.

As the first course was being cleared away, I took a moment to check my phone. There was a string of increasingly angry texts from Tom—maybe seven or eight of them. I scanned through them; the last one was positively abusive. It consisted of two words: **Selfish bitch**.

There was no way I was going to let him spoil my night. Instead, I powered off my phone and let Luke pour me another glass of wine. The conversation turned to our respective domestic lives. Luke was recently divorced and had no intention of settling down again any time soon. I told him about the difficulties Tom and I had been having, and he understood. He had been where I was not too long ago. As we chatted, I realised Luke was hilarious, and I was aware that I found him really attractive. The feeling was clearly mutual. I was drinking more than usual, but then so was everyone else. The noise level in the room was testament to that. When the food was cleared away and the music started, Luke wandered off to find the toilet, and Amanda turned to me.

'What an absolute tosser,' she said, her mouth pulled into a sneer. '"Plastic monsters?" Who the hell does he think he is? Droning on and on about his job? Look, I'm sorry I dumped him on you, but he was boring the arse off me.' This was classic Amanda. If a guy she fancied was not interested in her, then there had to be something wrong with him. I envied her, in ways. She didn't suffer the pain of self-doubt. Luke was history. End of. I knew Amanda so well and knew she would think no more of Luke Fitzpatrick.

'I actually think he is quite cute,' I said, with a coy expression. Amanda's mouth dropped open in mock horror.

'Well, listen to you, you naughty minx,' she said laughing and giving me a high five. 'Can't account for your taste, but do you know what? It would do you good to have a bit of fun, let your hair down for once in your life.' A minute later I watched as her attention locked onto another potential target, and she darted off to the dance floor.

The music was thumping, and Luke suggested we find somewhere less noisy to keep our chat going. At first, I told myself the unmistakable flirting that was going on was harmless. I was a married woman with two teenage kids—nothing was going to happen. Actually, I knew deep down that it would; that I wanted it to. Luke was a guy who wasn't looking for anything serious. He would be gone tomorrow. Tom was not the man I married. We hadn't had sex in months; he barely spoke to me except to give out about something. Was it so wrong to want to be wanted? We found a couple of quiet seats outside the function room in a small bar area. For the first time in hours Elena popped into my head again. I hadn't thought about her since the lift doors had closed downstairs, but I wondered now if she might still be wandering about the hotel. If I was too drunk to talk to her earlier, I was definitely not fit to face her now. I looked around outside the bar, left and right up the corridor, just to be sure she was not lurking somewhere. Then I plonked into my seat and finally relaxed.

Luke was flirting openly now. It felt so good to be desired again. When he reached over and kissed me, I kissed him back. My head was swimming with pleasure and alcohol. The kiss was tender and warm. My body was tingling, the feeling of his lips on mine was electric. I knew it was wrong, but it felt so completely perfect that I didn't want it to stop. I thought of Tom's words in the text—**Selfish bitch**—and I thought: *to hell with you.*

Sometime later a group of our classmates spilled into the little bar, and Luke and I broke apart abruptly. Amanda was amongst them. The guy she was with had started doing a Riverdance impression, and a crowd gathered. Everyone was standing around videoing his performance. He careered around the lobby like Michael Flatley on speed. In the chaos, Luke whispered to me to follow him, and I did. Once out of view, he took my hand, and we walked down the corridor outside the bar. There was a function room all in darkness and, without thinking twice, I slipped into it with him. The door was barely closed before we had pounced on each other. His hands were under my dress. The feeling was incredible. This was so unlike me, but I didn't care. Things became heated very quickly, and I found myself pulling open his trousers' belt. After a few seconds of fumbling with it, I managed to pull it open; Luke lifted me up onto a table, and his hands pushed my dress up around my waist and started pulling at my knickers.

At that moment I heard a door beside me shut. The noise cut through the delirious haze I was in, and I clattered back into my senses. Someone had been in the room with us. I pulled away from Luke and stood up, pulling my dress back down. This was far too risky—most of the people outside knew I was a married woman. We had to find somewhere more private. We took the backstairs down to the lobby and, from there, a lift to Luke's room to avoid being seen. Luke knew I couldn't stay long, but we spent a few sex-and-laughter fuelled hours together. Afterwards, we talked about Tom. I knew I needed to give things with him one more try. I wasn't ready to throw away the last fifteen years. Luke was a good listener; he seemed to understand. When it was time to go, he insisted on walking me down to find a taxi. He was flying home the following day. I was heading back to my husband and kids. As we said goodbye, a wistful 'what if' feeling stirred in me, and I think Luke was feeling it too. However, there were no regrets. Luke and I had shared a moment in our lives, but it was a moment, not a beginning.

Once in the taxi, I texted Tom to say I was on my way and saw he had texted me an apology.

I am so sorry. You deserve better. Enjoy your night. Tx.

A wave of guilt washed over me. I wanted to get back to my home and to my husband, where I knew I belonged.

* * *

A few days later I was driving home after work with the twins, Alex and Hannah, who I had collected from school. Alex was in his rugby training gear. I was still suffering the after-effects of the alcohol from Friday night, and the smell of muck and sweat and filthy kit which filled the car was making me queasy. I had arrived home the night of the reunion to find Tom asleep, which was a relief. I had undressed in the en suite and had slipped into bed without waking him up. The following morning, he was contrite about the texts which made me feel horribly guilty. I almost told him what I had done but stopped myself. Tom had a serious problem with jealousy. Up until now I had never so much as looked at another man, yet Tom's jealous feelings would emerge in periods of stress and cause bad feeling. I knew that if I told him he would never be able to get over it. It would be the end for us.

Right now in the car, the twins were fighting, but I was only half listening.

'It stinks in here,' said Hannah, rolling down her window. 'Why can't he shower after training?'

'Shut up, fat ass.'

'Mum, Alex just called me fat.'

I indicated right and pulled out onto the Rock Road. My head was pumping, my body still reeling with the abuse of two nights ago.

'Please stop it, guys, I've had a hell of a day.'

'Alex fancies the new teacher; he was sucking up to her in supervised study.'

'I was not. She's been helping me with my Spanish project.'

I suddenly remembered Alex's project. It was due on Wednesday, and I had told him I would help him. I had meant to look at it with him over the weekend, but I hadn't been able.

'Alex, I'm sorry. I can help you with it after dinner.'

'It's fine, the new teacher has been helping me. I have it nearly done.'

'*Oooh, Miss, can you help me?*' Hannah taunted.

Alex who was sitting in the back reached forward and smacked the back of Hannah's head with his knuckle.

Hannah shrieked.

'In the name of God, stop it, the pair of you. Not another word until we get home!' I yelled.

* * *

A few hours later I was brushing my teeth in the en suite. I was dying to crawl into the bed and close my eyes. That's when I heard my phone ping from the bedside table where I had left it. Tom, who was already in bed reading, looked up quizzically.

I finished brushing my teeth and went into the bedroom and looked at my phone. It was a text from a foreign number I didn't recognise. There was a photo. The image was dark, and it was hard to make figures out, but I knew what I was seeing. It was me and Luke in the small bar, and I was kissing him. My stomach lurched. I flipped my phone cover shut.

'Who's texting you so late?' Tom asked, dropping his book onto his lap.

I retreated again to the en suite, mobile in hand. I locked the door behind me.

'It's a work thing. A client,' I said. I looked again at the photo. Who could have sent it? The number was a +1 prefix, so it was from the US. It might be Luke's number, but he was in the photo. I couldn't work it out. Had someone sent it to him, and he sent it to me? Surely, he knew we couldn't be in contact? I was sure he had understood we couldn't see each other or contact each other again.

There was silence from the bedroom for a few moments.

'Why have you locked yourself into the bathroom?'

Shit. Why did I lock the door? I never locked it. I sat down on the toilet. Who could have taken that photo? I looked again at the photo and tried to remember everything I had spent the last few days trying to forget.

Still in the en suite, I flicked my phone onto silent just as another text message pinged in. This time there was a video. The text with it read:

Here's one for Facebook, not! Your Cheating Heart, the movie?

My heart started thumping as I clicked into the video.

The shaky video was of me and Luke in the dark function room. The raucous sounds of revellers could be heard in the background, but the camera was close in on me and Luke.

'Shit!'

I knew what was coming next, and the camera zoomed in on my hand fumbling with Luke's belt. My stomach lurched as, on-screen, Luke lifted me onto a table and pulled off my knickers. The video ended there.

My hands were shaking as I flicked off my phone. Someone had followed us into that function room, and stood there watching, filming. Panic roared through me. It crept up my spine as a horrible realisation began to dawn on me. How many people might see this video if it was posted on Facebook? I had a vision of Alex and Hannah seeing me like that. Their revulsion. This could not be happening.

From the bedroom, I heard Tom.

'Maeve, what are you doing in there?'

I couldn't reply, I could barely breathe. I froze. Who had filmed me? One of the group in the lobby? Why would any of them send me the video? Had Amanda been pissed off at me for snaring Luke? If she was, she did a good job hiding it. Maybe Tom had come into the Shelbourne that night looking for me? Could it have been him? Could he have filmed me? Could he be sitting in bed on the other side of that door, right now, taunting me?

Then the answer came to me. Elena. Of course! I had seen her in the bar downstairs earlier that night. She must have hung around watching me. She must have been in the lobby, had followed me into the function room. Filmed me. It was classic Elena. The threat to post on Facebook, that was classic Elena too.

A wave of anger surged through me. The years of working with her, supporting her as best I could. Fucking bitch! My mind went blank, and I found I couldn't work out what to do next. I had to protect my family, but how?

It must have been fifteen minutes later when I came out of the en suite. The bedside lights were still on, but Tom had turned away. I slipped into my side of the bed. I knew he wasn't asleep. The atmosphere was rigid with tension. I flicked off the lights and turned my back to him. My mind was racing. I could tell him everything now, but what if he could never forgive me?

It took hours for me to fall asleep and when I did, I slept fitfully. When the alarm woke me as usual at seven o'clock I could hear Tom downstairs making breakfast. I pulled out my phone. There was a new text, this time from Elena's number.

I have cancelled the meeting with Dr Nolan. I want to see you. Today.

So it *was* her. What choice did I have but to meet her? I looked at my diary. On Wednesdays I only worked until lunchtime as it was a half-day for the twins. If I got the kids to walk over to my office from school, I could fit Elena in for a few minutes after my last client. I couldn't risk provoking her. I knew what she was capable of when ignored. Derek would be on my case, as would Dr Nolan, but I had to engage with Elena until I could find some way out of this nightmare. I desperately wanted to talk with Amanda. I rang her number but was put through to her voice recording. Of course. It was the middle of the night in the Caribbean. I left a message.

Ring me as soon as you get this.

At twelve fifty I opened the door to Elena who brushed in past me. I felt the urge to punch her but kept my fists balled by my sides. Whatever she said, I had to keep my emotions under control. *You can do this.* She took off her coat and hung it as usual behind the door, acting as if everything was normal.

'My kids will be here soon, Elena,' I said. 'I can only see you for five minutes.'

She moved the brown chair to the window and sat down.

'I have to say I am disappointed in you, Maeve. It's

21

the double standard that gets me. You of all people.'

I felt my face flush with anger. I dared not look her in the eyes.

'If the people who bought your book knew how you behave yourself, well ...'

I took a deep breath to control the rage inside. I looked directly at her, steeling myself to keep my expression calm.

'What do you want from me, Elena?'

Elena smiled and sat back in her chair and said nothing for a few moments. She was enjoying her power. Finally, she spoke.

'I want to move past all that unpleasantness on Saturday night; leave it behind and get back to our normal routine.'

I felt myself exhale and the clenching around my heart release. If all she wanted was to keep seeing me then I could do that—for now at least.

Alex and Hannah walked past the window. They knew to stay in the waiting area until I was finished.

'The important thing is you saw sense in the end. There's no point in me starting with someone new; you know my history. I will just keep seeing you as usual every Tuesday at five fifteen.'

For the next five minutes, I listened to a tirade about James and his 'pathetic' wife, Katie. Elena had sent compromising photos of James to Katie, and James had phoned her to call her every name under the sun. As Elena spoke, my mind was getting to grips with the implications of continuing to see her. I was going against a treatment plan agreed upon with a psychiatrist and with my supervisor. Questions would be asked. Disciplinary action would be taken against me if I continued to see her. It was only a matter of time, but what else could I do? Five minutes later, I walked Elena through the waiting room to the front door.

'See you as usual next Tuesday,' Elena said, her wide smile revealing dazzling white teeth.

I locked my office door and indicated to the twins that it was time to leave.

'Is Miss Martinez a client of yours?' Hannah asked as she and Alex followed me out to the car park.

I felt the hairs on my neck stand up. I stopped dead and whipped around to face Hannah.

'What do you mean "Miss Martinez"? Do you know her?'

'The American teacher I told you about; the one Alex fancies. That's her.'

My heart sunk deep into my stomach, and my head was swimming. I had seen Elena's camper van parked outside the school. Of course. Elena had wrangled her way into the twins' school, and she had targeted Alex.

Jesus Christ, I've put my children in the path of a psychopath!

I waited until we were in the car and out of earshot of any of my colleagues who might be passing.

'Miss Martinez, how long has she been working in the school?'

'Just the last few weeks, I think,' Hannah replied.

I started the car engine and pulled out of my parking space.

'I don't want either of you talking to her again.'

'What?' Alex said. 'That's so unfair.'

I felt a tightness in my chest.

'Don't talk to her, either of you, do you hear me?' I said, my voice coming out louder and angrier than I intended.

An hour later, I was grating cheese over the pasta dish I had prepared for dinner. Cooking the meal had taken every bit of energy I had. I felt overwhelmed. I poured a large glass of wine. Maybe I should just tell Tom everything now? What happened with Luke was

23

meaningless—a drunken stupid mistake. I could explain the video; that nothing more had happened, in spite of how it looked. But telling Tom would only solve a small part of my problem. What would happen if Elena posted the video to Facebook? Think of all the people who might see it; all the people who had bought my book? All my family and friends who had watched me on the *Late Late*. All the clients I worked with? My practice could collapse; what would we do for money? How would we pay the school fees, the mortgage?

Over dinner I barely touched my pasta. I felt consumed with a sense of dread. A time-bomb was set to explode under my family and professional lives, and I didn't know how to stop it. I could see Tom exchange glances with the kids. They could all sense something was not right with me.

'OK, out with it,' Tom said, after he had finished the last mouthful of pasta. 'You could cut the atmosphere in here with a knife.'

'Mum lost it after school 'cos one of her clients is a teacher at school, and we saw her in her office,' Hannah said.

I needed to end this conversation.

'Hannah, Alex, you'll just have to trust me on this one,' I said, while I brought my plate to the bin and scraped the untouched contents into it.

Tom stood and opened the door to the lounge.

'Leave these plates kids; your mum and I will clear up.'

Hannah and Alex high-fived and headed into the lounge to watch TV. Tom closed the door behind them. I placed my plate into the dishwasher and started to wash up the pasta pan. Tom came behind me and gently took the washing up brush out of my hand.

'Come on,' he said, his voice full of kindness, 'I need you to sit down and tell me what's happening. I'm not blind. I know there's something up.'

I left the pot and sat down heavily. I wasn't ready to tell him, to destroy the life we had together. It would almost have been better if he weren't being so bloody nice. I didn't deserve his kindness; I didn't deserve him. I had to tell him something, anything to get him off my back.

'It's a client. Elena Martinez. She's that girl who was here banging the door in the middle of the night.'

Tom's brow creased now into a worried expression.

'That headcase—the American one with the slashes on her arms? You didn't tell me she was teaching in St Luke's?'

'I only found out this afternoon when the kids saw her at my office.'

Tom reached over and touched my hand. 'Has she got something to do with the texts you got last night?'

I pulled my hand away. His compassion was unbearable. I took a deep breath. Underneath the table my foot was tapping a stealthy staccato beat on the floor. *Don't tell him about Luke. Whatever you do, don't tell him.*

'She's been sending me texts; angry texts accusing me of all sorts.'

Tom's expression changed; he looked confused.

'Accusing you of what?'

'It doesn't matter, it's all made up. I referred her on to a psychiatrist, and she's incensed, that's all. You saw her the night she was here. Well, she's even more out of control now.'

'What did she say in the texts?'

I could feel the blood draining out of my face. My heart was beating rapidly.

'Nothing worth repeating. Honestly, I didn't want to worry you, I wish I hadn't told you now.'

Tom now looked desperately worried. He reached over and stroked my cheek.

'Maeve, I'm your husband. If you're in some sort of trouble, then I need to know. Maybe you should show me the texts?'

I flinched from his touch. My phone was charging beside the toaster, and I saw Tom glance at it. Without thinking, I lurched for the phone, powered it off and put it into the zipped pocket of my fleece.

'I would show you, but I deleted them.'

A dark expression passed over Tom's face. He knew I was lying. I couldn't deal with him now. I had to get out of the house.

I made for the door.

'Maeve, look at me. Do you honestly expect me to believe that?'

I spun around, but I couldn't look him in the eye. I grabbed my coat and ran out the front door, pulling it closed behind me.

It was freezing cold and starting to rain but I needed to get away from Tom and his questions. I walked down the lane towards the sea pulling on my parka, zipping it up and pulling up the fur-lined hood. I had to think. Elena was appeased for now but that couldn't last. My supervisor would be asking why I was still seeing her, as would Dr Nolan. Besides, she was so volatile; she could change her mind on a whim and post that video at any time.

I passed a group of youths drinking beer at the bathing place at Seapoint. One of them showed the others something on his phone, and they all laughed. I imagined the humiliation if that video was posted on social media; how Alex and Hannah would feel seeing my betrayal of their dad. A wave crashed out onto the path. I couldn't allow Elena to ruin my children's lives. Somehow, I had to get her phone, and then I had to put her where she couldn't get near my kids; where she couldn't harm anyone. There was one way I could protect them and that was to have Elena sectioned. Could I live with that? Elena was a loose cannon, a danger to herself and others. Wouldn't she be better off in a residential setting where she could get the care she needed?

Maybe this could work? As I walked, my mind went over the practicalities. Getting Elena's phone was a priority. She kept it routinely in the pocket of her coat which she hung on a coat hook behind the door of my office during our sessions. I needed to get her in for an extra session—tomorrow, if possible—and take the phone then. To have Elena committed, I would have to persuade two psychiatrists that she posed a real danger to herself or others. The woman was deeply unstable—that was obvious to anyone who talked to her for long enough—but would that be enough?

As I walked back past the Forty Foot, I dialled Dr Aoife Nolan, Elena's new psychiatrist. I apologised for the late call but explained that it was an emergency. I filled Dr Nolan in briefly on Elena's history. In my opinion, I went on, Elena was now completely out of control: psychotic, a danger to herself and others.

Dr Nolan sounded sympathetic but explained that it was not possible to have Elena admitted against her will at this point.

'As you know, if we are going to section her, we need evidence that she poses a serious threat to others or herself. I will personally make a new appointment with her tomorrow, and when I see her, I will be in a better position to see what needs to happen.'

I tried to press her.

'She's told me, in session, that she intends hurting this man she has been seeing. I believe her. I really believe she could do something terrible to him.'

I knew it wasn't enough, and that I was now sounding desperate. Again, Dr Nolan's tone was sympathetic but firm.

'Look, if she actually does something, we will act immediately, believe me; but what she has told you, it could just be fantasy, bluster or wishful thinking. It's not enough.'

I ended the call just as I arrived back to my front door. If Dr Nolan needed Elena to do something to prove she was a danger, then I knew just what buttons to press to make that happen. I texted Elena and asked her to come in for an extra session mid-morning the following day.

* * *

The next day Elena arrived and hung up her coat as usual. I stayed by the door, and as she turned her back on me to move her chair to the window, I snatched the phone out of her pocket and stuffed it into my trousers' pocket. My heart was beating so fast I thought I might pass out as I sat in front of her. She hadn't seen me. It took several minutes before my heartbeat calmed down.

There was a change in Elena—she seemed more confident in herself, cocky even. There was a trace of a smile on her face.

'Maeve, it's really good of you to offer me this extra session, but you don't look well; you look like you didn't sleep a wink.'

I realised Elena was enjoying her new-found power. *Well, not for long, you psychotic bitch.*

I had to chew on my lip to keep my expression neutral and hide my anger.

'I'm fine, Elena, but I've been worried about you. How you are coping with what's happening with James?'

Elena's expression changed, the smile replaced with a grimace.

'He hasn't been returning my calls. I think he's blocked me. How could he just cut me off?' She looked away briefly, pain etched on her face. Then she looked back at me, her expression hardening now.

'I won't let him, or anyone else, treat me like

garbage. He left me no choice. I had to send those photos to his wife. If he doesn't contact me today, I'll post them on Facebook; see how his kids like him then.'

As she said this, she looked at me with a faint smile. The implied threat was clear. *If you don't keep seeing me forever, I will send that video to your husband and post it on Facebook.*

I took a deep breath to dampen down the sense of panic building in my chest. I had no choice here. What I was about to do went against everything I had ever stood for, but Elena had left me with no other option. I had to protect my family. I leaned over and patted Elena's hand. Elena looked taken aback. I never, or at least rarely, touched her. I cleared my throat.

'I don't blame you Elena, for ... whatever you've done. He pushed you to it. You're desperate to keep seeing him. I get that. You don't deserve to be treated like this.'

I paused before playing my trump card and looked her straight in the eyes.

'I have to tell you something important, Elena; something that I know will hurt you, but you need to know,' I said.

Elena looked concerned. She sat forward in her seat.

'What? What do you need to tell me?'

I leaned forward too. 'You are letting James treat you like a loser.'

Elena flinched at the mention of the word 'loser', as I knew she would. She swallowed hard. I could see she was genuinely vulnerable. I had to press on now—seize the moment.

I pulled my seat forward until my knees were almost touching Elena's.

'You're not a loser. I have always told you that. That's what your father and James want you to believe, and you have to show them what you are made of. It's time to take a stand against your father. Against all the men who have treated you like a loser, and especially against James.'

Elena was looking directly at me, hanging on to my every word.

'But I have been taking a stand.' Her voice faltered. I had her just where I needed her to be.

I put my hand over hers and held it there.

'You need to take real action, Elena; sending videos, that's not enough of a stand.'

Elena was staring at me. She looked confused and a little frightened. Fighting back was not something I had ever suggested before.

'Really? But what about "an eye for an eye leaves everyone blind?"'

This was a saying attributed to Mahatma Ghandi that I had quoted a lot to Elena over the years. I had spent countless hours persuading her that by acting out revenge on others, she always ended up hurting herself.

'I think this is an exception, an important part of your recovery. You have been repeating a cycle with James, with all of these men who have treated you so badly. It's a cycle which was put in place by your father, where you allow yourself to be humiliated and cast aside because he made you believe you were a *loser* who deserved no better.'

Elena's chest was shuddering, and I could see my words had hit their mark. Tears streamed down her face. She was struggling to keep from sobbing.

'Only a *loser* hides behind emails, sends anonymous messages. You are not that loser, Elena. You are stronger than that. It's time for you to stop crying and start acting like a *winner*.'

Elena wiped at her tears with the back of her hand. She was taking the bait. A part of me felt empathy for her—like all narcissists, there was a very vulnerable core to her—but I had to remember the threat she posed to my children.

'That's more like it. Dry your tears. It's time James paid for how he has treated you; for how all those men and your father treated you. You need to confront him in person, in public; do something he can't ignore.'

'Maybe I should show up at his office,' Elena said, almost to herself, deep in thought. 'He would be so embarrassed if I confronted him there.'

Elena had told me James worked as a solicitor in a firm on Dawson Street in the city centre. They would not take kindly to Elena showing up. James might even press charges or seek some sort of court protection order against her. That would be perfect.

'Now you're talking,' I said. 'But you need to create a huge scene—throw some furniture around, cause a fuss. That will get everyone's attention'.

Elena was silent for a moment. She looked at her watch. Suddenly, she stood up and grabbed her coat. She didn't check her pocket.

'I'm going straight over there, before I have a chance to think about it, and I can promise you, Maeve, if he thinks what I've done so far was bad, then he has a surprise coming.'

A wave of unease shivered through me, but I resisted thinking about what Elena might be capable of.

'Remember, a public protest; something to embarrass him, but don't actually hurt him physically. That could lead to trouble.'

I could see Elena wasn't listening. She pulled me into an awkward hug.

'Thank you. This has been the best session I think we've ever had.'

After she had gone, I walked out to reception and poured myself a large mug of coffee, although what I really needed was a stiff gin and tonic. I was filled with a sense of dread and doubt. What had I done? What was Elena going to do to James? The guy was a shit by all accounts, but he didn't deserve the public humiliation that Elena was about to throw his way. I went to look through her phone, but my first clients had already arrived—a couple coming for their first relationship counselling session—which meant I was tied up for the next hour and a half. When I finished with them, I looked at my phone.

There was a new message in from the US number. How could that be? I had Elena's phone, which I now pulled out of my trousers' pocket. I clicked into the message on my own phone.

> **Hi, babe. Sorry, just realised I sent you that video and the photo from the work phone I'm using in Puerto Rico. Hilarious! You must have been wondering! I know I shouldn't have filmed you, but I thought you might like it as a memento, you bold girl. Talk soon. Weather great. Axxx**

Relief flooded through me, and I jumped up and down with joy where I stood at the coffee machine. I smiled at the receptionist.

'Good news?' she asked.

'You've no idea. The best,' I replied, running over and pulling her into a quick hug.

It was then I noticed two missed calls from Tom, and a text message which read:

> **Look at the news. Incident in Dawson Street. Doesn't your client drive an orange camper van?**

There was a television in reception permanently tuned to Sky News. I snatched the remote and switched it to RTE. The *One O'Clock News* was on.

A reporter was standing at the junction of Dawson Street and St Stephen's Green. Behind him I could see a

Luas train and the remains of an orange VW Beetle camper van which had been crushed in the train's path.

'Witnesses say the camper van was parked on the double yellow lines here. A man came out of the office across the street, and as he stepped out onto the street to cross the road, the female driver of the camper van appeared to rev the engine and drive straight for him. The driver apparently didn't see the Luas train approaching which crashed into the side of her vehicle. She sustained massive head injuries and was pronounced dead at the scene.'

My legs gave way from under me, and I sat down.

The view from the office window became a blur. I slumped to the floor and let the two phones slip out of my hand onto the floor.

'Oh God,' I whispered, 'what have I done?'

Eleven O Two

Martin Keating

Conor, the boss had just flown in from Denver, replete with the latest good corporate stuff. He announced that he would be hosting a dinner for his team. Not compulsory, but a strong hint that it would not be a good idea to miss it. As far as Barry knew, his partner Lucy didn't have other plans for them, so he texted her, saying he would be late tonight and apologising for the short notice.

Just a few guys from work. no big deal.

She texted back.

Dinner???

That's so he would ring her.

'It's just dinner and a few drinks,' he told her. Bonding, he explained; the boss was recently big on bonding. Barry didn't necessarily want to go, but, 'Mustn't piss off the man who signs the pay check.'

Which Lucy chose to interpret as meaning it was OK to piss her off. She got teed off even more when he said he would leave his car in work and take the DART home. What if she needed the car herself tomorrow? She referred to it as 'our' car (the minefield of co-habitation). She had this way of twisting things to highlight her martyrdom. She was also acting as if Barry had been looking forward to breaking bread with his boss. As if he preferred to spend more time with the guys and less time with her. *Keep up the moaning, babe, and that could come true yet.*

Had he asked to spend the evening with the fucker, hearing about Denver and the exciting new corporate developments? Fuck sake, he'd rather bathe his eyes in vinegar.

* * *

Conor had an ulterior motive in getting them together around the 'chow bench'. The remuneration system was being changed in such a way that that the team's average commission earnings would be halved next year.

'We're moving to a more earnings-at-risk paradigm,' Conor explained.

'Earnings at risk' meant that instead of ten guys having half a chance of making 130 per cent of basic salary, one guy might make 200 per cent and the other nine were likely to end up with 90 per cent. Conor said he knew how they felt and had argued mightily against the changes. But his was only one voice, right?

Barry asked him how much *his own* remuneration might improve at the expense of the rest of the team. Sounding decidedly shifty, Conor said that no one understood the algorithm—except the maths professor in the University of Colorado who'd come up with it. Making a joke of it. Easing the tension—*we're all mates here.*

No one laughed, except Conor.

The team bet the boss knew just how well he'd be doing, otherwise why would he be so content, or prepared to be so persuasive?

So, they drank.

They wanted to spend his thirty pieces of silver for him. Fuck his plastic till it melted. The younger guys murmured treason, plotted mass defections. Only, hang about, hang about, the older hands advised in whispers. Get new jobs by all means, but don't leave any money behind you. Wait, collect the last bonuses under the old system. Don't give the fuckers a freebie.

And, in the meantime, mindfuck the fat bastard. Tell him you understand his dilemma; assure him of your determination to run gross sales at 200 per cent to earn the new bonuses. Show him that he's leading a team of winners. 'We don't grieve; we achieve.'

'You guys,' Conor said, tearful and gloopy, 'You

are some great guys.'

As the old hands said, cutting your head off is no cure for a headache.

Conor was eager to reward their loyalty. 'Whatever you want, guys. How about going on to a lap dancing club?'

Popular choice with the guys, who planned to ride the boss's credit card until it died under them.

Barry, though, felt like killing the whiny liar. The fat deceiver. Having him buy overpriced drink and lap dances with stale-eyed blondes was childish yah-boo stuff compared with strangling the bastard and eating his eyes. Barry took a pass on the club, saying he'd get the DART home.

* * *

When the circumstances are right, a train ride is just about the most romantic thing. When you're twenty and with a girl; and you're both a bit high, and you're experiencing your own irresistible maleness, humming a riff you can't get out of your mind; and she hums along, and you laugh together; and she gets a fit of the giggles and lies back against the window, with her hair flattened against the glass and her eyes blinking with sleepiness, or highness, or happiness, and the lights blurring past behind the foggy glass … mellow, blissful late-night journeys like that are memories to treasure.

On the other hand.

If you're business-suited and pissed off, and are looking at losing half of next year's bonus, and not wanting to think about what you need to cut back on; and are not quite drunk, and very definitely not mellow, then a train ride is just a drag, with a long walk at the end of it. You let your phone select the playlist, and you stand on the platform, head nodding like some care-in-the-community spaceman. You don't want to think. Because if you did, you might start crying.

He caught the eleven o two. It was right on time.

Shudder, hiss, phut, accelerate, rattle, brake; shudder, hiss, phut, accelerate.

Station to station: Tara Street, Westland Row, Grand Canal Dock.

Where she got on.

Unsteadily.

She had a short leather jacket and drainpipe jeans. All in black. A look Barry liked. A look that would be good on Lucy, who, lately, had gone all ethnic—jangly necklaces and bangles, and muddy brown floaty fabrics.

She had red hair, a mass of it, teased and piled up on her head. One eyelid struggling to stay up. Considerably drunker than he was. She reached where he was sitting when the train started again. The lurch into motion caught her unawares. Her shoulder bag swung around and hit Barry on the head. Christ, what had she in it? An anvil?

'T'sorry.'

He told her not to mention it.

'T'sorry.'

She went to the seat across the aisle, slumped into it, and her eyes closed immediately. Her head fell on her chest, the light material of her blouse stretched over her breasts and her legs formed a loose diamond, drawing Barry's eye to her crotch.

'Hello. Excuse me,' Barry called to her.

One eye flipped open.

'Are you all right?'

The eye closed again.

The train juddered into Booterstown. Two teenagers got on. Barry watched them nudge each other and go sit opposite her. They made some jokes. The braver one rubbed his shoe against the back of her calf.

She opened one eye. She said something to them. And drifted off again.

Her bag had slid off her shoulder and was lying on

the seat. An open invitation. The foot-stroker looked across at Barry. Barry held his stare. The automatic announcement for the next station boomed out. The would-be thief hit his mate on the shoulder and made a 'Let's roll' move with his hand. As they passed, he feinted towards Barry with his shoulder, and Barry gave him the hard eye.

They threw a few weak hand gestures from the platform as the train groaned away.

'S'thanks.'

She rolled to her feet and came across to the seat facing Barry.

'Thanks.'

'Where are you going? What station?' Barry talked to her in a slow, emphatic way, like you do with someone who mightn't know your language.

'D'leary.'

She gave him a heavy-lidded smile, before settling back into the seat. She sat modestly now, legs parallel, wrists crossed over the bag in her lap. She closed her eyes.

What it would be like to fuck her? Barry thought. Without caring if she had interesting opinions or told good jokes. Just plunge into her. What's the point of ethics and values? He lived in a decaying city, worked with stupid double-crossing bosses, lived with a controlling girlfriend. Why give a shit? Why not pick up this foxy drunk and, if she'd let him, fuck her addled brains out?

Why not—just once—do whatever he could get away with?

* * *

'Hey, Dun Laoghaire coming up.'

'Uhnn?'

'Your stop.'

'S'right.'

She looked about, up and down the carriage, blinked; looked at the overhead lights, at the route map over the window. The doors sighed open, and cold air rushed in.

He helped her to her feet, a steadying hand on her elbow.

'Thanks.'

She leaned into him. A strong tang of alcohol and stale cigarette smoke rose from the ticklish tangle of her hair. He sneezed. She pivoted towards him with a woozy smile. Her heavy bag rapped against his ribs.

'Sorry.'

Time to get off the train. She fished for her ticket in her bag. It was a big bag. Halfway between a handbag and a weekend bag. He saw a bottle of champagne in there. With a gold ribbon around it. And a lot of other junk.

She couldn't find her ticket at first. The search continued on the platform. At last, the ticket was found in a zipped pocket on the side of the bag. The doors behind bonged shut.

'S'thanks. Y'don' needa.' She made a vague gesture at the train moving away.

'I don't want anything to happen to you.' *Unless I happen to do it*, Barry thought.

She was wearing flats; she probably wouldn't have been able to walk in heels. The guy at the ticket desk peered out from behind his shatterproof glass and asked if everything was all right. As if he'd do anything about anything that wasn't— Well, maybe press a button.

Barry gave him a thumbs-up.

'Do we need a taxi?' he asked her. One was loitering outside with its sign lit. She shook her head and started to walk off. She turned and looked back. Beckoned.

'Y'cumm'n.'

They walked along, bumping together. Barry asked her questions. She gave long incomprehensible answers, half the time addressed to the locked doors and shuttered windows of the street. They reached a black-painted door.

A couple of faintly lit doorbells to one side.

She handed Barry her bag.

'S'keys.' She pointed to the bag.

He held up both sets that he found in the bag. She clasped his hand and brought her head in close to look at them before making a selection.

'Dem.'

He rattled the bunch she had chosen.

'Odders'r work keys. You can lose those.' This she found very funny.

He opened the door and stood back to let her in first.

'Thanks. S'coffee?'

She led the way in. Banging the door after her and giggling. She pushed past him on the narrow stairs, and then dipped and kissed him. A drunken kiss: hungry and not particularly pleasant. She led the way to her flat, pushing the door open, shrugging off her jacket at the same time as she turned back to kiss him. He didn't know her name, and she hadn't asked his.

'Mmpff.'

She talked while kissing. He rubbed her back and breasts, which she seemed to like. She was loud and sloppy, and her thoughts were flying about at a thousand miles an hour. When, to move things on, he started to undo her belt she said, 'Nuh-uh.'

She backed away, smiling, resting a finger on his nose.

'Coffee.'

She turned on the lights then and swayed off in the direction of the kitchenette. She hit her hip against the corner of a table, laughed and put a finger to her lips. She filled the kettle and banged around looking for stuff.

The flat was tiny and crowded; on the shelves she'd got books—not many, none good—and a picture in a wooden frame of her and a fat guy with a stubbly face.

He was an ugly mope, so Barry figured he was either a brother, or he'd got a ten-inch dick. There were drawings on the walls, abstract stuff, tortured women's faces, winged creatures rising out of flames, and so on.

'S'mine.'

She peered at Barry peering at the art. She slopped a mug in his direction, spilling hot coffee over the back of his hand.

'It's good,' he said.

'Think so?'

'I like them.'

She lunged at the photo. Picked it up and kissed the mope.

'S'mine. Pig.'

She pitched the photo onto the bed.

'He's fucked off. Le's drink to that.'

She grabbed Barry's coffee mug, went to the en suite and poured the drink down the toilet. She went to her bag and took out the champagne. She paused, then rummaged some more and brought out a plaque, which she rubbed on her T-shirt. She handed it to Barry.

He was in the company of Karen Flynn, Target Couriers' Employee of the Year.

Pop went the cork.

'Wow,' said Barry, pointing to the inscription, 'Congratulations.'

'Phoo,' she said. 'Gave us a dinner, but I'd prefer a bit of wedge.'

'Recognition is nice,' Barry said.

She laughed. 'Recognition is cheap.'

* * *

She poured champagne into the mug and handed it to him. Keeping the bottle in her hand, she went to the bed and lay down. She stood the bottle beside her on the floor and told Barry about her boyfriend and his leaving her. And how it was a pisser not having anyone to celebrate with. She'd got drunker than she wanted to at the dinner, and probably made a show of herself. She certainly said a few things to a few people. 'Home truth alert! Oh dear.' She snorted in amusement. ''M a bad girl. Bad, bad, girl.'

She was getting drunker. She knocked over the champagne bottle and spilled all but a small amount. She drained the bottle, took off her top, and invited Barry over to the bed.

When Barry touched her, she found she was ever-so-ticklish and laughed and kicked about. Getting her boots and socks and jeans off was a real hoot. Her pants came half off with the jeans. When Barry hooked his thumbs in the waistband to pull them off, she shook her head. 'No-oh. T'sleep.' She folded her legs back, leaving him holding empty air. She wriggled under the covers. 'Sleep,' she repeated.

Barry was left looking at the big tangle of red hair between the quilt and the pillow. What's more stupid than a naked man with a hard-on, standing in a strange room, listening to a drunken woman's snoring? He picked up the empty champagne bottle and hit her with the heavy bottom end, right in the middle of that rat's nest of red hair. He hit her again, and she moved. He hit her many more times until there were red spatters all over the covers and the bedhead.

He took a shower and dressed. He washed the champagne bottle and brought it with him. He brought the Employee of the Year award too, after he had prised the inscription plate off with a kitchen knife.

* * *

'Had a good night?' the cabbie asked.

'Work do,' he said, 'Employee of the Year.'

'Congrats, buddy,' said the driver. Barry asked the cabbie to stop by a bottle bank. 'If I came home with an empty champagne bottle, my missus would ask, "Who's the wan?"' the cabbie said.

43

After he had dumped the bottle, Barry thought he might go to the lap dancing club. He couldn't remember which one it was. He rang one of the guys, but his co-worker was already at home. The club proving a bit of a failure. The boss got the heebie-jeebies, when the barman told him that the credit limit on the card was blown. Then the guys had drained Conor's petrol tank, so he had no money and no way of getting home. His wife had to fetch him from in front of the lap dancing club. 'You missed the fun, Bar.'

'I can believe it,' Barry said.

Back in the taxi, he rang Lucy. He was surprised that she picked up and didn't let it go to voicemail. He told her about the dinner and the lap dancing club and draining the petrol tank and stranding the boss. As if he had done it all himself.

When Barry got home, he went up to the bedroom immediately to show Lucy the Employee of the Year award he'd been presented with. 'It was a surprise,' he said, 'so it was worth my while going to the dinner after all.' He made her come downstairs and help him clear a space for it on their mantelpiece.

You Must Be Good For Something But You Ain't No Good To Me

Martin Keating

Derek Dowdall thinks he's my boss. He'd like me to believe it and all. Derek's a big fucker and ugly, needless to say; so bulked up around the shoulders that he goes through ordinary doors sideways—that's steroids for you. Where it matters—between the ears and between the thighs—he's got nothing. He gives me a snide smile and says, 'Here's the Christmas list, Charlie,' sliding a folded paper across the desk. 'A nostalgic trip for you; for the season that's in it.'

I unfold the sheet and see the names. And I think: *Oh fuck! This I don't need.*

'You go, Derek,' I say, prepared to fight about it.

'I've got the Christmas Eve party tonight. All that organising.'

'Fuck.'

'You're coming tonight, yeah? Angie will be expecting you.' And he gives me more of that sneery smile.

'Fuck off.'

'That's disrespectful, that is.'

I grab my tool bag and go out the door of the Portakabin. His laughter follows me down into the yard. I throw my tools into the boot of the jeep; Molar, meantime, has climbed into the front passenger seat.

'Where to, boss?' he asks.

'I can do this shit on my own, thanks,' I tell him.

'Derek says it's safer if I come.'

'Derek is not my fucken boss.'

'He's my boss, *boss*.' Molar laughs.

I start the jeep, and we squirt off in a cloud of dust and gravel. I'm tired of explaining things to this big Polish

45

fucker. Let Derek be *his* boss if that's how Molar wants it. Derek is a partner in *our* business. These days he's abandoned finance in favour of running his gym and dosing himself with steroids and diuretics and oiling himself up. And posing in his little leather ball-pouch and making like he's fucken Ray Liotta's love child by Ray fucken Winstone. He does what he does, but I bring home the earnings, and in a couple more years, my share will be better than fifty per cent. And then, if Derek wants a bareknuckle, scratch and kick, fight-to-the-finish, I for sure will give him one.

I take a sharp turn out of the yard, and Molar has to clutch the armrest in the door and brace himself against the dashboard.

'You know, you wreck the gearbox driving like that,' he tells me.

* * *

We sweep down on my old hometown, under a sky the colour of an old bruise. Like villains in a movie. There's a guy emoting on the radio. The vulnerable and the marginalised. It's a real weep session—him, the presenter, and some politician bitch. Yadda, yadda, yadda.

Right on, man; the vulnerable and marginalised!

Deadbeats one and all. You can always find them at handout time, but when it's time to pay their debts, it's a whole different matter.

I should know; I'm their banker.

I hate this fucken town. I left it, swearing never to come back. But I guess I'm like the dog and his vomit. Even the Christmas lights, and the big tree in the square and the bunting can't brighten the place. Molar looks out the window and makes a 'phut' noise. *Welcome home, Charlie,* the dirty windows wink at me.

First call.

I go to the boot while Molar rings the doorbell. I come up to the house and let them see Mr Sledge through the glass panel beside the door. A thin female face appears and disappears. I squat down and push up the letter flap. 'I haven't got the fucken time for huffen' and puffen', little pigs. You come out or the door goes in. Your choice.' I pause, then start the countdown. 'Five, four …'

The woman shivers back and lets me in. Showing a properly respectful attitude, but my debtor is shouting from the front room. Nasty personal stuff and bullshit about rights that he must have read in some anti-austerity leaflet.

'You pricks can't come in here,' is the gist of his argument. 'Fuck off, or I'm calling the coppers.'

He's splayed on the sofa, the fat fuck, instant noodles drying on his chin, and this big plasma screen front and centre of the cosy nest he's made for himself.

I bring him up to date.

'Your partner invited us in. We're here in regard to an instalment payment that might have slipped your mind. With your hectic schedule and all.'

He's watching Molar, who has eased into a ready stance. He is thinking that my associate could do him some serious soft tissue damage. He is concerned about the wrong person.

'I will take a payment of two hundred euros now, Mr M——,' I say.

His slack jaw forms itself into an aggrieved look.

'Hey, fuck you, Charlie Currie, the payment is one hundred euros.'

'*Was*,' I correct him. 'Until you made me come here today. It's a long drive, and I need compensation for the emotional damage I suffer being in your fat and futile presence.'

'You can fuck off; I haven't got it. And if you touch me, right … If you touch me, you'll get done.'

'Do I look like I want to touch you?'

Molar moves closer, and the guy twists himself

into a defensive position. He rabbits on about how he'll have it in a couple of weeks. He's had an injury—he points to the dirty bandage on his ankle. He is going to get compo and disability, and then he can settle up. Meantime, I have to be patient.

That big-screen TV tells me he's settled his claim already. I know there's money in the house. I know by the way his wide-eyed woman is hanging around, ignoring the whingey baby in the blue bath on the kitchen table. Fuckers like these think they're smarter than me. God, how I hate their fucked-up places; their hopeless scams; their neglected children.

Who, I mean, who do they think they're fooling?

Not me.

Christmas is a time for giving.

Lessons, in this case.

The Family Shiftless go whoo as Mr Sledge flexes his long hard shaft. Crash, the TV goes over. Whup, Deadbeat Dad scores some genuine ankle trauma. While he's rolling around on the floor, waiting for the shock to pass and the screaming to begin, I make Momma a proposition.

'Perhaps you would give me the two hundred now, so we can leave you to enjoy the rest of your day in peace.'

'Don't ...Jesus ... Christ ... give him nothing ... call the cops! Call the fucking cops.'

Old Deadbeat lies there screaming. His woman stands there quivering. I really haven't got time for this.

'The back door, Molar.'

I hand him Mr Sledge as we move to the kitchen. Molar turns the key and pushes the door out. As I pick up the bath, the scabby infant gives a resentful frown.

'Nothing personal, kiddo.' I assure him, 'It's the price of picking the wrong parents.'

Momma is hearing the call to action loud and clear. While I limber up with a few mild practise swings, she scampers through to the back yard. 'No, please, don't,' she's saying, not taking her eyes of the blue bath.

'Three. Two. One. Blast off,' I say.

Whoo goes the blue plastic bath.

Whoo goes the big-eyed baby.

Up in the clear blue air.

'AAAAGH!' Momma dives to the left. She catches the kid just before the bath whacks her on the head.

'Good guess.' I give a respectful clap. 'Good catch.' If she hadn't taken the path of scrounging and having ugly children by useless men, who knows, she might have had a career as a rugby fullback. Deadbeat Dad is getting the picture in Technicolor now. 'Oh, shit, shit … You dirty cunts. It's in the airing cupboard. You bastards … you—'

We take two hundred euros. No more. The family are clustered together, wailing, as we come down.

I pause at the door to remind him.

'You still owe four hundred euros. Next time, you bring it to me. Or, better still, send the kid.'

It would make you weep, really. The amount of shit in this world caused by stupidity. The moronic fuck had an easy choice and a hard one. And guess which he took? I was going to get my two hundred anyway, but now he's gotta get himself a new TV, and the doctor's visits and physiotherapy, and neither the kid nor his woman is gonna sleep for a week. And it will be next Christmas before he gets fucked in a good way.

Molar closes the front door ever so softly and shakes his big Pole head. 'I dunno you should bust up that guy's leg and throw the kid about like so.' A conscience isn't part of his job description, but, all the same, it's kinda cool that he has one. I reassure him.

'She was always going to catch that brat.'

'How so?'

'She had the motivation. If I threw your kid up in

the air, Molar, you'd catch him.'

'Yeah, and then I'd kill you, man.'

Like this would ever arise. He's got a job, a normal life and stable family environment. He doesn't need crisis finance, so no call for his kid to get flying lessons.

'For real, Charlie. For fucking real, if you ever touch my kids.' Molar says, looking majorly pissed off. I tell him that if he's so concerned for our clients, he should think of becoming a social worker.

'Phut,' he says.

* * *

Thirsty work it is, in the old informal financial services sector. I suggest we have a bevvy at Kielty's; let word of our presence percolate through the town.

Molar drinks neat vodka—all the Poles got tin guts. We clink glasses.

'Cheers, Molar, mate.'

'Why you call me that instead of my name?' He's rightly cranky.

'I can't pronounce your name, mate.' It's Zbigniew Molyzywyzicky (or something). 'Were vowels, like, rationed back in the good old commie days?' I ask him. 'Or did the party only give them out to members?'

'Oh, ho-ho.'

I dribble water in my Bushmills. He drains his glass in a single swallow. Some of my future customers are playing poker for brass money. If I'd stuck around that would be my regular table, with the rest of the futureless fuckers. One catches my eye, blushes like a girl and looks away again. I know him from somewhere, way back. He knows my name, and I couldn't give a shit what his is. There's a moral there.

I used to come in this gaff, back in the day, when I had a thing for Kielty's daughter, Deirdre. She was a sweet kid with a gentle nature and soft skin that bruised easily, and she told me all his secrets. Speak of the devil, and he appears. I say 'Hi', and he glares at me. Brave of him, considering what I know about his fatherly affections.

'This is, like, your home place, boss?' Molar asks.

'You must have your share of shit-holes back in Poland.'

'This is more like Russia, you know; everyone drinking, and all depressed all the time.' I laugh. He thrusts out a thoughtful lower lip. 'Maybe I exaggerate. The bums here dress better.'

As we leave, we see a cop car is pulled up outside. I wave, but they don't wave back. Unfriendly lot, the fuzz. I wait for them to get out of the car, come across and ask us to blow in the bag, if they dare. They sit and stare at us, like kids stare through the glass at the dangerous animals in the zoo. They watch us drive off.

'You brought your licence?' I ask Molar. I made him get an Irish licence when he started working for me. 'See, my name is spelled out there,' he says, holding up the licence to point this out to me.

'I know how to spell it; I can't fucken say it.'

He tells me how to pronounce his name.

'I prefer Molar,' I say. 'It has bite.'

He makes another 'phut' noise.

We finish our morning rounds. The sink estate social media have been active, and our next client is waiting at the top of her cul-de-sac. Three hundred in old notes. She listens humbly when I explain to her the bit that she missed in maths class about compound interest. And how, if you don't watch that fucker, it will go all geometric on you. Defaulter number three has his balance and the hundred over all ready. I like to see that sort of responsible attitude, so I rebate him a tenner to get his kiddie something for Christmas.

It's not all about punishing.

'You're a real Santa Claus,' Molar says.

Cheeky prick.

'You have Christmas in the Third World, do you?'
I ask him.

* * *

Last call is on the top of the hill overlooking the town. I'm
thinking: *Get it done and finish the fuck with this place.* Up here
the big houses look west, away from the mess and the
stench. The church is up there too; and the graveyard. In
my hometown, you make it to the top of the hill in the end.
One way or the other.

Another house call for Doctor Debt.

Toby is a gambler. He can't help it, he says.

Maybe I looked at his cars and his house and his fit
missus and thought here's someone who'll always be able
come up with the readies. But Toby had burned a lot of
cash and friendships before he rolled my way. So, big-time
as he looks, he's the same cheap goods I usually deal in.

Here there's no call for Mr Sledge. Rich folks are
far too well bred to barricade themselves in or leg it out the
back when obligations come calling.

Fran, his partner, opens the door. Fit Fran with her
slutty-barrister look going on.

'You, is it?' she hisses. She's a fine piece of ass with
a nasty attitude. Fuck knows why, as Toby's the tosspot
who's squandering the tampon money, and I'm the
legitimate businessman.

'Toby home?' I ask, in my best house-call manner.

She points towards a room from which the sound
of a sports commentary is coming.

Good old Tobe could give lessons on grace-under-
pressure. Getting on first names immediately. 'Charles …
Charlie. Hi. Come in. No need to call in person, my friend.
Everything is cool.'

He doesn't have my money.

'You were due yesterday, Toby. Is something
wrong?'

'Yesterday?'

Compared with the brain-dead mass of my clients, this guy is Stephen Hawking. This is where—if he were kosher—the money clip would be putting in an appearance. He lies back and looks at the ceiling in a thoughtful sort of way.

He, for sure, doesn't have my cash.

'I'm so sorry, Charlie. And you came all the way out here? You should have called me. I'm going to have it for you, first thing ... Monday ... oh, shit, no ... Monday I have to be in Cork to close a transaction. Tuesday, definitely Tuesday— Oh, wait ... I might have to overnight in Cork. Let's make it Wednesday. Wednesday, to be sure.'

I let him go on. That's nearly another week, and there are Premier league matches and the Christmas racing at Leopardstown. Not forgetting the online casinos in real time, all the time. Just like old fat fuck Hopalong, Toby is taking liberties. The deadbeats and their pathetic scams never surprise me, but I expect more from the top slice, considering that the field is tilted so far towards them in the first place.

Such is life.

I lay out the situation.

'You know Toby, due date is due date. There is only one twenty-third December in this year's calendar. Even for the rich folks. You're past due, which means you owe me a hundred a day surcharge. So, I wouldn't advise stretching it out to Wednesday. You'll owe a lot more money that you still won't have.'

These folks are trained from an early age to cope with sticky social situations. Bob on Benefits goes effing and arm-swinging. Private School Patrick gets depressed that anyone could think he would welsh on them, and puts on the proud-but-wounded voice.

'Oh, that's uncalled for, Charles. (Nice touch.) I made a simple mix-up with the dates and didn't go to the bank. My bad. If it really is that vital, I'll go in on Monday. But you're making such a bloody fuss. I don't see why I should have to pay another three hundred because of an oversight.'

His pocket is as empty as his promise. He knows that. I know it too.

'I need money, or I need security that I will have my money on Monday.'

Another wounded look.

'How long have we been doing business? You know me.'

'I do know you, Toby. Which is why it's a case of cash now, or security.'

He used to bathe in brandy, and he's sipping own-brand water. Who's he kidding? The cupboard is bare. Only one car outside.

That's an idea.

'I'll take the Beemer.'

It's worth far more than the debt, and easily convertible into parts. He can report it stolen—assuming that he's carrying insurance on it.

'Come on, Charles, don't be ridiculous. A forty-nine-grand vehicle for a one-and-a-half grand debt? That's disproportionate. Plus, I need transport. To get your money.'

'I'll send Molar to get you in the car. He gets the money; you keep the car.'

He's screwed, and he knows it. There is no money—Monday, or any other day. He gives me a smile.

'Toss you for it?'

I suppose he thinks he's coming across as a sport and being strong under pressure.

All I'm thinking is: *Twice fuck-all is still fuck-all.*

'Toss me the keys instead.'

He doesn't reach for his pocket.

'Hey, listen. Sit a mo'. I've got a proposal for you.'

He's got a light in his eyes, like an alky who's seen a woman made out of rum. Listening doesn't cost anything, so I sit down.

'You know Fran?'

Sure, I know Fran.

'I see the way you look at her.'

'A cat can look at a queen.'

He tells me it's not a problem for him if Fran and I get together. Matter of fact, he'll set it up for Fran to be waiting for the bald postman's knock. If I just give him a minute. Before he leaves the room, he stops. 'Of course, one favour begets another. How do you feel about a little interest-free period on my obligation? Let's say Wednesday next, I still owe just one and a half grand.'

I go wide-eyed. He goes huffy. As if I have impugned his honour.

'Fair's fair. I mean, I'm not looking to repudiate the loan. I will pay you what I owe you.'

He goes out, and I go search his desk for the second set of keys. My back is turned when I hear the door open. It ain't Foxy Fran standing there in her Agent Provocateurs; its good old Toby in his PRLs and loafers. Sporting a fresh hand-shaped weal on his cheek. So, it seems Fran wasn't cool with getting on her back to get me off Toby's.

I toss the keys into the air and catch them.

'I tried, you know. I gotta get credit for that,' he says.

'Toby, you're all out of credit.'

'Hey, you can't leave me without a car.'

'It's only till Monday. Then we'll be square again. Right?'

We both know that ain't true.

'Right.'

He's pretty deflated showing me out, and Fran doesn't come to say no hard feelings. I think I'll let Molar take the Beemer—seeing me behind the wheel might make Toby want to throw himself in front of it.

I come out, and there is my jeep, and there is Molar.

What I can't see is Toby's 5-series BMW.

'What the fuck,' I shout. 'Where's the Beemer?'

'Woman has taken it. She has flat battery, so I give her a push to get it started. "With my big muscles," she says.' He flexes his biceps, real pleased with himself.

I rattle the key at him. 'I was going to take the fucken thing for security.'

'How I know that?'

'You should have fucken stopped her.'

'She don't owe us money. The guy owes us money. You don't tell me before you go in, you're gonna take the car.'

'Fuck sake.'

'I assault lady, I get arrested. Christmas in jail? No way; I got a family. You tell me to hold on the car, I hold on the car. But you didn't tell me that. I don't touch no woman, no account. She shout rape or something.'

'I've called the cops,' shouts Toby through the letter slot. 'You'll get your money Monday.'

I tear the holly wreath from Toby's front door and kick it onto the lawn.

Molar stands in my way when I go looking for Mr Sledge.

'OK, we come back Monday. Monday, I don't let anyone go anywhere. Don't fuck this up, OK? For Christmas, OK?'

'This is not over,' I shout at Toby's eyes, which are watching us through the letter slot. He knows the shit he's in; I can see the tears forming already.

'Leave it, boss.' Molar pulls me towards the jeep.

* * *

The fuzz has a checkpoint at the bottom of the hill. A big

Guard in a hi-vis jacket and sergeant's stripes holds up his hand. We establish Molar's identity and my identity and ownership of my vehicle, and the fact that it's taxed, insured and etc. He invites me to step out of the vehicle.

Actually, he says, it isn't a traffic stop; he wanted to have a chat. A chat? Back in the day, I'd had lots of chats with the local Guards. Sometimes, just for the hell of it, they'd give my balls a yank. But now that I'm a success in life, a chat is just a chat.

We walk around the back of my jeep. I lean against the tailgate.

'I believe you were visiting here today?'

'Back to the old place. Yeah. Hasn't changed much.'

'You went to visit an old friend, was it? Mr M——?'

'We were at school together. Years ago.'

The copper shakes his big head. Were we now? Yes, we were. Cop Junior, who is looking on over the roof of the squad car, is picking his nose. He burrows away industriously while his senior colleague briefs himself on my busy day.

'Were you congratulating him on his wee boy?'

I smile.

'Just the spitting image of his father. Actually, I went to see Mr M—— because I heard he'd had a bit of an accident. Busted up his ankle quite bad.'

'You were commiserating.'

'I was, Sergeant.'

Seems, the old sarge says, that a neighbour woman had reported some very strange goings on and a lot of shouting and crying. I tell him that it was an emotional reunion. I ask if my friend has complained.

He says no. He shakes his big cop head regretfully, and says no.

'Well, time and tide, Sergeant. Until the next time.'

I watch the cops in the rearview mirror until they merge into the brown and grey background. Until they are just dots.

* * *

Derek's party is well under way, and his missus, Angie, wants to get jiggy. She's got fishy eyes from all the gin, and drinking makes her sweat. Angie tells me all the stuff that Derek gets up to, that he thinks he's keeping really secret. She likes to fondle my balls even more than the cops used to. And, believe me, they could be gentler.

'Hey, baby,' I tell her, 'take it easy.'

A conger eel devours a crab with less violence than Angie gives head. I'm not kidding.

'Oh fuck,' I shout.

'Oh, baby,' she squeals. 'Oh, baby.'

Just the two of us, all cosy in the Portakabin. I'm helping her bring in another case of wine for the party. Except there is no wine in the Portakabin. Just me and Angie and a sound like an iron lung on its last legs.

Later, while she's swigging mouthwash, she says, 'I'm leaving him.' Her face is all shiny with hope.

This is not a plan I approve of.

I ask (though I know the answer), 'Why would you do that, Angie?'

'To be with you.'

'But we are together, baby.'

'Not really. Not like we should be.'

'You need to be patient, baby,' I tell her. 'You don't want to lose all this?'

I don't mean the Portakabin. I'm thinking the ranch house Derek had built for her and their butthead kids, Regal and Destiny. I'm thinking the black credit card that gets her respect from shop assistants and doormen worldwide.

'I'm going to tell him tomorrow. That I can't stand him, and I'm leaving, and you will look after me.'

'How, baby?' I slide my hand up her thigh, and she groans. She pops a tit out in case I want to blow on it. 'You know all the money is tied up in the business; just be patient until I take control. And then we'll be together?'

We'll be like sausage and skin.

'I have no inner life with him, Charlie. He starves my soul.'

What! Did she really say that? She did. She even repeats it. 'Derek starves my soul.'

'I know, baby. I hate him too.'

'You don't know what it's like to be ass-fucked by him.'

'Believe me, I do.'

'No, you don't. I mean actually getting it in the arse. I want to be with a real man; not a gay one in denial. I want to be with *you*.'

She cries a bit, and I tell her to be brave.

'He wants us to go to Lanzarote on Stephens's Day for a family holiday. I won't go. I hate him.'

'Look, go on the holiday, and I promise we'll be together after.'

'Promise?'

'Promise. Just don't piss him off right now.'

'You know, when he's doing his sicko stuff, I'll be thinking of you, Charlie.'

'And I'll be feeling it with you, baby.'

We go back to the house, and Angie goes upstairs to change and put her face back on. Molar knows that I've been giving my partner's wife something to chew over. It worries him.

'You know, you don't think things out so well sometimes.'

'I can't control my urges, Molar. But if you want to help me, introduce me to your wife's friend, Margareta.'

Margareta works in the local Lidl. She's got those classic Polish features: blonde hair that goes all the way to

59

the roots, cheekbones you could fold paper over, that cheeky curl in the mouth.

Molar shakes his head, 'I don't think so. She's a nice person.'

'Ain't I nice?'

Molar does his 'phut' face.

I could ask Margareta out myself, but I prefer having fun with this sombre Slavic fucker. I know he'll tell his missus, and she'll get freaked. You ever see how those Polish women get into their men folk. Like when a little terrier gets after a big dog. Arr-arr-arr-arr-arr-arr.

'She'll love me.' I clap him on the back. 'And she'll be so thankful to you for introducing her to a real man.'

'No, this is another of your bad jokes. Serious now. Stop it.'

I blow him a kiss and wander away.

And wander right into Derek, host of this evening's entertainment. He is circulating through the lounge in a spangly red velvet jacket—the kind a gay cocktail-bar pianist would wear to his own wake—with a crystal brandy balloon in his hand. As if the overall effect isn't laugh-out-loud enough, he's toting a cigar thick enough to hammer nails with. He gives me a friendly wave, 'You enjoying the party, Charlie? Anything you need, I'm sure that Angie will see to you.'

Derek's too stupid to mean anything by that. I wave, and, *shit*, what does he do but come over.

'Didn't go too well today, I hear.' He breathes halitosis and cigar smoke over me, moaning on about GBH, cops, terrorising the community, yadda, yadda, yadda.

'I prefer to do my business unobtrusive, like.' He tells me this, dressed like he is.

'Unobtrusive? Derek, they could sit you on a slice of angel cake to scare the tarantulas away.'

'That supposed to mean something, Professor?' he

laughs. He's an uneducated fucker, is Derek. 'What I mean is, you're slipping my friend. You send one of our clients to hospital, and you go away from another call with your hands empty, and your face as long as your dick.'

'Angie's been talking to you then?' I shouldn't have said it, but he gave me the opening. And fuck it, he was annoying me.

He pulls back like he's thinking of hitting me, does some more thinking and says, 'You ought to watch yourself, Charlie. You think you're clever, but really, you're getting sloppy. Sloppy. Sloppy.'

He blows a raspberry at me, like a kid would.

That's the truth of it: he's a big, dopey, stupid kid.

Soon after, Angie appears at the top of the staircase in her beach wrap and announces hot tub cocktail hour. This the signal for all except the most depraved to grab their coats and leave. Not that I don't like a bit of water sports now and then, but I have stuff to do tomorrow.

* * *

Christmas Day. The day when peace reigns throughout the world. The day they even stop wars for. I've made my list and checked it twice. And top of the naughty side is old Toby Loafers, so today he'll be visited by the Anti-Santa.

I ring Molar.

'Job on.'

'Huh.'

Old Molar sounds like he's giving the brain cells that didn't drown in vodka some mouth-to-mouth resuscitation.

'Job on. I'll be rolling your way in a bit.'

'Huh,' he says again.

I'm bright and breezy this fine cold winter's morning, zipping down to Poletown. Quiet streets, light traffic. Just the perfect conditions for the quick incursion I've got planned. *You ought to see me, Derek, you fat fuck. Bet you're on your knees in your marble bathroom right now, talking to Jesus on the Great White Telephone. Sloppy, eh. Just you wait!*

'An hour tops,' I tell an angry Mrs Molar, who is giving me grief, which being in Polish, is not really grief as such, just background chatter (though she's got some fairly easy to understand sign language going on too). Seems to me Molar is happy to get a couple of hours out of the firing line. The little Molars are cuties: girl and boy, blonde and blond. I tell Mrs Molar that she has lovely children.

Molar doesn't say much on the journey. We stop once so he can spew in the ditch. Old Wise Charlie knows what's up. 'You got in the hot tub with Angie, Molar. Don't deny it. I can tell by the look of shame on your face.'

'Oh, God,' he says.

'Ask Margareta to go on a date with me, and I won't tell Mrs M.'

He groans.

'Bet Angie lured you into one of her aquatic scenarios? American nuclear submarine trapped in the undersea cavern? Right? She loves that one.'

'Shit.'

'I bet she got all the seamen out safely.'

'Fuck off, serious. Not funny scene. No way.'

'You up to driving?'

He holds his hand out and flutters it. 'So-so.'

We zoom on up to Toby's place, and I stop a short distance back from the gate. 'OK, Molar, you take my jeep back to yours, take Mrs Molar and the kiddies for a Christmas drive. Make it up to them for being such a filthy boy last night.'

I get out and wave him away.

I pop Toby's keys up and down in my hand as I stroll up. Taking my time, this is one to savour.

Old Hard-Luck Toby is not so hard up after all. To judge by the profusion of executive style transportation gathered in front of his little castle. Sounds of merriment waft out to me.

Plip.

The BMW winks four little amber lights at me, like it knows that it's time for drivies.

Toby's given the car a wash and valet. Summer pine forest fragrance inside. I approve. A full tank of fuel, too, generous Tobe. I start the engine and engage reverse. I reverse right up to the door.

Two toots of the horn, people come to the windows.

I wave.

Now this is the sort of party I should be invited to.

No fat old gits in shiny togs.

No flabby tarts overflowing their spandex.

Gentlefolk in high grade occupations fitted out in designer ensembles.

I give another toot of approval.

They wave back.

I see Fran. In figure-hugging blue, showing a thin slice of perfectly tanned bosom.

I approve.

I blow her a kiss.

Fran starts running for the front door

I see Tobe.

I make a finger pistol and go 'pow'.

Tobe drops his drink.

Tobe starts running for the back door.

The guests are looking first one way, then the other. I bet not one of them guesses who I am.

The front door opens and out comes Fran. Waving her pretty little fist, jangling her bracelets and shouting her disapproval of my crashing the Christmas shindig. This piece of grief not being given in Polespeak, I get the key points right away. Fran is certainly forthright and concise.

Love to chat, but time presses.

The silky 200-brake horsepower BMW overhead

cam powerplant engine eases me smoothly away. Fran hitches up her skirt and does a pretty good job of keeping up over the first ten metres or so. Fabulous legs, I must say; everything about her is class, class, class. People cluster at the windows, looking on, mouths open. What an intriguing talking point I've provided for dessert time. This'll have them queuing for invites to next year's Yuletide at Toby's.

I soon catch up on Toby, who's haring off down the hill. I give a friendly toot-toot and he dives into a drain.

There's a gift-wrapped bottle of brandy in the glove compartment, which is really too much. So sweet and unexpected. A little bit of me hopes that, when Molar comes calling tomorrow, Toby will have the cash on hand.

Derek is waiting outside my gaff when I pull up in the Beemer. Fran seems to have gone all the way to the top of the organisation with her customer service complaint. I'm surprised that a gangster like Derek is in her contact list, but those posh birds do like a bit of rough.

Fran is also a cheeky little liar.

'It's not her car, it's his.' I show Derek the registration, which Tobe keeps in the glove box, with the insurance cert—along with a box or Strepsils and a three-pack of ridged condoms. (Somehow, I don't see Fran as a French tickler sort of girl, but lately I've been wrong about a lot of things.)

'She says she's got the money and wants me to bring the car back right now.'

'She doesn't, unless she's taken up a collection at their Christmas party.'

'Come on, Charlie, be nice.'

He holds his hand out. Having gone to the trouble of getting the car, a part of me feels like arguing. But another part of me is saying that it's about time that the fat fucker did some actual on-the-street business. And I quite like the image of Fran giving fat Derek an uppercut with her diamond-encrusted fist when he tries to take the car away again. He doesn't ask me to tag along. He's either supremely confident or supremely deluded.

I swap the BMW keys for those of his car and tell him I'll see him Monday.

* * *

Stephen's Day I go to the races. Come out about even, which is not bad for a day at the track. Not a tinkle on the phone from dawn to dusk, which is even better. Not Derek with more orders. Not Molar with some stupid work query. Not Angie with her need for affection. Every day should be like this.

Monday rolls around. And guess what? There is Tobe's BMW sitting in the yard by the Portakabin. Derek left a voicemail that he and Angie have gone to the Canaries for some quality family time. I think about ringing his mobile and teasing him about Tobe and Fran. With whom I now have a pressing appointment.

'You want I come too?' Molar asks.

No way, Ho-zay; this victory is mine to savour alone.

'No need. In the unlikely event that Tobe has the money, he can give me a lift back.'

'You want I get your tools from the jeep?'

'No, I think I've got this covered.'

'You're not going to hit him, right?'

It's amazing how little the guy knows about the class system. I guess it's only lately that these former commie countries have got theirs back up and running. They're learning again that the poor are like children—to get them to do what you want, you have to smack them. A middle-class boy like Toby, on the other hand, only needs to be asked. You have to be insistent, of course, but in a nice way.

As I'm driving over, I can't help thinking about Fran and Tobe's little party that I gatecrashed. If I find out that they paid cash up front for the canapes and champagne, then I really will be miffed. Because that means that when he and Fran were giving me the run-around on Christmas Eve, they actually had my money. Naughty, naughty.

I never get to ask them about this, because who should be waiting for me at the top of the hill, but good old Sergeant Hi-Vis and sidekick Cop Junior. Chests pushed out and right hands held up to stop me.

'I heard you were coming back again,' the old copper says. 'You can't seem to get enough of us.'

'I been away so long, and now I can't stay away, eh?' I say, keeping the mood light.

'This is not your car, Charlie.' Top detection there, Sarge.

'It's a loaner. I got stuck at Toby's Christmas Day party, and he saw me right for a ride home. Did me a real favour. He's a proper gent, is our Toby.'

'Well, now, Charlie,' says the copper, 'it's Toby asked us to keep an eye out for you. He's worried that you might represent a danger to him.'

'Oh.'

'People say you're inclined to swing a sledge around when there's no demolition to be done.'

'Someone is lying to the police. Isn't that an offence?'

'You wouldn't mind if I take a look in the boot, just to make sure that the only tools back there are the ones that came with the car.'

Cops Do Comedy. That's a reality show just waiting to happen.

'Knock yourself out,' I tell him.

So, he pops the trunk, but I don't hear him have a rummage.

A minute later, Cop Junior is asking me to step out of the car and come around to the back with him.

Old Derek, the skinflint, hadn't taken Angie to the Canaries with him after all. Angie usually has a lot to say for herself, but just this moment, it looks like I'll have to explain to the cops how it is that she's got all tied up and dead and riding around with me in a borrowed car. And industrious Cop Junior finds another friend of mine is keeping Angie company. Mr Sledge—way in the back and out of sight under a travel rug. And all bloody too, like Angie.

Goodbye Bella Bailey

Alix Moore-O'Grady

Friday, 9 March 2018
Jubilee Line, London Underground, 7.10 a.m.

Tom was lucky to get a seat that morning. The train was packed to capacity and reeking with that combination of stale air, sodden overcoats and body odour that is peculiar to the London Underground.

Shutting his eyes, he remembered how Sophie had looked when he left her earlier, fast asleep, curled up like a field mouse in their bed, clouds of dark hair veiling her face, her arms folded protectively around her belly. A sudden and unexpected wave of emotion surged through his body, forcing an audible sob from his throat. Feeling the hot scald of tears gathering behind his eyelids, he shook his head like a dog to try and rid himself of the feeling that suddenly swamped him. An increasingly familiar feeling that he was adrift; that all was not as it should be.

Frowning slightly, he gave himself a mental ticking-off for this ridiculous show of weakness. He was thirty-eight years old, happily married, about to become a father for the first time, and everything in his life was perfect. Sophie was happy and healthy, looking forward to becoming a mum, loving their new home in Kew and working hard to grow her catering business. Tick those boxes.

'So, how am I?' he wondered, reckoning that all the ingredients for his guaranteed wellbeing had already been covered by the 'Sophie checklist'. If she was happy, he was happy—that went without saying. Sure, he sometimes—actually often—missed their mad, crazy London life: the trendy loft in Chelsea, the Porsche Boxster they'd recently swapped for a Renault Scenic, the buzz that came from stepping out of your front door straight into the mad, intoxicating hubbub of the city. But the anticipation of becoming a father and raising his family in safe, unpolluted suburbia where the neighbours were unlikely to be drug trafficking or doing moonlight flits every five minutes, well, that was all good. Wasn't it? And there he was again: the doubting version of Tom who kept asking those same difficult questions. Was he ready to become a father? Was he quite as happy about the baby as Sophie was? Had he been as supportive to Sophie as he should have been?

Irritated with himself for indulging in what his late father would have described as 'self-serving navel-gazing', he scrubbed his fingers through his carefully gelled hair, trying to ease the tension in his scalp. In doing so, he created a series of tiny, stiffening spikes which would later resist all of his attempts to flatten them into submission when preparing for the Friday lunchtime partners' meeting. The feeling of dread that accompanied this latest thought was like a physical blow; he swallowed hard to prevent the re-emergence of his breakfast. Pulling his case from the floor, he flicked through its tightly packed contents until he found the email from Gil Cooper, his CEO, outlining the arrangements for the coming evening.

The Annual Wealth and Finance Awards
The Savoy Hotel, Strand, London
19.30   Drinks Reception
20.30   Dinner
22.00   Awards Ceremony

'Christ!' he thought, remembering the same event taking place at the Savoy last year as if it was yesterday; and the year before that, and before that. As the train screeched and shuddered its way into Southwark station, Tom realised that he was bored. Not just slightly bored but catastrophically, monumentally, terminally bored with his dream ticket of a job with its watertight contract, excellent salary and index-linked pension. Bored with his perfectly planned and privileged life and terrified because he didn't have the faintest idea what to do about it.

* * *

Friday, 9 March 2018
The Lancaster Room, The Savoy, Strand, London,
10.50 p.m.

Tom tried not to sob into his glass of claret as he watched his nemesis, Peter Crawley, flash his nicotine-yellow teeth in a self-satisfied smirk as he received the Wealth Manager of the Year award. OK, Tom had to admit that Crawley had managed to sign off a few more deals than him that year, but that was mainly because the other man's patch included all the private nursing homes in the affluent Home Counties. Tom imagined that the sight of Crawley's vulpine face and his boisterous, bullying presence would be enough to frighten many of the captive, moneyed residents into signing on the dotted line without too much pause for thought.

Tom, by contrast, had spent the past endless year slogging his way through the client backlog of a colleague who had left the company in disgrace. It had been a thankless task, requiring every ounce of his considerable charm and charisma to win back the confidence of the clients and restore the reputation of the company. But he'd had to concede defeat on several occasions, which had severely knocked his confidence. He had been brought up by his father to believe that second-best wasn't good enough, and that failure was unacceptable. No wonder he felt so bitter and morose. The evening had been a nightmare thus far, and all he could think about was the twenty-five years or so that lay ahead of him before retirement or death—and at this particular moment he didn't much care which—released him from this corporate version of purgatory.

As he sat trying to ignore his pissed, self-congratulating colleagues fawning around Golden Balls Crawley in sycophantic adoration, he noticed Gil Cooper leave the table to talk to a couple who were sitting at the bar. The man was tall and thick-set, his tuxedo hanging on him like a flour sack and his bow tie askew. He looked like a boxer or a scrum half, his nose bent and flattened, an ugly scar under his left eye. But the woman next to him, perched on a bar stool laughing at something he'd just said, was beautiful: blonde, slim and with eyes so pale that they shimmered like silver in the dim lighting of the room. It was obvious from the amount of handshaking and back-thumping that was going on between the two men that Gil was being congratulated, and Tom watched for a minute hoping that his boss would settle in with them and give him an opportunity to escape and go home.

Suddenly, the woman glanced over and smiled at Tom. It was a sexy smile. The sort of smile that Sophie, in the halcyon pre-pregnancy era, used to give him before enticing him into bed and administering the full works. Lost in the memory, he smiled back at the woman, mentally awarding her a nine out of ten. She held his gaze for a minute before sliding off the bar stool and walking over to a small alcove at the side of the room. Settling herself onto a velvet sofa, she beckoned him over. Intrigued, Tom tossed back the remainder of his claret and walked over to her. Close up, she was slightly older than he had first imagined—late thirties, maybe—but so stunningly beautiful he found himself unable to stop looking at her, and he adjusted his score to ten out of ten.

'Hello,' she drawled, her voice low and cultured, her smile slightly cool, as if she was trying to decide whether he deserved the full effect.

He held out his right hand. 'Hello, yourself. I'm Tom Wright.' His eyes automatically flicked down to her left hand. No wedding band, no diamonds. Tick those boxes.

Placing her slim hand into his, she murmured, 'Delighted to meet you, Tom Wright. I'm Bella Bailey,' and gently pulled his hand until he was sitting next to her.

Her touch triggered a weird sensation in Tom's stomach which burned its way up his torso and made him blush like a schoolboy. 'Good to meet you, Bella. What brings you here this evening?'

She gave him a mischievous smile, 'I'm talent-spotting.'

Tom grinned back. 'Have you spotted any?'

She studied his face for minute and said, 'I have.'

He knew he should put on the brakes, but couldn't resist asking, 'What are you looking for?'

'Someone who knows this business inside out. Someone who doesn't mind pushing back the boundaries and isn't scared to take a risk or two. Someone looking for a bit of excitement.' Widening her eyes, she asked, 'Do you know anyone like that, Tom?'

He laughed. 'Wow. That sounded like a proposition.'

'It could be.'

Finding her extreme scrutiny suddenly uncomfortable, Tom asked, 'Which company are you with?'

'Bailey's Wealth-Care. I own it with my brother Jeremy over there.' She nodded towards the bar where Gil was still talking to Mr Ugly.

Tom frowned. 'I haven't come across the name before.'

'That's because we don't advertise like the big companies. We work with high-worth clients and businesses who value their privacy. Most of our new business is by word-of-mouth recommendation.'

'Sounds interesting,' Tom said politely.

'Seriously, Bailey's *is* different,' Bella said. 'A bit

more—let's say—exciting.' She leant closer to him, releasing a fragrant burst of expensive perfume, and whispered, 'Do you find the thought of taking risks exciting, Tom?'

'Life can get pretty boring if you're not prepared to take any risks.'

'Do you like working with Gil?'

'Gil's great.' Tom was extremely fond of Gil; he appreciated his blunt, no-nonsense management style which was so typical of his boss's Yorkshire heritage. 'I've known him for years. He worked for my father back in the day, and he's been really good to me. But …'

'What?' breathed Bella.

'… the consultancy's a bit old-school. We've just won the top award tonight on the back of providing advice to old codgers, for Christ's sake. What does that say about us?'

Bella shot him a sympathetic look. 'Tell me.'

Tom sighed heavily. 'We play it by the book, straight down the line, with very little room for creativity.'

There was a short silence, and then Bella said, 'I spotted you the minute I walked in.'

Tom waited for the usual flirtatious platitudes.

'You're the image of my late father,' she continued.

Surprised, he asked, 'Is that a good thing?'

'It is. He was the most beautiful man in every way. I miss him.'

Seeing the genuine pain in her eyes, Tom asked gently, 'When did he die?'

'Oh, a long time ago. I was very young.'

'I'm sorry. That must have been hard.'

'Harder than you can imagine.' Unexpectedly, she gently cradled his hand in hers and started to draw circles in the centre of his palm with her forefinger until Tom, finding the sensation so shockingly intimate, so intensely erotic, tried to pull his hand away. Giving a low, throaty laugh, Bella stroked her finger up the inside of his wrist, resting it for a moment on the place where his pulse leapt and jumped, before releasing his hand and saying lightly, 'I hope I haven't embarrassed you with my ramblings?'

He gazed at her. 'Of course not.'

She sighed. 'How disappointing. I must be losing my touch. Ah well, an early night, I think.'

As they stood, Tom turned to her and said, 'It was good to meet you, Bella Bailey. You've been the only bright spot in an extremely dark and gloomy evening.'

Bella regarded him seriously. 'There's a bottle of vintage Dom Perignon waiting in my suite. Would you share it with me? There's nothing lonelier than drinking champagne on one's own.'

Still reeling from the shock of her touch, unable to keep up with her mercurial changes of mood and wanting to feel her skin against his again, Tom simply nodded.

As they waited for the lift, standing carefully apart from each other, she asked, 'Is there somebody waiting for you at home?'

He hesitated for a beat, before replying, 'My wife. No doubt she'll be enjoying having the bed to herself and watching something on Netflix.'

'Do you have to rush back?'

'No,' he replied, knowing he wouldn't return home that night, already composing a suitable lie that he could text to Sophie, telling himself that this was just what he needed—an exciting but casual interlude with no strings on either side.

Bella said calmly, 'I wonder whether you'd consider meeting my brother and me sometime soon to discuss a role that we're currently developing? I think you'd be perfect for it.'

'What sort of role?' Tom asked curiously.

'Reeling in the clients,' she said with an enigmatic smile, as she effortlessly reeled him in.

* * *

Saturday, 10 March 2018
River Room, The Savoy, Strand, London, 7.26 a.m.

Tom rolled onto his side and winced as sharp pain flashed through his head. Opening his sleep-glued eyes, he groggily registered acres of velvety carpet and a gleaming mahogany dressing table on which sat an ice bucket containing a couple of upended champagne bottles. A fleeting memory of pale, naked skin and cool, confident fingers flickered through his mind before an intense wave of nausea overwhelmed him. Struggling upright, he swung his legs over the edge of the bed, sucking in a deep breath as the sudden movement caused his head to throb with a sickening intensity. Glancing round the room, he saw his clothes were neatly folded over the back of an armchair and that somebody, presumably Bella, had placed a glass of water and a packet of aspirin on the bedside table. Reaching out, he picked up the glass and saw the folded sheet of paper that had been tucked neatly under it.

> **Dear Tom,**
> **Sorry I had to leave without saying goodbye.**
> **Last night was a wonderful treat, but I don't want you spoiling the memory by getting an attack of guilt. So let's pretend it never happened and start again as friends. I never mix business with pleasure, and I was serious about that job I told you about. I'll be in touch.**
> **Bella xx**

He went into the bathroom and stood under the shower, allowing the powerful jets of warm water to ease the pain in his head. After scrubbing himself from top to toe, he shrugged on one of the heavy towelling robes hanging on the bathroom door, went back into the bedroom, lay on the bed and finally allowed himself to remember.

They'd had sex twice—the first so fast and urgent, their hands and mouths greedy with need, there hadn't been time to remove their clothes or get onto the bed. The second, a while later, had been slow and sensual, punctuated with champagne-perfumed kisses and feather-light touches which seared the skin, creating such an exquisite tension that when it was over, they just lay and gazed at each other.

Tom smiled as he remembered how assured she had been, calmly telling him what she liked, how she wanted it and how—once she was satisfied—she'd turned her back on him and instantly slept like a well-fed cat. He'd turned away from her then and checked his mobile for messages, a sudden stab of guilt making him fearful that Sophie may have been trying to contact him. But there were no messages, and he'd briefly imagined his wife tucked up safely in their marital bed before turning back to Bella and carefully folding himself around her.

He picked up Bella's note and read it again before screwing it up and throwing it in the direction of the wastepaper basket, laughing out loud as it landed bang on target. Last night had been fun, the sex had been great, and Bella had chased the clouds away. Her job offer was flattering, but he knew he couldn't risk seeing her again. Satisfied that his equilibrium was fully restored, he lay back on the pillows and waited for the rush of relief that would surely follow this decision.

* * *

The longed-for feeling of relief eluded him for the remainder of the weekend. At first, he put it down to the lingering after effects of his hangover, and to the fact that Sophie was sofa-bound and listless with the daily sickness that attacked her as soon as she got out of bed, and hung around like an unwelcome guest for the remainder of the day. By Sunday afternoon he was once again experiencing that sense of being disconnected, of yearning for greener grass and to be rid of the enveloping boredom.

He and Sophie went to bed early that night, and as he lay next to her in the darkness, breathing in the scent of lemons and vanilla that lingered on her skin, he said, 'I'm sorry I've been such a misery this weekend. I hate to admit it, but watching Crawley get that award crucified me. I'm dreading going in to work tomorrow and having to listen to the odious toad bragging about it all.'

Sophie switched on her bedside light and turned to look at him, her eyes full of loving concern. 'Stop beating yourself up, darling. Why do you care about the stupid award or creepy Crawley when you've got so much more going for you?' She began to gently stroke her hand up and down his chest, murmuring, 'You're young, good-looking, clever, successful …' Her hand moved lower. '… and you're sexy.' She giggled. 'Actually, you're very sexy…' Until Tom stopped her words with his mouth and finally found the relief he so desperately needed.

* * *

Monday, 12 March 2018
Jubilee Line, London Underground, 7.52 a.m.

As he sat on the train the next morning, a text from Bella pinged provocatively into his phone.

> **Come to see Jem and me at ten on Wednesday morning. I've sent you an email with our address, etc.**

He thought for a few minutes before replying.

> **Hi Bella, it's good of you and your brother to take such an interest in me, but I've thought about it over the weekend, and I've decided to stay in my current job. All the best, Tom.**

Satisfied that he'd concluded the matter, he unfolded his paper and tried to distract himself by reading an article by Boris Johnson describing the pleasures of cycling in London. He had just finished reading the second sentence for the third time when his phone pinged again.

> **Tom Wright! You absolutely have to come on Wednesday. I won't take no for an answer! I haven't stopped talking about you all weekend, and Jem is so excited to meet you. Don't let me down!!! PS Don't worry about Gil—I can square it with him.**

Fuming, he shot back:

> **I'm perfectly capable of dealing with Gil myself!!!**

To which she immediately replied:

> **I find touchy men so sexy! See you on Wednesday.**

He spent the rest of the journey stewing in a mixture of indignation and lust, while conducting a silent, irate conversation with himself. How dare she be so presumptuous, assuming that he would just drop everything to go and work for her and her ugly brother? How dare she refuse to take no for an answer—he'd made himself clear, hadn't he? How dare she accuse him of being touchy? How dare she be so fucking sexy that he didn't know how he was going to wait until Wednesday to see her? Not that he was going to take things any further— he'd simply listen to what she and Jem had to say, thank them for their interest and walk away.

* * *

Wednesday, 14 March 2018
Bailey's Wealth-Care, 14 Compton Square, London,
W1, 10.50 a.m.

Bailey's Wealth-Care's headquarters was an elegant Georgian house in a quaint little square tucked away between Bond Street Tube station and Hyde Park. It was a seriously wealthy area, and Tom imagined how impressed Bailey's clients would be by the house, which must be worth millions.

He felt a surge of excitement as he strode up the short flight of steps leading to the imposing front door. Just as he reached the top step, the door was flung open, and Jem Bailey appeared clutching a doughnut in one hand and a large white cake box in the other. He looked as if he'd rolled out of bed and into his jeans and polo shirt without bothering to shower or brush his hair, although he'd clearly made some attempt to shave—as evidenced by the large wad of bloodstained tissue stuck to his chin.

Much to Tom's amazement, Jem stepped forward and pulled him into the sort of man-hug usually only given by close family members at Christmas and funerals and exclaimed, 'Good to meet you at last, man.' This was followed by arm-punching, hysterical yelps of laughter and a non-stop stream of chatter which was impossible to follow given the fact that Jem was busily working his way through the jam doughnut without bothering to shut his mouth or, as far as Tom could see, swallow between bites. It was a truly extraordinary welcome.

Tom followed Jem into the entrance hall and looked round in admiration at the huge oak staircase and the vast expanse of highly polished black and white floor tiles.

Jem swallowed his latest jammy mouthful and mumbled, 'Kind of cool, isn't it? We kept a lot of the original features when we were renovating it. There's a servants' staircase and a dumb waiter which we use for transporting the client files. The kitchen has the original bell pulls. I'll show you round later.'

'Tom! You're here!' Bella's voice echoed across the hall as she walked down the stairs. She was wearing a jade green silk dress, cut high in the neck, with small cap sleeves. It should have been a demure little dress, but the way it clung to her high, round breasts, its swirly skirt showing off her long, shapely legs, meant that it was—in fact—brazenly provocative. Stepping into the hall, she walked over and shook his hand. 'Welcome to Bailey's. When are you going to join us?' she said, smiling at her own boldness.

He couldn't help but smile back, and decided that he'd never seen eyes quite like hers—silvery, pellucid and almost other-worldly. Suddenly—shockingly—he remembered those eyes gazing into his that night at the Savoy and felt himself becoming aroused. He turned away from her abruptly and made a nonsensical comment about a murky, uninteresting watercolour of a simpering female that was hanging nearby, while sternly willing his body not to betray him.

Bella laughed and said, 'It's completely ghastly! Part of a job lot we inherited when we bought the place.' Glancing at her brother, she cried, 'Good grief, Jem, what on earth do you look like?'

Jem gave her a jammy grin and held out the box of doughnuts. 'Have one; they're still warm!'

Ignoring the box, Bella looked pointedly at his feet. 'Did you forget your shoes?'

Giving an almighty swallow, Jem put the box down on a side table, saying vaguely, 'My feet get hot when I'm thinking. Not sure why. Anyway, I was just going to tell Tom about the bank in Nauru and my idea for—'

Bella interrupted him sharply. 'Tom's not going to be involved in that side of the business. He'll be working with me on the individual wealth clients.' Touching Jem's face gently, she said in a much softer voice, 'You appear to be bleeding, darling. Go and freshen up while I have a chat with Tom.'

Showing no signs of being annoyed at his dismissal, Jem touched his face absently, saying, 'Will do. See you later.' He grabbed the doughnut box and disappeared through a door at the back of the hall.

Bella smiled at Tom. 'Apologies for Jem's unconventional appearance. He's a complete genius. I never know what he's going to do or say from one minute to the next, but the clients love him, especially the Chinese!' She stood for a moment, as if she wasn't sure what to do next, and then said hesitantly, 'I wasn't sure you'd come.'

Tom grinned at her. 'Neither was I until I arrived!'

She shook her head and laughed. 'You're just like my father; can't resist a challenge. Fancy that tour?'

* * *

Half an hour later they finished the tour in Bella's office, which was small but comfortable and furnished with an antique partners' desk and a couple of matching chairs. Bella led Tom over to a battered leather chesterfield which had been placed in front of the dormer window.

'Wow!' said Tom, taking in the distant view of Hyde Park and the Serpentine, its water glittering in the bright morning sunshine.

'Quite something, isn't it?' said Bella, sitting down next to him. 'Anyway, I'm glad you decided to come today. I was scared that I'd put you off with my shameful behaviour at the Savoy.' She gave an embarrassed laugh. 'I don't normally go around picking up married men. The only excuse I can give is that it had been a long time, and I found you so …'

Tom looked at her as she sat, head bowed, long blonde hair concealing her face, and said gently, 'We both wanted it, Bella. You're incredibly beautiful, but I shouldn't have done it. I have a wife whom I adore and a baby on the way. I'm totally committed to them, and if that is in any way a problem, then there's no point in taking this discussion any further.'

Bella gave him a wistful smile. 'A new baby—how wonderful.' Looking down at her tightly clasped hands, she said quietly, 'Thank you for being so honest. I meant what I said in my note about not mixing work with pleasure. It's a particular rule of mine.' Looking back up at him, she said hesitantly, 'Are you still interested in the job?'

Tom regarded her seriously. 'I could be, but I'm still not entirely sure what it involves.'

* * *

For the next hour Bella described what she and Jem had created. 'Jem's the financial wizard. He's worked for some of the top private banks, knows all the key players. What he doesn't know about asset management and growing wealth isn't worth knowing. Once clients are signed up, Jem and his team work with them to decide how best to invest their money and ensure they get the best return for it.'

Tom asked, 'And what is your role?'

'I suppose I'd describe myself as the "scout". I do a lot of networking and socialising, attend loads of conferences, seminars and parties. It's amazing what you can pick up when you know the right people.' She laughed. 'I'm a bit like one of those specially trained dogs who can sniff out truffles; except, in my case I sniff out people with money.'

Tom decided that he loved the way her eyes crinkled at the edges when she laughed and covered his resulting confusion by asking, 'Who are Bailey's clients?'

'They fall into two distinct market segments. Firstly the super-rich—and, believe me, there are plenty of them—who are happy for us to take the pickings from their table so long as we employ enough smoke and mirrors to minimise their tax liability.'

He frowned. 'What do you mean by "the pickings"?'

'As you know, the money markets constantly shift up and down by a percentage or two. Jem follows those shifts and tries to ensure that he catches the crest of the wave when he invests clients' money. That's where the magic comes in because he is amazingly accurate. We shave a percentage off the top as our profit.'

Tom nodded. 'That makes sense. What sort of percentage do you take?'

'It varies depending on size of investment.'

'And the second market segment?'

'It tends to be people who experience sudden and unexpected wealth, either by inheriting it or winning it on the lottery or through some other type of gambling activity. Many of them have no idea what to do with the money and are at risk of blowing it or becoming sitting targets for being ripped off.'

'How would I fit into all of this if I decided to join you?'

'Your role would be to lead these newly rich, highly confused individuals to the "promised land", otherwise known as Bailey's Wealth-Care.' Bella picked up her coffee cup and took a sip before saying casually, 'Would you like to know the package we'd be offering you?'

Tom thought about Sophie who had no idea that he was thinking of changing his job; considered the financial security that he had with Gil and the consultancy; and contemplated the risk he would be taking if he came to Bailey's to work closely with Bella. He said, 'Yes please … although I'm not at all certain that I'm ready for such a move,' and listened intently as Bella made him an offer that nobody in their right mind would ever refuse.

* * *

Later that day Tom told Gil he was leaving the consultancy. Gil immediately waived his three-month period of notice saying, 'If your heart isn't in it anymore, you're no use to me. But a word of caution, if I may?

'I'd welcome your opinion,' answered Tom.

Gil continued. 'I'm not saying that there is anything necessarily illegal about what they do at Bailey's. Despite his scruffy, uncouth appearance, Jem Bailey is one of the most brilliant financial magicians I've met in a long time. But he sails close to the wind, and word on the street is that Bailey's push risk to the extreme when investing their clients' money. Let's just say that I'm not sure how closely they adhere to the regulations laid down by the Financial Conduct Authority, or how well they'd stand up to scrutiny.'

'Noted,' said Tom. 'What do you know about Bella Bailey?'

Gil said bluntly, 'She's a bundle of badly damaged goods disguised in fancy packaging. I'd say that she's the one to watch carefully.'

Tom asked, 'Can you be more specific?'

Gil face was grim. 'Come off it, Tom. You know how conservative our industry is, and that there are rarely "specifics" given when it comes to market intelligence or—as I prefer to call it—"gossip". At the moment, you're squeaky clean. You have a good reputation for being an honest broker. That's worth a lot in our industry, and once your integrity is gone, there's no getting it back. But ... you're old enough to make your own judgement, and I sense that you've clearly made your mind up to go and nothing that I'm going to say to you is going to change that, is it?'

Tom shook his head. 'I'm sorry, Gil. I think I need a change.'

Gil sighed. 'Fair enough. I can't tell you how sorry I am that you're leaving us. But if things don't work out, please don't be too proud to come and tell me. I'll always try to help you the way your father helped me.'

Tom hesitated for a minute, feeling a flicker of doubt, before standing and offering his hand to Gil.

The older man pulled Tom into a warm embrace. 'Keep in touch.'

* * *

That evening he told Sophie about the new job. His timing was bad because she'd been sick as a dog all day and looked thoroughly out of sorts—her hair dull and lank, face slightly puffy and the waistband of her jeans held together with a safety pin.

She listened to him without interruption, looking increasingly worried, and, after he finished speaking, had assumed a hurt expression and said, 'Why didn't you discuss this with me before making your decision? Honestly, Tom, I hardly recognise you these days.'

Surprised by this uncharacteristic outburst from his normally supportive and sympathetic wife, Tom stared at her silently and thought: *Right back at you, Soph. I hardly recognise you! Where the hell has my gorgeous, sexy wife gone?* and wondered whether he'd ever get her back again.

* * *

April 2018
Bailey's Wealth-Care, 14 Compton Square, London, W1

Tom soon discovered that working at Bailey's was an informal affair compared to his previous job. Jem treated the place like a cross between a playground and a sweetshop and had furnished the building in an eclectic style—which seemed to chime in with his eccentric appearance, but was somewhat out of keeping with the beautiful Georgian house. On his induction tour, Tom discovered that the boardroom didn't contain the usual meeting table surrounded by chairs but simply had a large empty space in the middle of the room where people would congregate for no longer than ten minutes because, in Jem's opinion, 'Any longer is a ball-ache for everyone.' The walls of the room were lined with gaming machines, and there was a full-sized trampoline in one corner. At the end of the short gatherings, the staff were encouraged to let their hair down for a few minutes before returning to work.

There were twenty or so staff in the company—all young and bright—and it occurred to Tom that, given his experience, it should be relatively easy to become a big fish in such a small pond. He seemed to be such a hit with Jem, who was constantly dropping into his office to 'shoot the breeze, man' as he put it. He was also amazed to find that Jem actively encouraged a nine-to-five culture and, when he was in the office, would run around just after five o'clock ringing a bell like a maniac, checking whether people had gone home and chucking out those that were still there.

In fact, the only formal thing about Bailey's was Bella herself. Tom spent an hour each morning in her top-floor eyrie while she briefed him on the various clients that she wanted him to court. These meetings were intense, focused affairs with little or no small talk. At first, he found it difficult to equate the professional, demanding and occasionally caustic version of Bella with the hot, sexy woman he'd bedded at the Savoy or the slightly vulnerable and apologetic version who had interviewed him a few weeks' before. But he told himself that it was better that she now appeared indifferent towards him as a man and only seemed to be interested in his potential ability to pull in new business, because he knew instinctively, that any personal involvement between them would not end well.

Tom got into the habit of arriving slightly early for these meetings, just for the sheer pleasure of spending a few minutes with Gideon Coyne, Bella's personal assistant.

Gideon had been temping for Bella for just over a year while 'resting', as he put it, from his career as an actor. At first, Tom couldn't imagine how Gideon had landed the job because his peroxide quiff and kohl-lined eyes gave him the appearance of an inconsequential piece of fluff with nothing but fresh air between his ears. But, in fact, Gideon was sharp as a tack and acted as Bella's eyes and ears, picking up the latest industry gossip, feeding back juicy titbits from the staffroom. Juggling her impossible diary commitments, Gideon supplied solutions to every challenge she threw at him, from where to get the latest Burberry handbag to jumping the waiting list for a table at the hottest new restaurant in town. Tom also discovered that he had the most amazing memory and was a phenomenal mimic with an ability to replicate voices and mannerisms with a wicked accuracy, often at the expense of his fellow workers. But, more importantly, he had Bella's measure and was able to shrug off her moods and coax a smile from her when nobody else could.

Tom quickly found himself genuinely enjoying the job, which involved meeting clients in their homes or giving them lunch in one of the many excellent eateries in the city and selling them the 'Bailey's dream'. Within his first month he had sealed five lucrative deals, presenting them like battle trophies to Bella, savouring each scrap of praise she threw his way and turning them over in his mind.

* * *

Thursday, 3 May 2018
Bailey's Wealth-Care, 8.32 a.m.

Tom wandered into Gideon's office, hoping for a bit of a chat and a coffee before his meeting with Bella, and saw Gideon standing with his ear to Bella's office door.

Tom crept up behind him and hissed, 'Caught you!'

Gideon swung round and clutched his chest, 'Jesus, you nearly gave me a heart attack!' Putting his fingers to his lips, he grabbed Tom's arm and pulled him into the small cloakroom area just outside his office.

'What's going on?' said Tom.

Gideon rolled his eyes. 'Bella and Jem are having one of their famous rows.'

'Really?' Tom couldn't imagine Jem rowing with anyone. 'What's it about?'

Gideon raised one plucked eyebrow and declaimed, 'You, darling! Jem wants you on his team.'

'Seriously?'

'Yeah. He thinks—and I quote his exact words here—"you'd be more suited to working on the corporate side with him than fannying around chatting up fat Cheshire cats!"'

'And I take it that Bella isn't happy about it.'

'Understatement of the year! The last thing I heard her say was "There's no way you're stealing another person that I've spent hours training up. It is so not happening!"' said Gideon in a perfect imitation of Bella's voice.

When Tom had stopped laughing, he said, 'Sounds as if I'll be staying with Bella, then.'

Gideon nodded vigorously, 'No doubt about that, my dear. What Belladonna wants, Belladonna always gets!'

* * *

Ten minutes later Tom was summoned into Bella's office and found her and Jem sitting on the leather sofa in the bay window. For somebody who'd just had a blazing row, Bella looked sleek and satisfied, her lovely face smooth and untroubled, mouth curved in a welcoming smile. In fact, she looked exactly like somebody who had just got their own way.

Jem, by comparison, looked flushed and rumpled, his hair unbrushed, his shirt buttoned up the wrong way and, although he had shoes on his feet, Tom couldn't help noticing that he was wearing odd socks.

'Hi Tom,' purred Bella, sounding like a cat mainlining on cream.

'Morning, man,' muttered Jem sounding uncharacteristically chastened.

Tom sat down in the armchair opposite them and waited.

'We've just had a chat about you,' said Bella. 'We think your skills would be better utilised if you moved over to work with Jem.'

Tom nearly fell off the chair in surprise.

'Is that OK with you, Tom?' said Jem. 'We'll have a blast, and I've got some interesting stuff planned for the next few months.'

Pulling himself together, Tom replied, 'I'll happily go along with whatever you think is best.'

Jem got up and shoved a battered baseball cap over his unruly hair. 'Great. See you later,' he said, and ambled out of the room.

Bella stood and smoothed down her skirt. 'That's sorted, then.'

Tom said hesitantly, 'I hope you don't think that I asked Jem for this move.'

She walked over and stood so close to him that he could smell her perfume, almost feel the warmth of her skin. Reaching out, she gently touched his cheek, her finger resting like a butterfly just above the corner of his mouth. 'Relax, Tom. Your transfer was entirely my idea.' She brushed her finger along his bottom lip. 'I was finding it increasingly difficult to keep to my rule about never mixing business with pleasure. So I kept telling Jem how brilliant you were knowing that it would be only a matter of time before he decided that he wanted to transfer you to his team. He finally asked me this morning. We had a bit of a tussle about it, and I let him win. Reverse psychology wins the day and everyone's happy … I hope?' She took another small step forward and Tom reached out and pulled her tightly against him, closing his eyes as his mouth found hers, feeling her lips moving under his, as she whispered, 'I always get what I want, Tom.'

A knock on the door parted them as effectively as a bucket of cold water, and Bella pulled away from him and walked across to the window calling, 'Come in.'

Gideon poked his head round the door. 'Sorry to interrupt, Bella. That German guy is on the phone wanting to check out a couple of things with you.'

Bella smiled at him. 'That's fine, Gideon. Put him through.' After Gideon had left the room, she said, 'This won't take long. Would you mind waiting for me in the orchard? It's through the archway in the back wall of the courtyard.'

* * *

The warm air was like a drug, and Tom felt disorientated and drowsy as he sat on a small stone bench waiting for Bella, his body still tingling and throbbing with the reaction to her kiss. He hadn't been in this part of the garden before; hadn't realised that it stretched beyond the small courtyard that was used by the staff for their coffee and lunch breaks. This section was full of fruit trees growing in a sea of lush, uncut grass studded with wildflowers. Leaning back, he took a deep breath, concentrating on drawing the scented air into his lungs and felt his heartbeat slowing as he calmed himself. Shutting his eyes, he listened to the rich, fluting song of a blackbird in the nearby apple tree. Tom thought about Sophie and how she would feel if she knew what had just happened: the effect it might have on her and the baby. He knew that he had to put a stop to this before it went any further. Then the sudden, urgent chitter of the blackbird's alarm call startled him and, opening his eyes, he saw Bella walking towards him.

Standing up, he said, 'I'm sorry, Bella; that should never have happened.'

Bella took a deep, shuddering breath and said, 'I know. It's just I … feel …'

Seeing her eyes fill with tears, he said more gently, 'Don't get upset. There's been no harm done.' He turned to walk back through the archway.

'Tom?' she said shakily, 'come into the house, and I'll make us some tea. I think we both need to calm down before we go back to the office.' She walked over to a door in the side wall of the orchard.

He stared at her in surprise. 'Where are you going?'

'Home,' she replied and disappeared through the door.

Curiosity getting the better of him, Tom followed her into the garden of the adjacent house, which was another Georgian gem, its mellow red bricks gleaming in the morning sunshine. Bella walked round to the side of the house and let herself in. Thoroughly intrigued, Tom entered the large, slightly old-fashioned kitchen which smelt deliciously of roasting meat. Leaning back against a counter, he watched her fill a kettle and place it on the hotplate of the Aga range. Watched her pour boiling water into a red teapot, take a blue willow-pattern plate from the oak dresser and arrange some scones on it. Followed her over to the faded chintz sofa in the curved bay window overlooking the garden. Thought to himself that it was a thousand miles away from the type of kitchen he would have expected Bella to have, and then—guiltily—that it was exactly the type of kitchen Sophie would love.

The new domestic version of Bella placed a loaded tea tray on the oak coffee table that stood in front of the sofa and sat down next to him. 'This was my parents' house,' she said. 'Jem and I grew up here. She laughed softly. 'What a pair! Partners at work and partners at home. He has the top two floors—all chrome and modern art—and I rattle around in the rest. This part of the house hasn't changed much over the years. I keep meaning to update it, but I never seem to get round to it, with work and all.'

Tom said quietly, 'I think it's perfect as it is,' stunned by this unexpected glimpse into Bella's private life.

Leaning forward, she poured the tea and offered him the plate of scones, saying, 'Try one. I baked them myself.'

He stared at her in amazement, unable to imagine her up to her elbows in sticky dough.

She laughed. 'OK, I confess! Our housekeeper Elaine made them.' Kicking off her high-heeled sandals, she drew her feet up onto the sofa with a contented sigh.

Glancing down, Tom felt his breath catch in his throat as he saw the delicate arches of her pale, naked feet so close to him and, reaching out, he gently touched one of them.

Pushing him away, she jumped up and yelled, 'Make up your mind, Tom. Either you want me, or you don't.' She stalked out of the room.

Unable to help himself, he followed her into a shadowy hallway and held her, waiting until her heartbeat slowed, and she let out a long, ragged sigh, before allowing himself to kiss her. Suddenly, a distant noise in the depths of the house made them jump apart like guilty teenagers.

She whispered, 'Don't worry, it's only Elaine,' and led him up the staircase and into a bedroom on the first landing. Locking the door she turned to him and said, 'I know you think you're being disloyal to your wife but ...'

'Shush ...' Tom pushed her back against the door and kissed her again, pushing his fingers into her hair, tasting her, savouring the feeling of her against him. 'Is this OK?' he murmured.

'Yes.'

'And this?' He started to unfasten the small pearly buttons on the front of her dress and laughed as she brushed his hands away to pull at the buttons herself, until she was able to push the dress off her body in a billowy puff of silk. For a moment she stood, her slim body silhouetted against the sun streaming through the long window. Looking at her, Tom knew he was lost.

* * *

May and June 2018

As spring gave way to a gloriously balmy early summer, Tom fell into a routine that incorporated his affair with Bella into his life so seamlessly that he rarely gave any proper thought to the rights and wrongs of what he was doing. It was as if he had been divided into two autonomous halves, each possessing a distinct persona.

The first persona was the loyal, loving husband and father-to-be who spent every weekend at home in Kew with Sophie developing his DIY and gardening skills and visiting the seemingly endless number of stores dedicated to the world of babies and their infinite requirements. This Tom made a real effort to be unfailingly kind and considerate to Sophie and even managed to get back from work in time to make dinner a couple of nights a week, with the result that the house in Kew finally started to feel like a real home.

Sophie was now well into her second trimester and beautiful again. Re-discovering his desire for her, Tom would make love to her with such exaggerated care that she would cry out in frustration that she wasn't made of china and wouldn't break. Her catering business was doing well, and she had taken on a couple of part-time staff which left her free to do what she really loved—going to private homes and boardrooms and cooking fabulous food.

He felt that all was good on the home front and, when one evening Sophie observed, 'You're so much happier these days—moving to the new job was definitely the right thing to do,' he took it as a sign that he had finally got his private life back into kilter.

The other persona—his alter ego—was the highly

polished risk-taker who was going to take Bailey's to new dizzying heights of success. He found working with Jem exhilarating and occasionally terrifying, but prided himself that he had the ability to temper the younger man's erratic brilliance with his own experience and judgement, quietly ensuring that their business practices were unlikely to attract any criticism from the regulatory bodies. So, when Jem asked him to become the initial signatory to all corporate deals and threw in a bonus of £10,000 for each one he finalised, Tom accepted it as vindication of his decision to move to Bailey's.

The affair with Bella continued to hold him in such thrall that he managed to convince himself that she was his rightful compensation for all of the changes he had been forced to make when Sophie had announced that she was pregnant.

They'd fallen in into the habit of meeting after work for an hour or so on a Tuesday and a Friday when Jem went out with his friends. Each of these encounters was different, and he never knew what to expect because Bella was mercurial, a creature of impulse who was in many ways a greedy and selfish lover. But other than expecting her physical desire to be satisfied, she made no additional demands on him, no crazy declarations of love; she was completely discrete about their relationship and showed no inclination to spend more time with him than she did. In fact, the whole arrangement suited him very well.

* * *

Friday, 6 July 2018
Bailey's Wealth-Care, 1.12 p.m.

Tom and Gideon were eating lunch in Gideon's office. It had been raining steadily all morning, and the air was heavy with the threat of thunder. Gideon had just told Tom a particularly filthy joke when the door was flung open and Bella flounced in, puncturing their laughter with a brusque, 'Get me a coffee, Gideon.'

Gideon retorted sassily, 'And what do we say?'

'Get me a bloody coffee. Now!' she snarled, adding, 'Come through, Tom. We need to talk,' as she stalked into her office.

Gideon rolled his eyes at Tom and whispered, 'OMG. PMT!'

Trying his best not to laugh, Tom followed Bella into the office and leant back against the wall.

Bella rummaged in her bag and pulled out a newspaper, rifling through the pages until she found what she was looking for and then thrust it at him growling, 'Why didn't you mention this to me?'

It was a tattered copy of the *Metro*, the freebie newspaper handed out to commuters on the Underground. His heart sank as he looked down and saw the photo spread covering a charity event that he and Sophie had attended the previous week. One of the photos showed them dressed to the nines, arms around each other, beaming into the camera above a caption which read:

Sophie and Tom Wright enjoy an evening at the Claremont Hotel in support of Cancer UK.

'I didn't think you'd be interested,' Tom said coolly.

Bella's nails tapped a peevish tattoo on the polished surface of her desk. 'Am I right in thinking that this event was partially sponsored by Bailey's?'

'Yes,' said Tom calmly. 'And Jem asked me to go and represent the company.'

'And you thought it appropriate to take *her* with you?'

Furious at her tone, Tom snapped. 'For your information, Jem gave me two tickets and suggested that my wife might like to go with me. What's your problem?'

Bella stalked over and jabbed a finger into his chest. 'I haven't got a problem, Tom, but you might if she finds out about us.'

Tom's voice was dangerously quiet as he replied, 'I don't appreciate being threatened,' and walked out.

He had just opened the door and seen Gideon standing there with a cup of coffee in his hand and a shocked expression on his face, when Bella screamed, 'And don't bother coming round for your Friday night fuck. I won't be there,' and slammed the door shut.

'Pub?' said Gideon.

* * *

Fifteen minutes later Tom perched on a narrow bench in the public bar of the Maiden's Arms and watched Gideon, resplendent in black drainpipes paired with a cerise silk smoking jacket, weaving his way through the crowded bar carrying a pint of bitter, a Campari and soda and various packets of snacks. Reaching Tom, he plumped himself down next to him and said dramatically, 'I didn't think I was going to make it back alive. There's a groper over there with as many arms as an octopus.' Setting his purchases out on the table in front of them, he handed Tom his pint, took a ladylike sip of his Campari and said, 'Tell me to mind my own business if you like, but what on earth do you think you are doing with Belladonna?'

Knowing there was no point in pretending he didn't know what Gideon was talking about, Tom quietly told him what had been going on with Bella, finishing with, and 'I didn't see that coming today. I thought Bella and I were tight.'

'Tight?' exclaimed Gideon viciously ripping open a packet of cashew nuts. 'Why would you want to be "tight" with a praying mantis who'll bite your head off as soon as she's finished with you, when you have a perfectly lovely wife who obviously adores you?'

Tom felt a hot flush of shame wash through him at the mention of Sophie and mumbled, 'I don't know. I'm not sure what I was thinking of.'

'Well, that's the point,' said Gideon meaningfully, his eyes dropping to Tom's crotch. 'It wasn't you thinking ... it was him!' Popping a handful of nuts into his mouth, he was silent for a minute before saying thoughtfully, 'I assume you know they're both completely bonkers?'

'Well, Jem's clearly ...'

'... fucking mental!' He's so far up the spectrum, they've probably had to extend it!' muttered Gideon, stuffing more nuts into his mouth.

'But he's brilliant at his job.'

'What's that, then? Being Bella's puppet?' retorted Gideon. 'If that man cut the apron strings and put his brain to something legitimate, he'd be the wealthiest man in London. And as for Bella. Don't even get me started!'

Something in Gideon's voice made Tom lean forward and ask him urgently, 'Tell me about her.'

Gideon snorted. 'Finally! The million-dollar question! I'll keep it short. Bella Bailey is a nasty piece of work who never gives a thought to the consequences of her grubby little schemes. It would never occur to her that wealthy people may have worked hard for their money or that someone lucky enough to win on the lottery actually deserves to benefit from their good luck. Oh no! She'd skin her grandmother for the tallow!'

Seeing that Gideon was getting really worked up, Tom laid a calming hand on his arm, saying, 'Steady on, mate; she's not that bad!'

Gideon's eyes glittered with indignation, and he hissed loudly, 'She is that bad—and more!' He shuffled nearer to Tom and whispered, 'When she and Jem were children, their mother ran off with another man, and their father topped himself.'

Tom stared at Gideon in disbelief. If this was true, why hadn't Bella mentioned it? She'd told him quite a bit about her father, showed him photos and said more than once how much he was like her father in looks. Surely, she knew she could trust him by now?

Gideon continued, 'The poor sod hung himself in his bedroom, and Bella found him. It turned her odd. Apparently, she spent years in and out of psychiatric care.'

'That's terrible,' said Tom. 'What on earth must it have done to her?'

'Made her into the hard, manipulative, moody bitch she is today,' answered Gideon.

'How do you know all of this?' asked Tom.

'The housekeeper fills me in on the gossip.'

Tom frowned. There was something niggling away at the back of his mind, something about that didn't feel right. And then it clicked. 'Why are you still working for them, if you think they're such monsters?' he asked quietly.

Gideon shrugged. 'They pay well, and I have to make ends meet while I'm waiting for the next part to come along. I'm just part of the furniture to them. Good old Gideon who makes the coffee and does the filing. But you're vulnerable, Tom. You generate new business, sign off mega-deals and accept their generous bonuses. Hasn't it ever occurred to you that they're using you to add a veneer of credibility to the operation? After all, who would ever suspect you of being anything but kosher? The truth is, however much you try to clean up Bailey's, you'll still be up to your neck in shit! If I were you, I'd be saying, "Goodbye, Bella Bailey, and good riddance!" and going back to my safe, respectable job in Canary Wharf without a backward glance.'

Tom's mobile pinged and, dragging his eyes from Gideon, he glanced down at the screen.

'Is that her?' asked Gideon.

'Yeah.'

'Delete it!'

But Tom was already reading it:

I'd say sorry a thousand times if I thought it would make things right. I'm

at home.

Looking at Gideon he said grimly, 'She sounds in a bad way.'

Gideon rolled his eyes. 'That's because she's a better actress than I am.'

A sudden weariness overwhelmed Tom, and he scooped up his jacket saying, 'I'm off. Thanks for the advice, mate. And don't worry! I'm going home.'

* * *

Outside the storm had finally broken, and within a minute he was soaked to the skin, hair dripping into his eyes and steam rising off him into the warm, sultry air. Lifting his face to the sky, he revelled in the sensation of needle-like drops of rain stinging his flesh and cleansing away the last of the anger that had clung to him following his row with Bella. Feeling a sudden, overwhelming sense of having escaped some nameless, faceless threat, he set off briskly for the Underground station, looking forward to the uncomplicated pleasures of a weekend at home with Sophie. But, rounding the next corner, he remembered she was spending the night with her parents and hesitated for a moment, wondering if he could bear to go back to an empty house. Telling himself not to be pathetic, he walked on past an overflowing drain belching out a gassy stench redolent of death and decay and, without warning, an image of a lonely and despairing Bella skittered across his mind.

* * *

Twenty minutes later Tom knocked gently on Bella's bedroom door and walked in. The clothes she'd been wearing earlier were tossed in a careless heap on the bed, along with her mobile phone and handbag. Noticing that the door to the en suite was ajar, he called out, 'Bella? It's me. Are you OK?'

'Tom?' she answered, her voice sounding husky, 'I'm so glad you came. Come in.'

There was a vulnerability in her voice, something he'd never heard before and, taking a deep breath, he walked through the door and into the bathroom. It was a large room, its mirror-lined walls reflecting the candlelight from two antique candelabra which sent smoke-shadows dancing across the ceiling. A haze of exquisitely scented steam rose lazily from the huge Victorian roll-top bathtub in which Bella lay, hair slicked sealskin-smooth against her head, lustrous skin gleaming like silk, eyes half-closed in the steamy heat, her lashes tangled and damp as if she'd been crying.

Walking further into the room, Tom sat on a chaise longue next to the bath and raked his fingers through his rain-soaked hair, saying wearily, 'I don't know what to do.'

She sat up, rivulets of water cascading down her shoulders and breasts, and said, 'I can't believe how stupid I am. I shouldn't have threatened to tell Sophie about us. It was seeing the two of you looking so happy together in that photograph. I hadn't realised how young she is. And she's expecting your baby. For the first time in my life, I felt jealous of another woman and I just lost it. I'm so sorry.'

Tom leaned forward and gazed at her. He knew that Gideon had told him about her past in the hope that it would warn him off, but looking at her now, all he could see was a beautiful, troubled woman whom he desired more than anyone he had ever met. He said awkwardly, 'Don't feel jealous of Sophie. What she and I have is completely different to what you and I have.'

Bella said urgently, 'Tell me about her. I need to understand.'

Tom said, 'I've known Sophie since I was in my early twenties. We've been married almost ten years, and she knows me better than anyone else.' He swallowed hard. 'She's the finest person I've ever met. She's decent and honest and loving. She's supported everything I've ever done and I'm never going to leave her.'

After a moment Bella whispered, 'You didn't mention love? Do you love her?'

'Very much,' said Tom, without any hesitation. 'And I don't understand why I'm doing this. If she ever found out about this, she'd never forgive me. It would be the end of my marriage.' He laughed harshly. 'Jesus! I must be going through an early midlife crisis or something!'

For a long moment Bella looked at him silently, and then said slowly, 'So ... if I promise you that I won't ever tell Sophie about us ... would that mean we can carry on seeing each other?'

'With no complications?' asked Tom.

'With no complications,' she confirmed. 'Just an uncomplicated affair between friends who like each other.'

Tom walked over to the bath. Kneeling down he brushed his forefinger over her lips, down her neck and further down into the soft valley between her breasts. 'That sounds too good to be true,' he murmured, as desire washed away any lingering doubts and made him feel that it was possible that he could have it all.

'Take off those wet clothes and get in,' she said, reaching for him. 'I'll never do anything to hurt you.'

* * *

Friday, 3 August 2018

South Western Railway, 6.12 p.m.
One Friday evening a few weeks later, Tom was on his way home when the Tube came to a juddering stop just outside Clapham Junction, and a disembodied voice announced that there would be a delay due to an obstruction on the tracks.

'That'll be some poor bleeder topped himself,' muttered the elderly man sitting across the aisle from Tom.

Still floating on a post-coital cloud following a

particularly steamy session with Bella, he ignored the man and rang Sophie to tell her that he may be later than usual, concluding the call with, 'I'll pick up a takeaway. It'll save you cooking.'

'That's a nice idea,' she said, 'but I've got a special dinner planned for us.'

Tom laughed. 'Have I forgotten something? An anniversary perhaps? The first time we kissed? Oh my God, please don't tell me we're expecting triplets!' he teased.

'Stop it!' she scolded. 'I've some really exciting news. So get yourself home in double-quick time.'

After he'd finished the call, Tom relaxed back into his seat and reviewed his latest mental checklist. Sophie sounded really happy. Bella was satisfied. He was back in control of his life. Tick those boxes.

* * *

Friday, 3 August 2018
Tom and Sophie's home, Kew, 9.27 p.m.

Later that evening Tom looked longingly at the last bit of rhubarb and ginger crumble before waving his white napkin in the air and groaning. 'I surrender. There isn't an inch of space left in my stomach.'

Sophie giggled and used a large serving spoon to scrape the last morsels from the dish before stuffing it in her mouth.

'Classy!' said Tom.

'I'm eating for two!' she retorted in mock indignation as she licked the spoon clean.

Tom grinned at her. 'You're very pleased with yourself tonight.'

She grinned back. 'And why shouldn't I be? I am the world's most fabulous cook after all.'

'This is undoubtedly true. And modest with it.' Tom got up. 'I'll load the dishwasher.'

'It can wait,' said Sophie, her eyes sparkling with excitement. 'Sit down and pour yourself another glass of that lovely wine that I can't share with you, damn you!'

Tom sat down and poured himself another glass of Rioja. He took a sip and studied Sophie who was wearing a red halterneck dress, her hair falling in glossy waves over her bare shoulders.

'You look gorgeous,' he said. 'And very happy.'

Sophie beamed at him. 'That's because I am. I feel amazing. In fact, I am amazing.'

'You'd better tell me before you burst.'

The words tumbled out of her mouth. 'I've been asked to do the catering for a very prestigious client. It's her birthday party, and there'll be loads of important people attending. She's asked me to choose the menu, select the wine and source the staff. The event will be covered in one of the glossies. I'll be famous! What do you think of that?' She looked over at Tom, her eyes shining with delight.

'It sounds brilliant!' said Tom proudly.

'You haven't heard the best bit yet,' said Sophie. 'Guess who it is?'

Tom smiled, vastly amused that his usually cool and calm wife was acting like an over-excited child. 'Hmmm, is it Katie Holmes?' he teased.

'No! Guess again.'

'Is it ... Nelly Furtado?' said Tom, shooting her an evil, lustful grin.

Sophie leaned across the table and slapped his hand saying 'Stop it! You're just picking out celebrities you fancy.' She winked at Tom. 'If you're not careful I'll take Jamie Dornan up on his offer. As you're being a bit dense, I'll give you a clue. It's somebody real. Someone you know.' Her face took on a look of delighted anticipation.

An icy chill of foreboding crept up Tom's spine, tightening all of the muscles around his mouth and freezing the stupid grin so his lips were hardly able to form the words, 'I give up.'

Sophie crowed gleefully, 'It's Bella Bailey!'

The grin melted down Tom's face like candle wax as he stared at his wife in disbelief.

'Tom?' she said uncertainly.

He wiped his sweaty face with his napkin and croaked feebly, 'She kept that quiet.'

'I asked her to,' said Sophie. 'I wanted to tell you myself.'

Tom took a deep breath before carefully saying, 'Is it wise to take on something this ambitious when you're almost seven months pregnant? How are you going to fit it in with your other work?'

Sophie said confidently, 'It's all down to careful planning. I'll make sure I have enough staff and a lot of the food can be prepared in advance. Bella wants an Italian feast served the traditional way with lots of small courses and—'

Tom interrupted her. 'It's a bad idea ... I-I don't want you to do it.'

She walked round and stood behind him, her arms around his neck, her chin resting on his head and murmured, 'You worry about me so much, and it's really sweet of you. But it'll be fine.' After kissing the top of his head, she sat back down opposite him before continuing to speak. 'Bella and I met last week and agreed everything down to the last detail. She's a powerhouse. And so stunning! You never told me how beautiful she is, Tom Wright. And she's clever,' mused Sophie. 'I could learn loads from someone like her.'

'Don't be daft! You've got nothing in common,' snapped Tom, horrified that Bella had contacted Sophie and arranged to meet her without his knowledge.

Sophie retorted indignantly, 'Actually, we really hit it off. She's good fun and an extremely successful woman.

Of course, I could learn from her. In fact I think we could become good friends. Anyway'—she brightened up—'she thinks so highly of you, Tom. She wanted to know all about you. And us. She asked me loads of questions: How did we meet? What sort of house do we live in? What do we do at weekends? How are we preparing for when the baby comes?'

As he watched Sophie enthusiastically ticking Bella's questions off on her fingers, he felt a terrible stillness envelop him as he remembered Gideon's warning, and swallowed hard to prevent the hot bile churning in his stomach from erupting into his throat. He wondered what the hell Bella was playing and what she might do next.

Sophie looked at him and started to laugh, saying, 'Oh Tom! Your face! Bella said you'd be speechless when I told you the news.'

* * *

Saturday, 4 August 2018
Tom and Sophie's home, Kew, 7.10 a.m.

Tom lay in bed, hollow-eyed and dry-mouthed after a sleepless night, trying to work out why Bella had betrayed him by meeting with Sophie behind his back so soon after reassuring him that she would never do anything to hurt him. He could only conclude that she was deliberately trying to unsettle him, and he was terrified that Sophie would find out about the affair. To make matters worse, Sophie was delighted that Bella had asked her to do the catering for her party and appeared to be as fascinated by her as he had been at first.

At some point in the endless, sleepless night, he'd decided to go and see Bella today to tell her that he was resigning and that their affair was over. He also intended to tell her to find another caterer for her party. Sophie would be devastated, but it was too risky to allow her to spend more time with Bella. He had no idea how Bella would react and realised that she may tell Sophie anyway, but he had no choice.

Dropping a kiss on Sophie's forehead, he whispered, 'Sorry, love, I've just got to pop into the office. I need to pick up some photocopying for my breakfast meeting on Monday. Won't be long.'

* * *

Saturday, 4 August 2018
Bella's home, Compton Square, 8.53 a.m.

Tom quietly let himself into Bella's kitchen, which was fragrant with the smell of baking bread and nearly jumped out of his skin at the incongruous sight of Jem standing at the breakfast bar whisking egg-whites in a bowl.

Jem, equally startled, looked up and exclaimed, 'Christ, you nearly made me knock all the air out of this meringue! What are you doing here?'

Tom blinked rapidly, as his fatigued brain tried to think of a suitable excuse, and heard himself say feebly, 'I didn't know you could cook.'

Jem grinned. 'Someone has to! Our housekeeper keeps us going during the week, but if I relied on Bella for sustenance at weekends, I'd be a goner.'

Tom watched as Jem spooned the shiny meringue mixture into a piping bag and expertly piped it onto a baking sheet. 'What are you making?' he asked.

'Raspberry Pavlova.' Bella's away, so I can eat as many sweet things as I like without getting a lecture.' Jem carefully slid the meringue into the oven. 'Coffee?'

'Yes, please,' said Tom as he digested the fact that Bella wasn't there.

Jem started up the coffee machine and said, 'Take a pew.'

Tom wandered over to the snug area, slumped into an armchair and stared morosely out of the window at the garden beyond. The grass was still dewy where the sun hadn't yet reached it, and a noisy gang of blue tits fought for a place on a peanut feeder hanging from one of the apple trees. Where the hell was Bella? She hadn't said anything about going away this weekend. But, there again, she hadn't mentioned that she'd been in touch with Sophie; hadn't told him about her birthday party plans. He wondered what else she might be hiding from him.

His thoughts were interrupted as Jem walked over and set a laden tray on the coffee table in front of him, saying, 'The flapjacks are fresh from the oven. Help yourself.'

Tom shook his head and murmured, 'No, thanks. I'm not hungry.'

Jem studied Tom for a moment. 'I know what's going on.'

Tom felt every muscle tense as he tried to gauge Jem's mood.

Jem continued. 'I saw you creeping in here yesterday afternoon, and I figured you hadn't come to discuss the stock market. Bella filled me in on the rest.'

Tom exhaled loudly. 'I'm sorry. We shouldn't have sneaked around behind your back.'

Jem shrugged. 'You're both adults.'

'Where's she's gone?' said Tom abruptly.

'Jersey. We've been in discussion with a small, privately owned bank about the possibility of opening up an offshore branch of Bailey's. Bella's looking at a few properties over there.'

'Was it a planned trip?' asked Tom.

'Yeah. It's been planned for weeks.'

'I see.' Tom looked down at his hands, trying to take in this further example of Bella keeping things from him. It felt as if she wanted to keep him constantly on the back foot. 'How long will she be over there?'

'A couple of weeks,' said Jem. Adding casually, 'I take it that you have no intention of leaving your wife for

Bella?'

Tom looked him in the eyes and said, 'That's correct, and Bella knew that was the case before we started the affair.' Reaching into his jacket pocket, he pulled out a sealed envelope and put it on the table saying, 'My letter of resignation. I'm sorry, Jem. I've enjoyed working with you, but there's no way I can stay on under these circumstances.' Tom turned to leave.

Jem called after him, 'That would be a real pity, Tom. I was going to ask you to step up and manage Bailey's London office while Bella and I get the Jersey project up and running.'

Tom spun round and looked at him saying, 'Are you serious?'

Jem nodded. 'Would you be up for it?'

'Of course! But what about Bella? Will she be able to work with me, given what's happened between us?'

Jem said abruptly, 'Leave Bella to me.' Picking up a flapjack, he bit into it, chewing vigorously for a couple of seconds, before adding, 'Don't try to contact her while she's away. Give her time to adjust to the fact that your future relationship will be purely professional. I'll make sure she understands that's the deal. We can discuss your new role when she returns. And make sure your wife gives my sister the best party she's ever had. No expense spared. OK?'

'Of course.'

Jem took another mouthful of flapjack. 'One more thing, Tom.'

'Yes?'

'Grab a cloth and pull that meringue out of the oven. Bloody thing's burning.'

* * *

The next couple of weeks passed so slowly Tom felt he would go mad with the weight of worry that was pressing heavily on him. Bella was still away and hadn't tried to contact him. All he could hope was that Jem would be able to persuade her as gently as possible that the affair was dead in the water.

Gideon had offered his own theory for Bella's absence saying, 'I reckon that she's testing you. She's dropped the depth charge by asking Sophie to do the catering for her party, and now she's waiting to see the explosion. She'll know that it will put you under a terrible strain, particularly as you can't challenge her face to face. I bet she's hoping that you'll break down and "confess all" to Sophie and that Sophie will kick you out.'

* * *

Thursday, 16 August 2018
Tom and Sophie's home, Kew, 7.45 p.m.

One warm summer's evening towards the end of the second week of Bella's absence, Tom and Sophie were about to eat dinner in their garden. Tom had had a couple of beers and was feeling more laid back than he had in a long time, his body free of tension, his mind calm.

Sophie walked onto the small patio carrying a bowl of salad in one hand and her mobile in the other, a puzzled look on her face.

'Everything OK?' asked Tom.

'I've just had a message from Bella.'

Forcing himself to remain calm, he said, 'What does she want?'

'Just a few things that she wants me to do for the party. There's a message for you as well. She says, "Tell Tom I've got a surprise for him when I get back." What's that about?'

Tom shrugged. 'Something to do with the new job, presumably. Trust her to make a drama of it.'

Sophie squinted at him, shading her eyes from the glare of the sun. 'Is everything OK? You look really pale.'

Feeling his heart flip at her anxious expression, he

said, 'Of course!' and walked over to give her a long, lingering kiss, his hand caressing the swell of her belly. 'I love you both so much,' he murmured.

'And we love you,' said Sophie, stroking his back, 'but I know something's wrong. Have you and Bella fallen out?' She gazed at him, her eyes full of concern. 'Come on,' she said gently. 'Tell me what it is, and we'll sort it together … like we always do.'

For a split second he was tempted to tell her everything, just for the relief it would bring, but, instead, he said vehemently, 'I wish Bella would butt out. I work with Jem now, and frankly she's doing my head in with her constant interference.' He kissed Sophie again. 'Don't worry, darling. It's all good.'

* * *

Saturday, 18 August 2019
Tom and Sophie's home, Kew, 6.47 a.m.

Tom woke with a throbbing headache which made lifting his head from the pillow seem an impossibility. Sophie lay next to him in a slumber so deep and peaceful that he held his own breath for what seemed like a full minute to check that she was actually breathing. He lay there for a while thinking through his strategy for getting through the party without any nasty surprises. Bella had returned from Jersey the previous day, but he still hadn't seen or heard from her and had no idea how she would have taken the news that their affair was over. He was confident that, if the need arose, Jem would do everything that he could to keep Bella in line, and he knew that he could count on Gideon to provide dramatic diversionary tactics at the drop of a hat. Even so, the potential for things to go wrong was high, and he felt his heart revving up a notch or two at the thought.

Silently sliding out of the bed, he stood for a minute looking down at Sophie who lay on her back, arms flung above her head, a gentle smile upturning her mouth. Tom imagined her dreams would be very different to the nightmares he had suffered last night. Leaning over he gently stroked her belly and sent a fervent plea to the universe to protect her during the coming day, praying it would be a huge success and promising whoever may be listening that he would never let her down again.

* * *

Saturday, 18 August 2019
Bella's home, Compton Square, 7.30 p.m.

Tom and Gideon stood in the kitchen of Bella's house watching Sophie and her team of cooks put the finishing touches to the feast.

Tom was so stressed he could hardly stand still and, leaving Gideon salivating over a platter of crostini, he walked over to the window and looked out at the garden. Every tree had been strung with lanterns and wind chimes which shimmered in the gentle breeze. The grass formed a lush green carpet for the long tables draped with muslin cloths and set with huge candelabra, pottery vases full of wildflowers and an esoteric collection of hand painted plates, antique cutlery and jewel-coloured glasses. He was reflecting on how wonderful it was that Sophie had created something so enticingly beautiful when he felt the lightest brush of a hand on his shoulder and whirled round to find Bella standing there.

She looked stunning, her skin lightly tanned and her silvery eyes dancing with suppressed amusement. She wore a long, pale blue dress shot through with silver which complemented the colour of her eyes, the crystal drops in her earlobes and her flat Grecian sandals. He tried to drag his eyes away from her but failed. It was as if he was hypnotised. 'Bella,' he said, forcing her name through lips that suddenly felt as dry and brittle as paper.

She gave a low, throaty laugh and whispered, 'You look terrified! Don't worry I'm not going to bite you … yet!'

Glancing round the kitchen he saw that Sophie was

deep in discussion with one of the chefs. 'Can we talk?' he said in a low voice.

'Of course,' she replied in a loud, carrying voice.

'Not in here,' muttered Tom uncomfortably.

She laughed again and purred seductively. 'So you want to get me on my own?' and then, to Tom's horror, turned and called, 'Sophie, darling!'

Sophie walked over to join them and said, 'Happy Birthday, Bella! You look amazing.'

'Thank you, darling,' replied Bella in a sickeningly saccharine voice, adding, 'But you shouldn't have dragged yourself over here, you poor love. You look so dreadfully tired and uncomfortable. I just wanted to tell you that everything looks wonderful. I hardly recognise my garden. You've transformed it. And the table settings ... just fabulous! The people from *Celebrity Lives* magazine are in ecstasy.'

Sophie's face relaxed, the small dimple in her left cheek appearing as she gave Bella a tremulous, relieved smile and said, 'I'm so pleased you like it.'

'Like it?' warbled Bella, 'I love it darling. Anyway, your lovely husband is kidnapping me for a few minutes. Apparently, he's desperate to talk to me about something, so, I'll catch up with you later.'

'OK,' said Sophie.

He saw the smallest change in Sophie's smile. No more than a flicker, but enough to tell him she'd detected something 'off' in Bella's tone. Throwing her a reassuring smile, he followed Bella out of the kitchen and down a short passage tucked away behind the stairs to a pair of French doors which opened onto an enormous conservatory.

It was clear that this part of the house was never used. The room was cold and damp, its glass walls and ceiling coated in a film of mould which dyed the feeble sunlight filtering through it a sickly shade of green. Tom shivered and felt a sudden childlike inclination to run back to the cosy sanctuary of the kitchen and Sophie.

Bella carefully shut the doors, walked over to him and laced her hands around his neck, gently pulling him towards her until their faces were so close that he could see tiny reflections of himself in her eyes and smell the warm, musky perfume on her skin. Mesmerised he watched her moisten her lips with a snake-flick of her pink tongue and closed his eyes as she began to place moth-like kisses all around his mouth.

Even as he thought *I mustn't kiss her back*, he was tangling his fingers in her long hair, kissing her neck, her cheeks, her eyes and finally her mouth. But as soon as he deepened the kiss, she pulled away and smoothed her ruffled hair, saying coolly, 'What did you want to talk to me about?'

He looked at her in astonishment, his body still responding to the kiss, his brain trying to process what had just happened. He felt drugged, as if Bella was somehow controlling him. Taking a deep breath, he eventually said, 'Why did you go behind my back and ask Sophie to do this party?'

Bella snapped sarcastically. 'For heaven's sake, Tom! We're not at school anymore. I promised I wouldn't tell Sophie we were having an affair, and I haven't. I knew that she was trying to build up her catering business, and I thought I'd give her a helping hand. Where's the harm?'

A flash of fury made Tom snap back, 'You must have known I wouldn't be happy about it; that it would mean we wouldn't be able to carry on seeing each other.'

'Poor Tom. Always wanting it all,' taunted Bella. 'But you needn't worry, I've got what I wanted from you. We're done.'

It was as if she had taken off a mask and, in that moment, Tom realised how stupid he'd been thinking that he could have a casual affair with this cold, calculating woman. Feeling his temper flare, he yelled, 'What the hell does that mean?'

She was quiet for a moment, as if choosing her words carefully, and then said, impassively, 'It means you've given me a baby, Tom. A little half-brother or sister for Sophie's child. Isn't that lovely?'

Tom recoiled from her. 'I don't believe you.'

She pulled a small folded card from her bag and offered it to him. 'See for yourself.'

He snatched the card from her and opened it, looked at the image of the tiny foetus curled up like a shrimp, and said, 'This doesn't prove a thing.'

'I can get a paternity test done once it's born, if proof is required, but, given the circumstances, I don't think that's going to be necessary. The baby's due on the ninth of March next year—the anniversary of our first meeting. Such a romantic coincidence,' she sneered.

Tom's bowels turned to water as he realised she was telling the truth. 'What are you going to do?' he asked, his voice heavy with dread.

She gave him a Madonna-like smile and said, 'I'm going to tell people that the baby's father is someone I met abroad. That we had a brief fling, and I got pregnant.' Her smile faded. 'I'll tell them that when I got to know him better, I found out he was married and realised he was a weak, shallow liar, not the sort of man I'd want to be involved in my child's life. I'll say that he was nothing more than a sperm donor. You know the type.'

'What do you want, Bella?' said Tom numbly.

'I want a baby, and you've provided me with one. All you have to do now is concentrate on your shiny new job and keep your mouth shut about the child. That's the deal.'

'What about Sophie?'

'I pity Sophie. I see no need to bother her with this.'

'And will Jem go along with it?' asked Tom in disbelief.

'Jem will do exactly what I ask him to do. He always does.' Bella glanced down at her watch. 'What are we doing here? It's party time!' With one last mocking smile, she turned away from him and walked to the door, pausing at its threshold to call out, 'Cheer up, Tom. You've got off lightly and—who knows—it could all work out fabulously well.'

* * *

An hour later the garden had taken on a magical glow, lit by hundreds of candles and torches, the lanterns in the trees casting mysterious shadows on the lush grass, the music from the live band almost drowned out by the excited buzz of the champagne fuelled, rich, bejewelled guests.

Tom sat at the table nearest to the kitchen, feeling as if he'd been eviscerated, his eyes constantly darting around the garden as he tried to keep track of Bella. He kept replaying the scene in the conservatory over and over in his head as he tried to make sense of it. Was it possible that Bella had been serious when she'd said that all she wanted from him was the baby, and that she'd keep her mouth shut about whose it was? Could he continue working at Bailey's with this terrible lie hanging over him like a sword of Damocles? He shuddered as he imagined what would happen if Sophie ever found out. He really wanted this new job but, for the first time in his life, he was questioning whether he could have everything he wanted regardless of the consequences.

Gideon was oblivious to all of this as he sat next to Tom, providing a running commentary on each new arrival. 'Ooh, that's that actor from *Downton Abbey*. The one who played the footman who ran off with the scullery maid. Or was he one of the sons? Anyway, he hasn't aged well.' He paused for a micro-second to drag some oxygen into his lungs before giving a low shriek, 'OMG, I don't believe it! It's ... look, Tom, the plump piece in the purple caftan. What's her name? She's on that morning TV show. The one with the theme music that goes "da da, de de de DAH". Gideon stopped abruptly and nudged Tom hard, exclaiming, 'You haven't heard a word I've said, have you?'

Startled, Tom gasped, 'What's happened?'

'Nothing's happened,' snapped Gideon irritably. 'I was just talking about all of this, and you seem a million miles away. You're no fun tonight, and I assume that Belladonna is at the bottom of it. Roll on Jersey is what I say! Giving an extravagant sigh, Gideon flung his arms wide as if he wanted to gather the garden and all of its occupants into an embrace. 'It's completely magical, isn't it? It reminds me of the time I played Aladdin in the Bournemouth Pier panto. Now there was an exotic stage set, if ever I saw one.'

Tom looked at him properly for the first time and couldn't help smiling because, in honour of the party, Gideon had dyed his hair in the colours of the Italian flag.

'Is it over the top?' asked Gideon anxiously.

'No,' lied Tom, 'It's very you.'

'Sweet,' said Gideon, preening a bit before whispering, 'Have you noticed the photographer from *Celebrity Lives*?'

'No.'

'He's over there by the apple trees. Completely scrumptious, isn't he?'

'Not my type.'

'You know what I mean!' said Gideon, with a toss of his head that made his tricolour quiff quiver. 'Anyway,' he confided, 'I've just done something a little bit naughty.'

'Oh?' said Tom absently, catching sight of Jem coming towards them, shirt hanging out of his jeans and a bottle of Becks clutched in one hand.

'Yep,' continued Gideon. 'I've changed the place

cards so he'll be sitting next to me. It mucks up Bella's boy-girl-boy-girl arrangement a bit but, there again ...' Gideon gave Tom a suggestive wink, '... if I've read things correctly, maybe it doesn't! Actually, I think I'll go and ask him if he'd like a coffee or something,' he said and hurried off.

Jem dropped into the chair next to Tom. 'Good to see you, man. Everything cool?'

'Fine, thanks,' said Tom searching his face for any signs of anger or disapproval. But Jem looked his usual crumpled, affable self.

Jem raised his bottle in a mock toast. 'It's a great party. Sophie's done well.'

Feeling a flare of hope at Jem's friendly tone, Tom said hesitantly, 'I've just seen Bella, and she's told me her news. It's one hell of a shock, to be honest.'

'For us all, man.' said Jem, calmly taking a swig of his Becks.

Tom pressed on, the words tumbling out of his mouth in an unstoppable flow. 'She seems to think that we can all carry on working together. But I'm ...'

Jem cut across him, saying, 'It's Bella's call.' He stood up. 'I need another drink. I'll catch up with you later after the fireworks.'

'Sophie didn't mention any fireworks,' said Tom, in surprise.

'Bella arranged them. Bit of an afterthought,' said Jem vaguely. 'Don't miss them. They'll be a blast!' and he shambled off in the direction of the small bar that had been set up in the archway that led to the office garden.

A few minutes later Gideon came back to the table and sat down next to Tom saying dejectedly, 'Well, that's that. He's straight. I'll never be a bride!' Catching sight of Tom's face, he exclaimed, 'What's up?'

'Nothing,' said Tom glumly.

'OMG, it's catching! I've just seen Belladonna of

the many faces over there, and she completely blanked me when I wished her a Happy Birthday. She's so weird tonight. Weirder than normal, if you'll excuse the pun.'

Tom looked at him sharply, 'What do you mean?'

'She's got a dangerous, glittery look about her. Like a tiger that's about to pounce. I reckon she's off her medication.'

'What medication?'

'Whatever she takes every day to calm her down and make her resemble a human being. She's always popping pills in the office.'

Tom said urgently, 'What's she on? Tranquilisers or something?'

Gideon shook his head. 'Tranquilisers wouldn't touch the sides with a personality like hers. From what Mrs B. told me, I'd put money on her taking heavy-duty stuff.'

Suddenly the band stopped playing and a loud drum roll was followed by hushed silence as a torch-lit procession of waiters and waitresses appeared, bearing loaded platters which they carefully laid on the tables creating an elaborate mosaic of colourful Italian meats, cheeses and salads for the guests to select from. Dinner was served.

Glancing back towards the kitchen, Tom saw Sophie standing in the doorway watching the spectacle, her chef's whites straining over her belly, a few strands of hair that had escaped her cap hanging in wispy curls around her flushed face. She looked like a tired child at the end of Christmas Day.

'Sophie!' he called softly, smiling as she looked over and blew him a kiss. 'I love you,' he whispered, but she had already gone.

* * *

The feast was accompanied by increasingly loud and raucous laughter from Jem and Bella's table. A man, who was sitting with his back to Tom, had a particularly annoying laugh, which sounded like a cross between a donkey and a foghorn. It was a familiar laugh, but Tom couldn't place it and decided it must be one of Bailey's many clients.

He risked a glance at Bella and saw that she was staring at him. To his surprise, she gave him a brilliant smile and rose to her feet. The band immediately stopped playing and as the buzz of chatter died down, she started to speak.

'Good evening everyone! It's truly wonderful to see so many of my dearest friends here tonight to help me celebrate my birthday. Firstly, I have to thank my lovely brother Jem for organising this amazing party and planning it down to the last detail.' She leaned down and kissed Jem. 'And now, I have some exciting news ...' She paused dramatically.

Gideon slid back into the chair next to Tom and hissed, 'What a load of bilge-wash. I'd vomit instantly, if it didn't mean wasting Sophie's wonderful food.'

'Shush!' whispered Tom, dreading what Bella might be about to reveal.

Bella resumed. 'Over the last few months Jem and I have spent considerable time in the Channel Islands looking for new opportunities, and I'm delighted to announce that we've finally found suitable premises and will be setting up a branch of Bailey's in Jersey. We're finally expanding our empire!' She paused and smiled as applause swept round the garden accompanied by a buzz of chatter. Holding up her hand for silence, she continued, 'From next month, we'll be spending the majority of our time over there while we set up the new business. We've appointed an extremely experienced and capable man to run our London operation'—she looked over at Tom and smiled warmly—'but I won't embarrass him by dragging him up here tonight. Suffice to say Jem and I are looking forward to working with him and wish him well. Once again, thank you for making my birthday so special. Champagne and birthday cake are on their way out of the kitchen. Enjoy!'

Gideon turned to Tom and gave him a hug. 'Congratulations, Tom. You're going to be absolutely brilliant. I may even decide to give up my glittering stage career and work with you for ever.' He clapped his hands in glee. 'And we won't have to put up with Madam Bella and her mad brother for much of the time either. OMG, it's going to be amazing!'

'Thanks, Gideon,' said Tom feeling himself relax slightly for the first time in a long time. 'How would you feel about a pay rise and a proper contract?'

Gideon clapped his hands. 'OMG! I'll grab us some champagne.' He hurried off.

'Have you got a minute, Tom?'

Tom spun round as he heard Bella's voice behind him and froze as he saw the man standing next to her.

'I'm sure you remember Peter Crawley,' she said silkily.

Peter Crawley flashed his uneven yellowed teeth and held out his hand. 'Tom,' he drawled, 'Short time, no see.'

'How are you?' said Tom, reluctantly shaking Crawley's wet-lettuce hand for as short a time as possible, and then surreptitiously wiping his hand down the back of his trousers.

'Never better,' replied Crawley, smooth as an oil slick, 'and looking forward to my new challenge.'

'What challenge?' asked Tom, his gut twisting in anticipation of the answer.

'Peter's just agreed to be our new Chief Operating Officer. It'll be such a feather in our cap to welcome the Wealth Manager of the Year on board,' said Bella smugly. 'He'll be covering the London operation while Jem and I are in Jersey. We contacted him as soon as you resigned.'

Tom felt a chill creeping up the back of his neck as he remembered the letter of resignation he'd taken round to Bella's house and forgotten to retrieve in his hurry to get home and tell Sophie about his promotion. 'I thought we had a deal, Bella,' he said in a low, desperate voice.

'In your dreams!' she hissed vehemently. 'You were never going to cut it at Bailey's. Not enough of an appetite for risk.'

Tom started to remonstrate, 'But, you said everything was—'

Bella held up her hand to stop him. 'Let me spell it out before you humiliate yourself any further. Any possibility of a deal between the two of us died the day you referred to me as your "midlife crisis".'

'Dear me,' mocked Crawley at the stricken look on Tom's face. 'Sounds as if you've thoroughly blotted your copybook, Mr Wright. Whatever would your father make of this, I wonder?'

Gideon, who had returned with the champagne and had been listening to the exchange, shrieked indignantly, 'You can't do that Bella. That's Tom's job!'

Bella said coldly, 'You appear to have nailed your colours to the wrong mast, you ghastly little man. Don't bother coming in on Monday. Ask the temping agency to get you a job as a parrot's understudy or something,' and turning on her heel, she stalked off, Crawley crawling behind her.

'OMG! The bitch just sacked me,' screamed Gideon, looking at Tom in disbelief. 'What am I going to do? How am I going to make ends meet?'

Tom didn't hear him.

Tom was watching Bella, her lips curved in a malevolent smile as she told her brother how Tom had taken the news. Tom was hearing their loud, vindictive laughter.

Tom was watching Sophie proudly push a trolley

containing the perfectly iced, four-tier, flower-strewn birthday cake she had made for Bella towards the braying, spiteful trio.

Tom was watching Bella greet Sophie with a hug, pulling her close and devastating her world with whispered words of destruction.

Tom was watching Sophie stumble away from Bella, her hands pressed hard against her mouth, as if she was trying to stop herself from screaming.

Tom was watching Sophie standing alone, her face illuminated by an explosion of fireworks, her eyes frantically scanning the garden until she saw him and held his gaze for one long, terrible moment before turning and walking away.

Tom was running after everything he'd lost.

The Porkeen in the Pulper Shed

Mark Bastow

Killian Burke dreamed his sister Sorcha was there in the kitchen banging on at him and wrecking his head. Do this. Do that. The old fella walked in and shouted,

'Shut that woman up.'

Killian hit her with a hammer. She shattered as though she was made of china. Killian stood there looking at all the shards of Sorcha scattered over the floor.

The old fella was there cheering. 'You did it at last.'

The dream had seemed so real.

Killian struggled out of bed still wearing his clothes from the night before. As he went to find his shoes, he stubbed his toe on a hammer. He picked it up. His father always seemed to have a hammer in his hand.

He went into the kitchen. Sorcha was at the sink washing up. His sister that he had shattered in his dream. Not a mark on her.

Not a mark on her yet.

'Morning, Killian. I thought I'd pop over and do breakfast. There's dinner in the fridge for you to microwave, but you could come over to Ballymartin House and eat with me and Richard. He's always glad to see you.'

Is he? That's why he looks so miserable when I walk in.

They sat at the kitchen table. He ate in silence.

He had put the hammer down on the table.

He watched Sorcha look at the hammer and then at him. He looked at the hammer and then at her defiantly.

Go on whinge about the hammer.

She looked down at the table.

'This oilcloth has seen a few years, Killian. Perhaps it's time to get a new one. Would you like me to look up a piece in Shaw's?'

What is she going on about? She doesn't live here. Do I go over to her house and tell her what to do?

'No. It was good enough for the old fella, it's good enough for me. I want everything just as he left it.'

She shook her head, picked up the breakfast things and washed up.

He sat there in a sulk.

She went over and kissed him on the cheek. He turned in disgust.

'Killian. You might take a bath.'

There she is casting aspersions again. Am I dirty? Do I smell? Am I always to be humiliated?

'Poor Killian, you look so sad. Is there anything I can do?'

Do us all a favour and drop dead.

'Yes. You can come and look at this.'

'At what, Killian?'

'You'll see. Come quickly.'

Surprise time.

Across the yard and through the sheds they went.

'Look at that. Do you think it is a funny colour?'

She was looking at an open slurry pit.

In she'll go. No one will ever find her.

'It looks normal to me. Same as ours at home, but to be honest I don't spend much time looking at slurry. Are you feeling alright, Killian?'

Shit! I can't do it. What's wrong with me? Why can't I just push her in?

'You think it's OK? That's a relief. I just wondered. Thanks, Sorcha. You are such a help.'

Yuk.

'I need to be off, Killian. Look after yourself. If you need anything give me or Richard a ring.'

As she kissed him, she said it again,

'You look so sad, Killian. Is anything wrong?'

'No. I'm fine.'

He went back into the kitchen. He looked up at the picture of his dad.

Why did you hug her? You never hugged me.

His eye caught the blue circle for the next day on the wall calendar alongside his dad's picture. It was marked: **Kilkenny Mart**.

Fifteen ewes ready for the mart, and the trailer's broke. I'll have to go over to Ballymartin and beg Richard for the loan of one.

Killian took the short cut down by the ash trees his grandfather had planted crossing into Ballymartin estate by the back lane. He crossed into the first field taking little notice of the cows in the far corner.

Halfway across, he stopped. One of the cows had slowly moved towards him.

There is something odd about that cow.

Shit! It's a bull.

Richard's pedigree Angus bull—the Chieftain. That is some nasty bull.

He's standing completely still with his back arched.

He's shaking his head.

That bull is ready to charge.

God. Help me.

I'll never make it.

What is that? Oh, thank you, God.

Richard was at the other end of the field shouting and banging a bucket with a stick. The bull's attention was diverted.

Killian ran to safety.

'Are you trying to get yourself killed, you eejit?'

No need to shout. I'm not deaf and you're the eejit keeping that mad bull. I'd send both of you to the meat factory if I could.

* * *

'Well, Killian, what can I do for you?'

'I'm taking some sheep to the mart, and my trailer wheel has fallen off. Can I borrow a cattle trailer tomorrow?'

'No problem, Killian, and if you need a hand with the wheel, just say. Always ready to help when we can. Will you come up the house and see Sorcha? You know she's always pleased to see you. I could do with a break.'

'No. I'd better get back and get the sheep ready for the morning.'

Have tea with him after he spoke to me like that? No way.

I will kill Richard in this field. As he lies on the ground dead, I will open the gate into the next field and let that bull in. Everyone will think the bull killed him. Then they will kill the bull.

I never liked that bull. He never liked me. That bull will pay for being nasty to me.

I never liked Richard either, but he's got to die anyway. I can't have him inheriting Sorcha's estate when I kill her. Then I'll have the inheritance I was cheated out of, and I can jack in working at the supermarket.

* * *

Back home in Ballymartin House, Richard was telling Sorcha about his encounter with Killian.

'That brother of yours is an eejit,' said Richard.

'Don't call my little brother an eejit. I hope you didn't shout at him. You know how sensitive he is.'

'Of course not. I'd never shout at him.'

'Do you want me to say anything to Killian?'

'Best leave it, but be careful when that fool is about.'

'Don't keep calling him names. He is not a fool, but he was very odd earlier today. He took me to look at a full slurry pit and ask me if it looked the right colour.'

'What colour was it?'

'What do you think? It was the colour of shit.'

'That sounds right. I bet he wanted to ask you something else and then couldn't muster up the courage to ask.'

'Perhaps. I sometimes despair of Killian. My poor little Porkeen, as we used to call him.'

'I always despair of him. The man's nearly forty and has gone to seed.'

'He hasn't gone to seed, and he isn't nearly forty. He is nearly thirty, and the poor mite looks so sad. He must be lonely. We need to find him a wife.'

'A what? Who'd marry him?'

'Don't laugh. We'll get him a wife. It'll make the man.'

'It'll break the woman.'

'Don't be like that. I made a list of eligible ladies, and asked Dominic to discuss it with Killian. I'm expecting Dominic to call by.'

'You've got be joking. That sounds like match making straight out of a John B. Keane play. People don't get partners like that anymore.'

'At least, we'll have given it a try. Have you got any better ideas?'

'Have you suggested online dating?'

'I have, and he said it would look as though he couldn't find someone.'

'Well, he hasn't found anyone. Has he?'

There was a ring at the door. Sorcha's other brother—Father Dominic, parish priest of Ballyfrack.

'Well, Dominic, tell us all.'

'He ruled out all of the ladies I suggested. Mary B. was labelled as very quiet and boring.'

Sorcha asked, 'What does he say about the rest?'

'Breda goes into tantrums and rages if she can't get her way.'

'Well, that is true. I find her scary. What about Jane?'

'She's secondhand goods.'

'I don't believe I'm hearing this. She lived with that man over in Stradbally for a couple of years. That's the way of life these days. What does he expect, a bloody virgin?' Richard exclaimed.

'Apparently, he does.'

'Who else was there?'

'Quite a few. Joanne was too heavy.'

'He's a damn lump of a man himself.'

'The Webley girl is past her sell-by date.'

'Past her sell-by date! She's not a packet of pasta, and she's only a few years older than Killian.'

'Jenny South is too sickly and hasn't got the hips.'

'What on earth is that about? Hasn't got the hips?'

'He says you need good hip formation for childbirth. Jenny also fails because her parents are divorced.'

'Why?'

'Killian doesn't want a wife who thinks marriage is a temporary arrangement. Shall I go on?'

'I think we have heard enough,' Sorcha said. 'What do you think he wants in a wife?'

'He tells me he wants a young professional girl like a doctor or a teacher,' said Dominic.

Richard was shaking his head.

Sorcha intervened. 'Richard, Dominic. You mustn't laugh. The trouble is Aunt Julia drummed it into his head that he should get married to a professional lady. I can remember her saying that if he couldn't get a doctor or a teacher, he could make do with a nurse.'

'Make do with a nurse! Who does he think he is? What did Julia say about who you should marry?' Richard asked.

'Aunt Julia wasn't really that interested in me or Dominic. I remember her once saying I should become a nun. If you keep shouting, I may take her advice.'

'That Aunt Julia of yours has a lot to answer for. She seemed to have an enormous influence on Killian. Why was that?'

Sorcha ignored the question and carried on. 'Guys, have either of you any ideas how I get my little brother a wife?'

'What about getting him to join a club?'

'Well, we could try. Any ideas for a club?'

'What about a book club?' suggested Dominic.

'Has he ever read a book?'

'Richard! You can't say such things. You could take him along to the IFA meetings. He is a farmer, after all.'

'I suppose I could if I have to. There aren't many women at the meetings, though. Except, of course, there's that Jackson girl.'

'What's she like?'

'The rising star of the Macra na Feirme. Problem is, she scores a strong nine out of ten, and Killian scores a weak two or three.'

'Now, don't be cruel. Killian is a fine young man. Any other ideas?'

'You could take him along to your camera club.'

'I'll try,' said Sorcha.

'We have various groups associated with the church over in Ballyfrack. You must have similar groups in Portlaoise. Worth popping into the parish centre and enquiring.'

'Thanks, Dominic I'll do that. Please try and think about this. It breaks my heart to think that our little brother is going to end up a sad old bachelor wondering where his life went.'

'I need to disappear. See you later,' said Richard.

Alone with Dominic, Sorcha continued, 'Richard must never know the truth about Killian. You do understand that.'

'He won't hear it from me. However, I put this question to you yet again. Hasn't Killian the right to know the truth?'

'Certainly not. Killian's fragile enough as it is. It breaks my heart to see him looking so sad.'

'Well, if it was me, I'd want to know.'

'Well, he isn't you. He must never know.'

'But—'

'End of conversation. You'd better go.'

After Dominic had left, Sorcha went up to one of the guest bedrooms. She took down a small leather suitcase from the top of the old mahogany wardrobe. She opened it and took out a little grey shirt. She held it to her face. Tears welled up as she looked down at the contents of the case— the clothes of a ten-year-old Killian. Sorcha sat on the edge of the bed gently rocking while she hugged that little shirt.

* * *

Next morning Sorcha was down to the Coffee Cup in Main Street, Portlaoise.

Mary of Glenduff Drive greeted her. 'Hello, Sorcha. Oh no! That isn't. Is it? It is. The new Marc Jacobs shoulder bag. How on earth did you get one? They're like gold dust.'

'Brown Thomas to the rescue yet again. Enough about handbags, Mary. Sit down. I've ordered coffee. Now tell me is that brother of yours still looking for work in the summer?'

'No, he has a placement on a farm in Meath.'

'Pity. We're looking for help on the farm this summer.'

'Can't Killian help out? After all, he is just down the lane.'

'To be honest, Mary, he is not much help these days. He isn't himself. No get up and go. It's not been good for him being on his own all these years. I'm hoping marriage will improve him.'

'He is getting married? Wow! When's the wedding? Who is the lucky girl?'

'The wedding will be as soon as possible. However, first we need to find the lucky girl.'

'Where do you start?'

'I've no idea.'

'Well, Sorcha the first thing you must do is get rid of the pong. He has serious body odour.'

'I know, Mary. I feel too embarrassed to talk to him about it. How on earth do you say it? I can't.'

'You don't say it. You get his best friend to do it. Man to man.'

'He hasn't got a best friend.'

'He must have friends. What about those three I saw him with in Matthew's Bar. What are their names?'

'You probably mean Kevin and Steve, and I can't think of the other.'

'They're the ones. Get one of them.'

'I couldn't. They would just laugh and call him names. They aren't really his friends. They call him the big man because he's overweight. Poor old Killian thinks being called the big man is a compliment. They only have him around to buy drinks. Well, that's what Kevin's two sisters told me at Sonia Burke's confirmation.'

'I bet they said they were only telling you to help Killian.'

'Yes, but didn't they enjoy my embarrassment.'

'Well, that does it. There is only one thing for it.'

'What's that?'

'Richard will have to do it.'

'Richard! He'll never do it.'

'Sorcha. What did our teachers say about never?'

'Mary. You are right. Richard will not like it, but Richard will do it.'

* * *

Later that day Sorcha and Richard had words.

'You want me to tell Killian to have a bath? I will not. End of subject. I will not even discuss it.'

Richard immediately walked out.

Sorcha smiled. Round one went as she expected. She would win in the end.

* * *

133

Killian was at the supermarket. The morning shift was painful. He was on the checkout.

Mrs Flanagan appeared.

'I thought it was you, Killian, so I came to your till.'

'Thank you, Mrs Flanagan.'

'Tell me how is that lovely sister of yours, Sorcha? She was at school with my Mary. Lovely girl, my Mary. She's in Dublin at St James's. A nurse. She so wanted to be a doctor, but the points let her down. Not fair really. The only ones that are doctors are those whose daddies can afford to pay for the grinds. Look at yourself, Killian, serving in a supermarket. Do you know why you're working in a supermarket?'

'I don't know, Mrs Flanagan.'

'It's because of the grinds.'

'But I didn't do the grinds.'

'That's exactly it, Killian. You didn't do the grinds. If you'd done the grinds, you'd had enough points in your Leaving Certificate to be a doctor or a solicitor.'

Killian saw the manager looking at him and pointing to his watch. A queue was building up.

'Thank you, Mrs Flanagan. We've a bit of queue, so if you could pay, and I'll pass your regards on to Sorcha.'

'Thank you, Killian. You are such a gentleman. I'm very sorry about your grinds. I have plenty of change. I know shops are always short on change. My Richie always says shops are always short of change. Wonderful man, my Richie. Did I ever tell you about the day he—'

'Perhaps another time, Mrs Flanagan. There's a queue waiting behind you.'

With laboured precision she counted out the money. 'So, there is. Never mind, I'll tell you all about my Richie later.'

The next customer had been looking at her watch

and making loud sighs. She thumped down her shopping. A bag of flour burst. A cloud of flour spread across the till. Miss Heavy-Handed glared and with arms akimbo stood there like a sumo wrestler. She looked round to the rest of the queue shaking her head and making loud sighs while Killian cleared the mess and ran off to get another packet of Odlum's Self Raising Flour.

Miss Heavy-Handed turned to her fellow shoppers. 'He wouldn't make the Olympic sprint team, would he?'

Someone laughed.

Killian could see the manager looking and pointing at his watch again.

The mid-morning break eventually came. Up in the canteen, Merker Murphy was showing clips he had taken of Killian running around looking for the flour.

'Ha bloody ha,' Killian shouted. 'Stop taking the piss.'

'Come on then, big man, make me.'

Killian's anger was tempered by fear. Killian's only experience of fights had been at school where he was regularly on the receiving end of Chicken Delaney's punches.

Killian escaped into the kitchen and made his tea. His packet of chocolate tea cakes was gone. When he came back into the canteen, Merker and the others had left. Killian sat down at the table and picked up a screwed-up chocolate tea cake packet. It was empty.

Yappy Yeats appeared with Orla Higgins.

'What's up, Killian, you look depressed?'

'Just one of those mornings.'

'I saw you had Mrs Flanagan. Did she tell you about her knee operation?'

'No. She was going on about the grinds. I didn't do the grinds, and that's why I'm serving in a supermarket instead of being a doctor.'

'You know, Killian, she may have a point. I didn't

do the grinds either. Did you, Orla?'

Orla shook her head.

'Well, that's it, Killian. Case proven. People who don't do the grinds don't become doctors.'

They chuckled.

'Anything else pissing you off, Killian? I see you finished off a packet of chocolate tea cakes. Chocolate tea cakes are the summit of comfort food.'

Killian picked up the empty packet.

'Merker and that crowd took them from my locker and ate them all. They just laughed at me.'

'Have some of the supermarket own-brand biscuits. They're good, and they're free,' said Yappy bringing over the biscuit tin.

'I just fancied chocolate tea cakes.'

'Fair enough. Don't let Merker get you down. It's not worth it.'

'That's right, Killian,' said Orla 'He's shit. I'd like to push him down the toilet and flush him away.'

'I think Merker fancies you, Orla. He keeps staring at you,' said Yappy.

'Oh God. Imagine being Mrs Merker. It'd give you nightmares.'

'Imagine all the little Merkers running about,' said Yappy waving his hands in mock horror.

They laughed.

'Anyone fancy going to the cinema tonight. I'm going to see the new Gleeson film. I could pick you up,' said Yappy.

'Oh yes,' said Orla.

Killian looked at Orla. She was smiling like the proverbial cat with the cream. Killian knew that while Merker spent time looking at Orla, Orla herself was looking at Yappy.

Killian shook his head. As soon as he declined, he started to think of whether he should change his mind.

'OK, Orla, I'll pick you up about quarter past seven. I'll just need to pick up Anne first,' said Yappy.

Killian was now glad he had declined. Anne Yeats was, of course, Yappy's twelve-year old sister. If Yappy was yappy, Anne was worse.

'Oh. Sorry, Yappy, I've just remembered. I've something on tonight,' said Orla.

'No prob. I'll tell you all about it tomorrow. I'll do the cups.'

Yappy disappeared into the kitchen with the cups.

'I didn't want to be tagging along on Yappy's date,' said Orla.

Orla obviously thought that Anne was Yappy's girlfriend. Killian wasn't going to correct her.

'I could take you to see the film one night you're free. We could have a McDonald's after.'

'Thanks for the offer, Killian, but I'll give that film a miss. I'll catch it on Sky next year.'

As Orla sadly looked towards the kitchen, Killian took a good look at her.

'Tell me, Orla. Did you ever think about becoming a nurse?'

'No, Killian. I did think about becoming a mountaineer, but I've no head for heights. I enquired about becoming a marine biologist. I was told there weren't many opportunities for marine biologists in Laois. Something to do with having no coast.'

Pity. She'd look good in a nurse's uniform.

* * *

Killian had just finished cleaning out the big cattle shed. Mucky old job. In the kitchen, he kicked off his boots. Put the kettle on. At least, he could relax now. Then he heard a car in the yard.

Fucking Richard. What does he want?

'Good to see you, Richard. Come on in.'

Killian held out his hand. Richard just stared at

Killian's outstretched hand. Killian looked at his hand and wiped the muck off it on his green overalls. The overalls were splattered in cow muck anyway.

'Tea?'

'Thanks.'

They chatted. The weather. Lawlor's new hay sheds. The price of feed.

Killian took a barmbrack from the press.

Cut two slices. Thrust one at Richard.

What's he looking at my hands like that for?

Killian waved the fly off the butter and pushed it towards Richard.

'Good isn't it?' Killian pointed at the brack.

Richard nodded.

'Another slice?'

'No. No. One's enough.'

What's he doing coming in here and pulling faces at Killian's cake? What does he want?

Killian looked at the hammer.

Killian must be patient. Killian must wait.

After a silence, Richard spoke. 'Killian, I want to say something.'

'Well, say it.'

Richard put the plastic bag on the table. He took out two cans of deodorant, some bath soak and a bar of soap.

Killian guessed what was coming.

'Don't be embarrassed, Richard. Just ask. The water's hot. If you want a shower just go through to the bathroom and work away. There's a couple of bags of sheep nuts in the shower. Just put them in the bath with the others.'

'No, Killian, *I* don't want a shower.'

'Have a bath then.'

'Killian, it's not me that needs a bath. It's *you*.'

'What did you say?'

138

'You need a bath. You smell.'

Killian looked at the hammer.

'Well, that's not a nice thing to say.'

'I'm sorry if I've hurt your feelings.'

Killian glared at Richard for a moment. Then he looked at the hammer.

'Well, Killian, I am trying to help you. You smell. That will put people off you. If you shower or bath regularly, you won't have a problem. It hasn't been easy coming over here to say that. If it was up to me, I wouldn't have bothered, but Sorcha is worried about you. Women have very sensitive noses.'

'You come into my home and insult me. You say I smell. You'd better go.'

'Killian, don't take it so personally.'

'How else can I take it? It is very personal. Now piss off.'

'Killian, what can I say?'

'Nothing. Get out of here.'

'Well, I'll take these back,' Richard said, reaching for the deodorant and soap.

'No. Leave them but go. Go.'

Richard walked out.

Killian was thinking,

Who does he think he is? Saying I stink. It's bad enough getting it at work from Merker Murphy. Merker's always calling me smelly.

Killian picked up the knife. 'They'll be sorry they weren't nice to Killian.'

* * *

Back at Ballymartin House that evening over the steak casserole, Sorcha broached the Killian subject.

'Did you have a chance to see Killian today?'

'Yes.'

'How did he take it?'

'Quite well, really. I think I handled it rather well.'

'I'm so proud of you, Richard. Strong but sensitive, as always.'

* * *

Over at the Burke homeplace, the six bags of sheep nuts that had been in the bath were now blocking the hallway, but as everyone came in through the kitchen, it didn't matter. Lying back in the bath, Killian was enjoying a long conversation with himself. Like some people who live on their own, he often chatted to himself.

'There's no company like your own.'

The bath soak bottle said: **Relax in a beautiful fragrance**. It was very relaxing. The fragrance was very pleasing.

'Bet Sorcha chose it. I shall miss her.'

* * *

Friday night. Killian looked in the mirror. Last week the new barmaid in Ramsbottom's had asked him if he was a rugby player. He reminded her of someone she had seen on the telly. He supposed he had that strong look. Pity he couldn't act strong, and just do away with his sister and her husband. Never mind. Time to go in and have a few pints with the lads.

First stop was Matthew's Bar. There should be someone there he knew. There was.

At the end of the bar, Killian saw the huddle of Kevin, Steve and Fintan. Killian said that he was in the chair if they wanted a drink. His offer was taken up. It normally was. It was a favour rarely returned.

The three lads huddled together in such way that Killian was not part of the group. They spoke softly knowing Killian had difficulty in hearing what was said. Killian's hearing on his right was not good.

He stood there, pint in hand, next to his three friends, but alone and excluded. He downed the pint. He said in a loud voice he was off to meet a friend.

He went down the Main Street looking for a

friend. No friends in sight. Truth was, he had no friends as such, but any acquaintance he met would have served as a friend. Too early to go home.

Bag of curried chips and sausages?

Killian had just joined a long queue outside the Tasty Plaice when he heard them. They must have been up by O'Loughlin's Hotel. One each side of the Main Street shouting at each other. Sounded like the Madigans. Looked like the Madigans.

Don't let it be the Madigans.

Shit! It is the Madigans.

Perhaps they will turn off and go down Church Avenue.

Please go down Church Avenue.

On they came. The twin brothers, Connor and Rory. Early twenties. Shaven heads. Tattooed arms. The swagger. The jerky movements. The unpredictability. Their very appearance intimidating.

First, they didn't join the queue. They just stared at it from the pavement. Killian tried not to look at them. He stared at the back of the head in front of him.

Please don't cause trouble. Please go away.

Then Connor Madigan went up and spoke to one of the girls inside waiting for her order to be bagged.

Probably asking her the time. I've seen this done before.

Meanwhile, Rory Madigan went up to a man in his sixties near the front of the queue and tapped him on the shoulder. He turned and spoke with Rory. When the older man turned back to face the front, he found Connor Madigan in front of him.

'Hey, you. Get to the back of the queue.'

'You what?'

'You've just pushed in.'

The older man was gesturing for him to go back.

'I was here all the fucking time. You just didn't see me,' said Connor

'I saw you come in, walk up the front. Get to the

back where you belong.'

'Don't you tell me where I belong. I was here all the time.'

'No. He wasn't, was he?' The older man turned appealing to the others in the queue for support.

The queue shuffled in uneasy silence.

The older man tried to push the Madigan to one side. There was a tussle.

The owner shouted, 'Any trouble, I'll call the Guards.'

Now both Madigans were standing in front of the older man.

Rory Madigan told the older man to stop causing trouble.

The older man gave up trying to assert his place. A strained peace descended.

As the Madigans went out they stopped and stared at the older man for a few minutes. He looked frightened.

Then two paces down, they picked on Killian.

'What are you looking at?' slurred Rory.

'Nothing,' squeaked Killian.

Rory moved very close to Killian. Killian could feel Rory's breath. Smell the alcohol.

'Nothing,' Rory Madigan mimicked Killian's squeaky answer. Killian was terrified.

They laughed. They waited outside eating chips.

When the older man came out, they both screamed out, 'Fuck you!' as he passed them. The older man stopped. He was white-faced. The Madigans laughed, and then ran up the Main Street in the roadway shouting. Cars they met had to stop.

Killian sat on the stone bench outside Shaw's old shop to eat his food. He felt sick. Fear had that effect on him. The Madigans had frightened him. He finished the sausages. He decided to bin the rest of the chips. He walked over to a builders' skip opposite Hughes Pharmacy.

As he threw the remnants of his supper into it, he saw a short piece of piping amongst the broken plaster board and building rubble. He leaned over and pulled it out.

That'll come in handy round the farm.

He looked up Main Street. What had seemed exciting and inviting two hours ago now seemed threatening and sinister. He wouldn't have another drink. He'd go home.

* * *

Coming to Kavanagh's Bar, he popped inside to use the jacks at the back. The two Madigan lads were there in the bar. Rory knocked into Killian and said, 'What's your trouble.'

'Sorry. No offence meant,' Killian answered.

'Watch yourself or ...' Rory drew his finger across his throat.

Connor Madigan now joined in. 'It's Mr Nothing from the chipper.'

Rory mimicked Killian with a squeaky, 'Nothing.'

Killian could see everyone looking at him. He went red. As he walked on, he could hear them laughing.

Killian sat on the toilet seat. He was not happy. He didn't like being spoken to that way. He didn't like being laughed at. He wanted to kill those Madigans. Smash their heads. He felt inside his coat. He had that pipe from the skip. It was a foot long of galvanised steel with a welded elbow curve at the end. He could use it like a hammer to smash their heads. He was still afraid. He was especially afraid of the Madigans.

Bum wiped and hands washed, he made his way back through the bar back towards the Main Street. Thankfully no sign of the Madigans. Better play safe. Have a drink here and give the Madigans a chance to move on up the street as far as possible.

A few drinks later, Killian walked up an empty Main Street. It was well late. He knew he couldn't drive home, but he just wanted to check his car before ringing for a taxi.

He cut through the alley way by the Bank of Ireland going into Lyster Square, and there was Rory Madigan. Kneeling on the ground, retching.

Killian walked quickly hoping to pass unnoticed. Around the corner, Connor Madigan appeared.

Killian stopped. He felt trapped.

'What are you staring at?' Connor snarled.

'Nothing,' Killian replied.

'You think I'm nothing. Is that it?'

Connor stepped very close to Killian.

Killian was terrified. He closed his eyes. He had little memory of what had happened next, except his arm just going up and down. He had no recollection of pulling out the pipe. When Killian opened his eyes, Connor was on the ground. The pipe was in Killian's hand. There was blood on Killian's hand. There was blood on the pipe.

Killian stood there shaking. He needed to get rid of the pipe. Needed to wipe his prints off the pipe. He used a rag from his pocket that he had used to clean his hands when he came in from the yard. He used the rag to hold the pipe as he ran to the bins in the corner past the bank. *No, he wouldn't put it in there*, he thought; that would be the first place the Guards would look.

Then he remembered Rory.

Did he see it? Was he a witness? Do I need to kill him as well?

Killian ran back to the alley way.

Rory was on the ground huddled in the pet shop doorway moaning.

'Are you alright, mate?' Killian asked.

Rory muttered something unintelligible without looking up.

Killian raised the pipe to strike Rory, but the sound of voices distracted him. He ran and hid behind a parked car. The voices faded. He heard a door slam. Silence. He emerged from behind the car. He decided to leave Rory.

He was too far gone to have seen, and I need to get out of here fast.

He looked round for somewhere to dump the pipe. In the end, he took the pipe with him. He could throw into a ditch on the way home.

Killian ran to his own car over by SuperValu. He knew he was in no state to drive home. With blood on his jacket and shirt, he couldn't get a taxi. He'd have to drive. He drove off, narrowly missing a parked van. He came to a halt just before the kerb and the parking ticket dispenser. He reversed up and went the wrong way down Bull Lane. A mistake, but at least that way he could get to the back roads quickly. He got to the bend past Chicken Delaney's on autopilot. He pulled over and threw up on the verge. He was shaking, but he was sober now. He felt relief as he was almost home. Suddenly, he realised his achievement. He had killed someone. He smiled. He was still shaking, but he was smiling. He had done it. Now killing his sister would be a piece of cake. A piece of Battenberg, he laughed.

* * *

It was a good day for Killian. He woke feeling a strange combination of relief and achievement on killing Connor Madigan. He now knew he could kill. Now it was a question of time before he righted the great wrong done to him. He would kill Richard. Then he would kill Sorcha and claim his rightful inheritance.

There were no delays on the road. Parked in his favourite spot at work. No sooner had he parked than Orla Higgins's red car pulled in beside his. She had the looks, the walk, the wiggle of the hips, the swish of the dress, the flick of the hair.

He caught her up. They walked in together, chatting.

Damian 'Merker' Murphy was smoking by the waste bins.

'See you know your place, Merker,' Orla shouted across.

'What?'

'By the bins with the rest of the waste,' replied Orla

'Bitch.'

'Prick,' replied Orla.

* * *

Shelf-stacking can be a pain, but Killian was paired with Yappy Yeats. Yeats's yapping was entertaining, and the banter sped the time to tea break.

Killian saw Orla going up to the canteen and followed her up.

Killian and Orla were alone at first, but then Orla groaned,

'Oh no. Look what's come in.'

Merker had arrived.

Coffee in hand, he sat next to Killian.

'Shouldn't you be on the late break?' Killian asked.

'Who cares what break I'm on? The CCTV isn't working up here. I heard the manager on to the electrician to get it fixed. So Big Brother in the office downstairs won't know. He thinks I'm up in the stationery store getting ink cartridges.'

'You don't have to sit with us, Merker. We wouldn't mind if you sat over there,' said Orla.

'Now that's not very nice, Orla. I know you really want me to sit with you. Let's face it, you're going make no one jealous sitting with Killian.'

'What do you mean?'

'It's obvious. Look at him. Overweight, dirt under his fingernails and playing for the other side.'

Killian put down his tea mug on the canteen table.

'You what?'

'Killian's a gay boy.'

'What if he is gay? Are you gay, Killian?'

'No.'

'Killian's coming out. He's gay.'

'I'm not.'

'You leave Killian alone. If he says he's not gay, he isn't gay. It wouldn't matter if he was.'

'Well, look at him. He's not married. He's not got a girl. What else can he be?'

'I'll tell you something, Merker.'

'Yes, Orla.'

'As you are homophobic, I'm gonna tell everyone you're gay, and I saw you making a pass at Killian. Killian will back me up, won't you?'

Killian nodded.

Merker stood up, banged his mug on the table, and stormed off.

'Hey, Merker, come back. You've forgotten something.'

'What have I forgotten, Orla?'

'Your mug. Take it, wash it and put it away. You homophobic waste of space.'

Grabbing his mug, Merker muttered, 'Lash.'

'What did he call me?' fumed Orla. 'I've just about had all I can take from him.'

* * *

A few minutes later Merker reappeared at the canteen door holding two boxes of ink cartridges and said, 'Oh, the lovebirds. How sad can you get? Frigid Orla chatting up gay Killian.'

As Merker disappeared to go downstairs, Orla was out of her seat like a greyhound out of the traps.

'That does it. I'll kill him,' she screamed.

Merker was just stepping down the first step of the stairs when Orla caught up with him and gave him a shove in the back. He lost balance and tumbled down the stairs, the boxes falling and spilling out the cartridges.

Orla spun round and went back into the canteen saying, 'That'll learn him.'

Killian was left at the top of the stairs watching Merker collect up the spilt cartridges. Merker came back up the top of the stairs and said, 'What is that woman on? She could have fucking killed me.'

Fucking killed him? Well, that's an idea. Let's give it a try.

As Merker stepped forward to go down the stairs for the second time, Killian barged into the back of him with his full body weight. Merker went down at speed, banging his head on the stone steps, cartridges spilling out again. This time he didn't get up. A pool of blood appeared next to his head.

Killian smiled.

That went well. Better than expected. Doubt if it killed him. If it didn't, he'll think Orla pushed him again.

Killian returned to the canteen and joined Orla.

'Do you fancy a second brew?'

'Go on, then. Better make it a quick one.'

They chatted for a while. Killian retold the stories Yappy had told him earlier that morning about Mrs Flanagan.

'You are so funny, Killian.'

'Thanks, Orla.'

She is eating out of my hand.

The store manager came in speaking on his mobile to his area manager.

'Yes. He must have slipped on the stairs. The first-aider has been unable to resuscitate him. It's not looking good. The ambulance is on the way. I thought you ought to know as we'll have the Gardaí and health and safety crawling over the place.'

The manager returned to the ongoing emergency in the stairwell.

'What have I done?' gasped Orla. 'I gave him a good push. I never meant to kill him.'

'Orla, he must have tripped on the stairs. Whatever you say, say nothing. If he's dead, he's dead. Nothing will bring him back. If you mention the pushing him down the stairs, you'll only distress his family.'

'Do yer think so?'

'I know so. They'll be upset that he had an accident. They'd be more upset to think someone pushed him.'

'Oh God. I said I'd kill him. Then I pushed him down the stairs and killed him,' said Orla.

'I didn't hear you say anything about killing him. We were just here having a coffee.'

Through the flood of tears Orla managed, 'You are so good, Killian.'

She clutched at Killian's arm.

The manager came in with two Guards.

'Killian, you'd better run Orla home,' said the store manager who was clearly wondering why Orla was taking it so badly.

'We will need to question them,' said one of the Guards.

'No need,' said the store manager, 'I saw these two go up to the canteen before it happened, and they are still here. They would have seen nothing. Murphy wasn't in the canteen. I sent him to get ink cartridges from the storeroom. I warned him about running down two steps at a time. I told him he'd have an accident, and now the bloody fool has. Oh God, I shouldn't have said it that way. I didn't mean to sound uncaring.'

Then turning to Killian and Orla he said, 'Now you two get off, and Killian no need to rush back. You take the rest of the day off, Orla, and don't take it so badly. It wasn't your fault he played the fool going down the stairs. Killian, make sure she has some tea and stay with her a while.'

The Guard intervened.

'They will need to stay just while I get an initial statement.'

Orla was weeping. She became hysterical, convulsed with shaking and weeping, clinging to Killian's arm.

The Guard disappeared for a while. When he came back, he took Killian and Orla's details and a brief statement from them. Killian did most of the speaking.

Killian led Orla down the stairs past the lifeless Merker, past the pool of blood.

Not so full of yourself now.

When they got in the car, Orla kept saying, 'What have I done?'

Killian response was, 'Nobody saw anything, so keep quiet. Don't tell anyone what happened. Don't even tell your mother. Let's face it, you could spend the next twenty years in jail for what you did.'

Orla dissolved into a blabbering state.

* * *

Sergeant Morrisey chatted away to a colleague in the car park of Portlaoise Garda Station.

'I heard the inspector talking to the assistant state pathologist. There's nothing suspicious about the injuries the young Murphy lad sustained. They are all consistent with falling down the stairs. Apparently, he was carrying a big box of printing cartridges down, and, would you believe it, he was running down two steps at a time? Poor lad has paid for his stupidity in a big way.'

'His funeral can go ahead?'

'They're digging the hole as we speak.'

'Arrangements announced?'

'Reposing at his parents' home from 5.30 p.m. tonight, with rosary at 8 p.m. Mass tomorrow at 12 noon followed by burial in Saints Peter and Paul's cemetery.'

'Will you go to the Mass or to the house? We'll be missed if we don't go. We are both neighbours.'

'Let's go to the Mass. I'll OK it with the inspector. They'll be eating after at the Killeshin, so we'll get a good sit-down meal.'

'Are you going to the music over in Vicarstown on Saturday night?'

'No way.'

'You don't know what you'll be missing. It should be good.'

* * *

What a stupid idea.

Thought Killian when he heard that the store manager had asked the staff to form a guard of honour in front of the church when the coffin was received into the church, and then again to walk behind the hearse the next day as it went the mile from Saints Peter and Paul's church up to the cemetery.

'I will be perfectly all right,' said Orla, gulping down another glass of brandy.

'You had enough. You need to go home and rest. You're in no state to go tonight.'

'I'm in a state of readiness. Mr Hennessey, producer of fine brandy, has fortified me. It's time to go and receive the poor lad into the church.'

They walked down to the church like a couple who had arrived early for a wedding and spent too much time in the pub waiting. He held her arm to stop her swaying into the road.

The guard of honour was formed. The hearse arrived. There was the mingle. The crowding. The pall bearers—all big Murphy men—made light of the coffin but heavy of the occasion.

As the coffin went up the church steps past the guard of honour, Orla freaked. She fell. Killian caught her. She almost collided with one of the pall-bearers.

She was wailing.

Then as the family passed, she screamed,

'I did it.'

The Murphy mother, a great lump of a woman, stopped and stared at the sobbing wench. The rest of the mourners following the coffin stopped.

As the family halted, the pall-bearers and coffin disappeared into the church. At the foot of the altar, a bevy of priests stood watching in bewilderment as the pall-bearers and coffin came up the central aisle with no mourners.

Killian eventually spoke up,

'She was very close to Damian. They worked together. I think she's had an accident.'

'I think you'd better get her home,' said Damian's father, giving Orla a hug. 'Never mind, sweet lass, our Damian is at peace at last. It's just nice to know there was someone else who loved him as much as we did. You and your friend must come and sit with the family tomorrow. We'll always think of you as family now. See you, then.'

Orla was shaking by now. Her sobs were almost silent but continuous. When Killian got her into the car, she exploded into a fit, repeatedly shouting, 'I did it. I did it. I killed him!'

No one could hear her apart from Killian. He put the radio on and drove out of the car park. As he drove down the Stradbally Road, she kept up her hysterical screaming, 'I'm going to prison. Oh. My. God. I'm a murderer. Oh God, help me. I keep seeing him lying there. His head in a pool of blood. What did I do?'

When he got to the Block Road, Killian decided he couldn't take her straight back to the Higgins's homeplace. She'd still be screaming that she had killed the Merker. He turned and headed for the Burke farm.

When he got home, he sat Orla down at the kitchen table.

There was a silence at long last. Thank goodness.

Killian made tea. They sat both staring at the oilcloth.

Orla broke the silence,

'Do you think my mammy will come and visit me in the prison? She's on the Council, you know. She'll have to resign. I've disgraced the family.'

Then the heavy, uncontrolled sobbing.

He sat there not knowing what to do.

On and on it went. Repetitive moaning until Killian could stand it no more.

Killian stood her up and marched her to the spare bedroom door.

'Go and lie down. Pull yourself together.'

He went back to the kitchen and put Midlands Radio on.

Peace at last, even if was courtesy of the radio.

He waited an hour. Made tea. Took a cup into Orla. She was asleep. Her skirt had ridden up. She had nice legs. She looked so calm, so pretty, so helpless. He put the tea down and woke her.

She was in shock, shivering and almost delirious.

'Where am I? What happened? I didn't kill him. Tell me, I didn't kill him.'

Killian sat there next to her on the bed wondering what to do.

'I'm so cold. Please hold me.'

He held her like he would have held a sack of potatoes. She snuggled into him. At some stage they kissed.

Killian never quite knew how they had gone from kissing to making love.

Afterwards, she went into the kitchen and sat there weeping,

'You took advantage of me, Killian.'

Killian was confused.

What is she on about? We've just been to fucking heaven

and back. She was fantastic. Orla, you are one fit girl, but you'd better stop this nonsense about me taking advantage.

'You don't want to make accusations. Listen, Orla. You're a murderer. So, thank me. I'm the only one saving you from twenty years in prison. Do you want me to go to the Guards?'

'Of course not, Killian. You're right. Now please hold me. I feel cold. You've been so good to me.'

After a while in his arms, she looked up and said,

'Thank you for protecting me. Can you take me home, Killian, dear?'

Orla's mother, the formidable County Councillor Orla Higgins, was very questioning to Killian when he took Orla home.

'She's in bed now. Now tell me, Killian, why is she so upset at Damian Murphy's death? She often came home saying how nasty he was. He was always coming on to her, and then upsetting her. She couldn't have had a crush on him, could she?'

'No. He wasn't nice to Orla. He wasn't nice to anyone. He sneered at everyone. I think he was upset that Orla and I have got so close. I don't know if Orla has told you, but she's thinking of moving in with me.'

'Well, that is a surprise. It all seems very sudden. She said nothing about to me.'

'I'll drop by in the morning in case she wants to go to the funeral, but it might be best if she gives it a miss. Tell her everyone will understand if she is not there.'

'Thank you, Killian. You have been a great help to my poor girl. A real saint, you are.'

When he got home to bed, he couldn't sleep at first. He fantasised life with Orla—the marriage in Saints Peter and Paul's church, the honeymoon in Lanzarote, and their children: two boys and the girl. Now was his chance. She was eating out of his hand. If she changed her mind, he would remind her that she needed him to stay quiet.

The day dawned. The signs on the supermarket stated:

Closed for today due to the sad loss of Damian Murphy. A friend and colleague sorely missed.

With the requiem at noon, Killian presented himself at Orla's house at 11 a.m. Quick look at himself in the car mirror. Knock on the door.

'She's already gone. Dan Murphy picked her up about half an hour ago. He came in for tea. Ever such a nice lad. He's a solicitor, don't you know?'

'How is herself?'

'She was not good at breakfast, but when Dan arrived, she picked up. There she was laughing and giggling like old times.'

'Well thanks, Mrs Higgins; I'd better be off.'

'You couldn't give me a lift into Portlaoise to the county council offices? I'm going to the funeral, but I'm meeting Irene Walsh from the planning department first, and we'll go together.'

By the time he had dropped off Mrs Higgins, the churchyard was parked up. Killian had to go park down the Boris Road. He rushed in late. The church was packed. He squeezed in towards the middle next to David Dearing.

'Shouldn't you join your girlfriend?' asked David Dearing.

'Where is she?'

'She's up with the family. I didn't realise you were so matey with the Murphys.'

'I am not. I'll stay here.'

The service started. Killian kept waiting for an eruption from the front row when Orla started screaming. It didn't happen.

He listened as the parish priest gave his address, telling the congregation how Merker had been a friend to everyone.

After the Mass, they gathered outside the church to walk up past St Fintan's hospital to the cemetery. The supermarket workers formed two lines and walked behind the hearse after the family. Orla did not join the guard of honour, instead walking with Dan Murphy and the family.

After the burial, Killian and David Dearing stood chatting as they went to sympathise with the family.

Afterwards, David Dearing turned to Killian and said, 'I think your Orla has changed allegiance. She seems with be with young Dan.'

'I think you may be right.'

'Never mind, you could always go for the mother. She's not bad-looking and if you ever needed planning permission, she'd be the woman to get it. You know she's Chair of the Planning Committee?'

Chicken Delaney was listening with a smirk on his face.

Killian was not amused.

Off to the Killeshin they went for the afters.

Chicken Delaney nudged Killian,

'Aren't you going to join your girlfriend on the table with the family?'

Killian ignored the question.

David Dearing joined in the Killian-baiting.

'No, Chicken. Orla is Killian's yesterday girl. Today Killian's love is Orla's mother. He is going for the more mature lady.'

'I am not. I'm not listening to this rubbish anymore. I'm off to the jacks.'

Walking out of the jacks, Killian bumped into Orla.

'What do you think you are doing?' asked Killian.

'What do you mean?'

'I thought we were an item.'

'Us an item? Think again.'

'You were all over me last night.'

'I was not. You took advantage of me, you bastard.'

'Aren't you forgetting something?'

'What's that?'

'I know you pushed Merker down the stairs.'

'So what? Say anything, and I'll say it was you.'

'That's not true.'

'Killian, dear, it's what people believe that counts, not the truth.'

Her eyes glared, and Killian's face went white.

Killian grabbed her left arm as she walked away. She spun round. Her right fist flew.

'Look what you've done, you fucking bitch,' Killian whined with both hands on his bloodied nose.

Killian stared at the back of Orla as she disappeared back into the hotel lobby. He had lost her and along with her, the girl and two boys he had imagined fathering with her. Back in the toilet he cleaned himself up. The nosebleed wasn't too bad. A few spots on his shirt. He stood dazed in the corridor.

Killian became aware that he was being gently shaken. It was Mrs Higgins with the Walsh woman from the Planning Department.

'We thought as we'd missed the funeral, the least we could do was to turn up at the afters.'

She gave Killian a wink.

The Walsh woman asked, 'Are you alright Killian? You don't look well.'

'No. I've never been finer. Just a bit of a nosebleed.'

With that Killian strode back into the dining room, called a waiter to get two main courses for Mrs Higgins and the Walsh woman. He sat down and picked at his dessert of apple pie and cream.

* * *

It was a fierce evening. A gale blew through the yard. Metal sheets on the hay sheds banged and rattled. Rushing from one shed to another to avoid the rain, Killian slipped. He lay on his back for a second checking his limbs that nothing was broken. He was OK. He looked at his watch. Time for tea.

He walked into the kitchen and took off his wet clothes down to his boxer shorts. He went to put on the kettle. The kettle was hot, just boiled.

'Don't mind me, Killian. I made tea when I came in.'

'Well, Dominic, I didn't see thee sitting in the corner. You don't change much over the years. Still skulking in the corner. Remember dad always called you the Skulker and me the Porkeen?'

'Yes, I do remember. He should never have called us by those names. I hated being called Skulker.'

'I liked being called the Porkeen. Made me feel special being given a pet name.'

'Didn't you ever think Dad was cruel to you?'

'Certainly not. Hard but fair.'

'Come off it, Killian. He put you on that long chain in the pulper shed for hours on end. You were chained up like a dog. Sometimes he forgot about you, and Sorcha had to plead with him to let you out when it got dark. It was a barbaric way to treat a young child.'

'No. It wasn't. It was no different than putting a child in a playpen. It kept me safe. Farmyards are dangerous. He was learning me to toughen me up. Thought I was soft. Our dad was a good man. A better man than either of us.'

'Then why did he disinherit me when I went to the seminary?'

'Because you let him down badly. You should have stayed and helped him with the farm. He might have been still alive if you had pulled your weight instead of skiving off to Maynooth to polish your bloody halo. You don't know how badly he took your desertion. He'd go in the yard and shake his fist at the sky. He never forgave God for stealing you.'

'Well, dear brother, our dear father was going to leave you nothing.'

'That's not true. He would have left me the whole farm, but Sorcha poisoned his mind against me.'

'That is not true, Killian. He was excluding you from the will. When he told Sorcha, she pleaded with him to leave you half the estate.'

'Well, a fine half I got. A damp house. A few acres and no money.'

'Come off it, Killian. There was no money, and you didn't do badly. Think of me, I got nothing.'

'What does a priest want land or money for? Listen to me, Saint Dominic, you should read your damn Bible. Christ told the rich man to give all he had away to the poor.'

'Thank you for the sermon, Killian. Can we call a truce?'

'All right, Skulker.'

'Thank you, Porkeen. Now the reason I came was to invite you to dinner at the Old Money Tree. I've asked Sorcha and Richard.'

'The occasion?'

'My birthday. Don't worry. I had a lovely card in the post from you in Sorcha's handwriting, as usual.'

'Well, Happy Birthday, brother. Let's hope you age better in the next year than you did in the last, Skulker.'

'Let's hope we both have a good year ahead, Porkeen.'

'You'll stay the night afterwards.'

'I hoped you'd ask. My case is in the car.'

'Will I book a taxi?'

'Already done.'

* * *

159

Later at the Old Money Tree, the conversation turned to the family, and Dominic proposed a toast.

'Well, here's to us Burkes. Norman Irish. Proud and defiant. Say the Burke motto together.'

'Ung roy, ung foy, ung loy.'

'How can you say one king, one faith, and one law when we are a republic?' asked Richard.

'It's just tradition. Let's face it, we've got the name. We may not be lords and ladies. Our ancestors were probably just servants to the Burkes, but it's fun to pretend,' said Dominic.

'Mother always said that Edmund Burke was a distant relative,' said Sorcha.

'More like a distant hope,' said Richard.

'Why, Richard, do you always try to put the Burkes down?' asked Killian.

'I think it's silly all this fuss about a name,' said Richard.

'Spoilsport,' said Sorcha.

'Well, the family name is important to me, and you, Richard, should not disrespect it,' said Killian, pointing the finger. 'I'm a Burke and proud of it. We're not like you Martins, who got their farmlands handed to them on a plate courtesy of the Land Commission. We Burkes had to work for our property.'

'You've a bloody cheek,' responded Richard.

'Boys! Remember the rule. No fighting at the table. I'm sure both our families got their lands honestly,' said Sorcha.

'Pity we have no one to carry on our family names,' said Dominic.

'How about you, Dominic? Do you think the church will ever allow priests to marry?' asked Sorcha.

'It will happen. It's a question of when. Just like women priests. The tide of history will change all, but I expect to be an old man when it happens.'

'Why do you always want to be controversial, Dominic? If the church has never allowed married priests in the past, why should it start now?' replied Richard.

'For the first six centuries the Church allowed priests to marry. Remember, St Peter was married.'

'He wasn't.'

'He was. One of Christ's first miracles was to cure St Peter's mother-in-law. You don't acquire a mother-in-law without acquiring a wife. They come as a bundle.'

'Can't you leave the scripture lessons at the church door?' said Richard.

Sorcha saw one of those argumentative bouts between Richard and her brothers developing. It could spoil the evening. What could she do?

'Shall I tell them, Richard?' Sorcha whispered in Richard's ear.

Richard pulled a face and shook his head. Killian and Dominic sensed there was something to tell.

'What is it?'

'Come on. Don't keep us in the dark.'

'There's going to be an addition to our family.'

'You don't mean what I think you mean, do you?'

'Yes. A Christmas baby. A girl.'

'Congratulations. That's wonderful.'

'Oh dear. What's the matter, Killian? You've gone very pale. Are you unwell?'

Killian was in severe shock. He had no problem in justifying his intention to kill Richard and Sorcha. That was necessary to inherit his birth right. Now there was this unborn interloper. Could he kill her? If he waited until she was born, she would inherit instead of Killian. She would have to die in the womb along with her mother. Then he would be murdering the innocent unborn. It was awful. He visualised the unborn foetus. He felt sick.

'Speak to us, Killian. Richard, you had better get an ambulance. Killian's having a turn of some sort.'

'No. No. Don't get an ambulance. I'm all right.'

'What is it, Killian?' asked Sorcha.

Killian thought quickly. 'Stop making a fuss. I just thought I may have left the far field gate open and the cattle could get into the turnips, but I remember closing it now.'

'Thank goodness for that. You mustn't worry so much, Killian.'

* * *

Two days later Killian was thinking.

For everything there is a season, and a time for all matters. A time to kill. That time has come. I have dilly dallied long enough. First, I lay the trap.

Putting his size nine boots to one side, he put on his father's old size ten boots. He put his rigger gloves and a bucket of stock feed pellets in the boot of his car. He drove over to the Ballymartin estate. He left the car down by the road and walked up the trackway with the gloves and bucket. He stopped by the gate from the Long Meadow to the Home Pasture. He felt the length of rope in his pocket. He put a packet of rat poison by the gate in the Long Meadow. He waited.

Richard drove up. Ten o'clock on the dot.

'Hi Killian. Now what is it you wanted to ask me about Sorcha that is such a secret we have to meet out here?' said Richard

'Before I ask, what is that packet of rat poison doing there?'

'I don't know but I'll get it up. I can't risk the cattle eating it.'

Richard went over the fence. As he bent down to pick up the packet, Killian took out the rope. The noose was pre-knotted. Killian lassoed Richard's neck. Pulled hard and fast. There was nothing Richard could do. He was held against the gate by the tightening rope, and Killian was a metre away on the other side of the gate pulling.

Richard's face went very red. Killian eased the pressure a little to prolong the agony. He wanted Richard to taste death. Then he pulled as hard as he could and waited. Killian was surprised how quickly Richard's body went from frenzied struggling to limp.

Killian went over the gate with his bucket of pellets. Took Richard's mobile and texted Chicken Delaney.

Please come over asap if you can. I need help with the bull.

Chicken Delaney may not like Richard, but he would always respond to a request for help.

Killian removed the rope, opened the gate, and shook the bucket. He threw some pellets down into the next field. Then he threw the rest on the ground around Richard. Chieftain Angus and his ladies came running to that feeding sound of the pellets rattled in the bucket. He wiped Richard's mobile and threw it down in the mud by the body.

Killian smiled as the Chieftain and his companions walked over Richard's corpse.

Next stop for Killian was Chicken Delaney's yard. No sign of anyone. He threw his father's size tens inside the first shed along with the rope. Then Killian remembered he still had the piping he killed the Madigan man with. He threw that in with the boots and the rope.

Back to the Burke place. Eleven o'clock.

Made tea. Put on the radio. Opened a new packet of biscuits.

Knock on the door. Ten past eleven. Couldn't be the Guards this quick.

Door opens, and in walks Orla.

'Aren't you pleased to see me, Killian? Is anything wrong.? You look frightened.'

'What do you want?'

'Killian. You said you liked me. You said you fancied me,' she said in a little voice.

'I did. That was before you almost broke my nose.'

'Our little misunderstanding at the Killeshin.'

'Our little misunderstanding! You gave me a bloody nose. I was in agony. You killed Merker, and then you savaged me. You should be locked up.'

'Oh, poor Killian. Do forgive me. Let me see your poor nose.'

'Keep away from me.'

'You'll make me tea before I go.'

'I'll do no such thing. Get out of here before I call the Guards, and you'll spend the next twenty years locked up.'

'Do you want our baby born in jail, Killian?'

'You're having my baby? You're having me on.'

'You took advantage of me Killian. I was with drink taken and very distressed. I was unprepared. You didn't take precautions.'

He made tea. She sat at the kitchen table opposite him playing with the buttons of her blouse.

'I really like you, Killian. I tried to forget you, but I can't. I keep remembering the day poor Merker died. You were so masterful.'

'That isn't what you said at the time.'

She was playing with her hair. She had almost run out of buttons to undo on her blouse.

'You said one day I'd thank you. You were right. My masterful Killian.'

A knock at the door.

A Guard. Garda Sergeant Morrisey.

'I'm sorry to disturb you, Killian, but I've got bad news. Can you sit down? Richard Martin appears to have had an accident with the cattle.'

'Is he all right? Is he in hospital?' asked Killian.

'No, Killian, he isn't all right. I am sorry to inform

you that he's dead. You didn't see anything up by the Ballymartin fields this morning?'

'No, he couldn't have done. He's been here all morning with me, haven't you, Killian? We were late up,' said Orla.

'Well, Killian, do you by any chance know his wife's whereabouts, and do you have her mobile number?'

After Sergeant Morrisey left, Killian spoke, 'What a surprise. Poor Richard dead.'

'Tell me, Killian, was it a surprise? Was it really a surprise?'

'What do you mean? Did you see anything?'

'I didn't need to. You've told me everything.'

'I've told you nothing. You're mad.'

'Your face told me it wasn't an accident and, dear sweet Killian, I'm your alibi, so look after me. You best go up to see your sister when she gets home. She'll need some support. Don't worry about me. I'll still be here when you get home.'

Orla thought: *My feet will be well under this table.*

* * *

In Portlaoise Garda Station, Sergeant Morrisey was talking to Garda Siobhan Whelan.

'How are you feeling, Siobhan? Not easy being the first officer on the scene when the body is a mess.'

'I can't get the man out of my mind. It was just a mess of blood and mud. Has the autopsy been completed?'

'Interim report. It's bad news. Richard Martin was strangled before the cattle trampled him. It's a murder investigation now.'

'So, the bull wasn't to blame. He'll get a reprieve.'

'No. The bull has already been put down. It's a sorry business. No release of the body for burial yet, and when it is released it certainly won't be an open coffin wake. Have you had your first counselling session?'

'Yes.'

'Make sure you go to them all. Your first corpse is bound to be traumatic and when it's like this one you need all the help you can get.'

* * *

Detective Inspector Jack Carney twiddled his thumbs.

Who killed Richard Martin? Not his wife. She was in Dublin. Confirmed by ten different people.

Near male relative? The nearest thing to a near male relative was his brother in law, Killian Burke, who was at home with his girlfriend. Girlfriend could be lying to protect him. Sergeant Morrissey thought she seemed truthful. Plus, his mobile phone was recorded as being home all that morning.

All that leaves is the man who discovered the body as the prime suspect. The only suspect. One Chicken Delaney.

'Well, what have you got, Sergeant?'

'Looking through statements taken from local farmers there was ill feeling between Richard Martin and Chicken Delaney. Most recent recorded incident last week over a dispute over right of access down a lane. Furthermore, he can't account for his movements on the night Connor Madigan was killed. He said he was at home with his wife and child, but we checked she was up in Belfast visiting her aunt on that night.'

'That does it. Search warrant for Delaney's house and farm. Get that underway.'

* * *

Six weeks later.

'What's wrong with you, Killian?' asked Sorcha.

'You know what today is?'

'Yes Killian. It's Wednesday.'

'It's the anniversary of Dad's death. There was no mention of it in this week's *Leinster Express*, and there was no mention of it at Sunday's Mass.'

'Oh no. I am sorry, Killian. I forgot.'

'You forgot. You got all his money. You got most of his land. Then you forget about him?'

'I'm sorry. Since Richard died, I've been struggling. The farm, the businesses, and on top of all of that I'm due in under two months.'

'Excuses. Nothing but excuses. You were always huddled up with the old fella, feeding him lies about me.'

'You've got it all wrong, Killian. I've always loved you.'

'Loved me. You loved me like you loved Dad. You murdered him. You stole my inheritance.'

'No, Killian, I didn't.'

'I know you killed him. Healthy men like our dad do not die of heart attacks in their forties.'

'He had a genetic heart defect.'

'He had you as a daughter. A daughter who poisoned him. A daughter who proudly pointed out all the poisonous plants in her garden that would bring on a heart attack.'

'If you think that you are mad.'

'Did you call me mad?'

'Killian, you're frightening me. Please calm down.'

He rushed at her. His hands to her neck. He pressed as hard as he could. She struggled on.

She should be dead by now.

She hit him in the groin. He let go. He looked round. Candlesticks on the sideboard. He grabbed one. Sorcha was bent over coughing.

Once, twice the candlestick went down.

Now justice has been done. Evil sister and her unborn offspring killed. Her arrogant husband despatched. And that evil bull sent off to the meat factory.

* * *

Dominic discovered his sister half an hour later.

Dominic pulled out his mobile and dialled 112.

'Ambulance. My sister. Unconscious. Looks as though she hit her head on something. She's not moving. I think she may be dead. I can't feel a pulse. Wait. I can feel a pulse now. It's very faint. She's still alive, but please hurry. She's seven months' pregnant. Ballymartin House, Ballymartin, Portlaoise ...'

* * *

DI Jack Carney stood on the steps of Ballymartin House. Another murder investigation. Sorcha Martin died in Portlaoise Hospital after an emergency caesarean section. A baby girl delivered.

Jack Carney confided to Sergeant Morrisey. 'I've a bad feeling about this one. The crime scene has been badly contaminated by her brothers and the ambulance crew trampling across it. You say the woman was well liked. Her husband recently murdered by the Delaney man who is in custody, and therefore not a suspect. The two brothers. One's a priest, and you reckon the other one, Killian, could hardly harm a fly.'

'Well, Jack, I am sure you will solve this murder just as you solved the murders of Richard Martin and Connor Madigan. Chicken Delaney proclaimed his innocence so strongly, I believed him at first, but you went and found the evidence to prove him guilty. Finding the boots and rope used in the murder of Richard Martin and the piping used to kill Connor Madigan in Delaney's sheds was conclusive. His alibi on the night of Madigan's murder falling apart.'

'That Delaney man will go down for a long time. Believe me, Sergeant, there are some people you just know are guilty, and he is one of them.'

* * *

Killian and Dominic were in the drawing room of Ballymartin House saying their farewells.

'How does it feel to be a married man?' asked Dominic.

'Great, and thanks again for officiating. I hope it didn't mess up your travel arrangements.'

'My pleasure. Not every day do you get a chance to marry off your younger brother. How's the bride?'

'Happy it's over. She was a bit upset about walking up the aisle four months pregnant.'

'People don't worry about that anymore. You and Orla still OK looking after little Sorcha?'

'Yes. Happy to do so, and soon she will have little Killian to keep her company. They will be like brother and sister. You ready for your posting to Rome?'

'Yes. I will be sad to leave. I go tomorrow. Which means I have to raise the painful subject now.'

'You've referred to this before, but never said what it was. Now you must tell me, Dominic, what this dread skeleton in the Burke family cupboard is.'

'Aunt Julia had a child in the Mercy Hospital in Cork.'

'That's a coincidence. That's where I was born.'

'She was in a desperate state. Unmarried, not knowing who the father was.'

'Good God. Aunt Julia of the holy rosary and endless novenas was sleeping around?'

'Well, that's not how it happened. A stranger forced himself on her.'

'She was raped?'

Dominic nodded. 'To avoid a family disgrace, it was agreed that Aunt Julia would go and stay with our cousin Rose in Cork, masquerading as our mother. When the baby was born, it was registered as having Mum and Dad as the parents.'

'Wow, there is someone out there who is Aunt Julia's son or daughter. Which was it? Boy or girl?'

'Boy.'

'Oh no. Now I see it. It was you, wasn't it? That was why Father wouldn't leave you anything?'

'No, it wasn't me. It was you, Killian.'

'No. There must be some mistake. I am a Burke. The old fella's son.'

'Look in the mirror. You don't look like us. Mum, Dad, Sorcha and I are fair-headed. You were black haired. We're all tall. You're short.'

'This is a lie you and Sorcha concocted. She told Dad lies about me to stop him leaving me all the farm. Then she killed him. She killed with one of those poisons from plants in the garden.'

'That's not so. Sorcha always looked after you, Killian. She would plead with Dad not to lock you in the pulper shed. She got you your inheritance. Dad was going to leave you nothing until Sorcha intervened. The truth is Killian that Aunt Julia was your biological mother and—'

'And, according to you, my father was an unknown rapist. It's all a damn lie made up to cover the murder of my father.'

Killian rushed at Dominic. He tried to strangle him. Dominic broke the hold, pushed Killian away. Killian returned and knocked Dominic onto the floor. Killian took the poker from the fireplace. Dominic rose dazed and unaware that Killian was about to strike from behind.

As Killian raised the poker, he saw their reflection in the mirror over the fireplace. Dominic looked exactly like a younger version of the old fella. Killian looked nothing like the old fella. Killian dropped the poker.

Killian knew he wasn't the old fella's son. That was why the dad never hugged him. Sorcha hadn't poisoned the dad's mind. She didn't kill the old fella.

Good God! What have I done?

Dominic turned and hugged Killian.

'Whatever happens, whatever has happened, you, Killian, are still my brother. We are still Burkes. Proud to the end.'

'They gave you a bloody good halo in Maynooth. I

must go. Bye, brother.'

Killian turned and walked out to his car, tears in his eyes. He had walked in to Ballymartin House proud, confident and justified. He walked out broken.

* * *

Four years later, on a visit from Rome, Dominic stopped at Portlaoise Garda Station.

Sergeant Morrisey got out the shortbread biscuits.

'Sugar, Father?'.'

'Thanks. Great to have some proper tea again. Now tell me. Any news about my brother?'

'There isn't much to tell. Nothing new. You know the story. According to his friend, Yappy Yeats, Killian had been suffering from depression in the weeks before his disappearance. One Monday he didn't come home from work. His wife reported him missing. His car was found parked on the hard shoulder of the motorway by the bridge over the River Barrow. Extensive searches were made of the river and its surrounds. Nothing was found. I felt desperately sorry for poor Orla. She was distraught. Only married two months and six months pregnant. You had to feel for her.'

* * *

After his chat with Sergeant Morrisey, Dominic drove up to the Burke farm.

'Come in, Dominic. Great to see you. You know Yappy Yeats. He was a friend of Big Killian. Yappy just popped in to see Little Killian and Sorcha.'

'Yes. I do. Good to see you, Yappy. Orla, you've certainly made some changes.'

'Yes, Dominic. Redecorated throughout. In the farm, we've gone organic. Free range pigs and poultry. Bought sixty acres of Chicken Delaney's land.'

'Well, I congratulate you, Orla. I don't know how you managed it.'

'The sale of Killian's land that was rezoned by the

council made it all possible. That was such a surprise. It was like a lottery win. Little Killian is in the drawing room playing with his cousin Sorcha. Why don't you and Yappy go in and see them?'

In the drawing room, Little Killian was sitting on the floor hitting a rag doll with a toy rubber hammer. He looked up, smiled and carried on hitting the doll. Little Sorcha sat in the corner motionless with a blank stare.

Dominic looked at fair-haired Little Killian and then at the fair-haired Yappy Yeats. Little Killian was like a miniature Yappy.

Dominic spent an uncomfortable hour with his niece and nephew. He politely declined the offer of supper and left.

After supper, Orla emptied the leftovers into the swill bucket for the pigs.

'I won't be long, Yappy. You put the kids to bed then we can have an early night. I'll just take the bucket to feed my Porkeen.'

She walked over to the pulper shed.

Number Five

Susan Rodgers

Daniel noticed with disgust the two trenches created by the wheels of the black bin in the neatly raked gravel as he dragged its heavy black bulk to the front of the house. It was Saturday, late afternoon, the summer sun hung high in the clear sky without the companionship of clouds. This addition of the bins to the footpath in front of his terraced yellow-brick house was the only thing that set it apart from the dozens of other homes on either side of his in the Honeymount housing estate. The bins were his last task before he got in the car to make his way over to Kerry. He wanted to get an early start the following morning. He hoped the weather was as good on the Dingle Peninsula as it was in Dublin. He had plans to hike Mount Brandon in the morning.

He had thought to put the bins out before he left. Monday was collection day for their street, and he knew he would be wrecked when he arrived back late the following night. They had been saving up rubbish, accumulating recycling for almost three weeks. Another week of household waste simply would not fit into the jaws of the black bin. It just wouldn't do to hoard what wouldn't fit in bags in the small hallway. He couldn't count on Amy, his wife, to remember to do it. Amy was going to have the whole bedtime routine with the girls, Emma and Maya, by herself, two nights in a row. At six and four, the girls were savvy enough to realise they outnumbered her, and he could only imagine the rebellion that would take place during what Amy called the 'witching hours'. Usually, he and Amy would take turns with the baths, brushing of teeth and hair, reading the chapter of *The Magic Faraway Tree* and tucking in. They were a good team when it came to household chores and childcare duties. They rarely fought over who left plates in the sink or whose turn it was to run the bath. He knew that Amy would miss his presence. Daniel liked that they needed him so much. From what he heard from Amy, some of her friends' husbands were complete assholes. They didn't seem invested in the raising of their children—not like Daniel.

When he went in to kiss Amy goodbye and give the girls one last cuddle, Amy's eyes belied the jealousy she was feeling for his night away. He thought of telling her that a night in a cheap hostel in Castlegregory was not something she should envy, but he did not want to have an argument right before he left. Amy was sweet and light, but she did have her limits. She was constantly telling him how lucky he was that she let him have his Sundays free of family responsibilities.

He was so looking forward to escaping the concrete footpaths and identical structures of their housing estate. He longed for the smell of grass tinged with peat and sheep manure. His heart two-stepped with excitement about doing the last few hikes on his list before the summer was over. There was such beauty in the Irish countryside. There was so much in Ireland that had lost its lustre over the years, especially in Dublin, with ghost estates, incinerators and bands of traffic-infested motorways. He wished people would realise how blessed they were to get into the countryside and hill walk through land untainted by man, the same as it was hundreds of years ago.

He had packed his car earlier in anticipation and to make a quick getaway. His sturdy boots still muddy from last week, stuffed with the *Irish Times* newspaper and in a plastic shopping bag. His backpack was loaded up with everything for the next day—first-aid kit, compass, trail map, snacks, tissues, an extra pair of gloves and even the water bladder was filled and ready to go. He just added his overnight bag with his gear for the morning and toiletry kit to the boot and went to tell his family that he was off.

'Daddy, can we come with you?' little Maya asked.

'No. I'm afraid not this time. When you are older, we'll all go hiking together. You don't want to miss the next chapter in *The Magic Faraway Tree*, do you? Will you tell me what happens?'

'But Mummy doesn't read as good as you,' Emma, the older and more critical of the two, commented. 'You make them have the voices, and it is so much better. Mummy reads too fast.'

'Now don't tell her that, Emma,' Daniel warned. 'You will hurt her feelings.'

'She already knows it. I told her,' she said.

He worried that little Emma was so critical of Amy. He knew it upset his wife.

'But, Daddy, I will miss you!' Maya's voice pitched high in the range of near tears.

'And I am going to miss you both so much. I need you to stay here and take care of Mummy, and I'll be back with a special surprise when you wake up on Monday morning.'

It was so easy to appease children, Daniel thought. They were so quickly caught up in the idea of a surprise that the quality of the item or goodie he brought home rarely mattered. It could be a bun from the village shop, a bar of soap if he splurged on a hotel room rather than a hostel, a packet of sweets from the garage, or a children's magazine with the cheap plastic toy taped to the cover. Anything simple would delight the girls. Amy was a much trickier customer.

She was not so easy to placate. He would have to do better with her surprise. She grumbled into his embrace while trying to finish the girls' dinner.

'I'm going to miss you, Mummy, but I'll bring you home a special present,' he said.

'Don't try to sweet-talk me now,' she said, batting him away. 'As soon as you get in that car, all you will be thinking about is weather conditions and getting up the mountain. Just think about me here with the kids while you are enjoying your fresh air and freedom.'

Daniel didn't want Amy to get emotional in front of the girls.

'You know I love you, and I'd do anything for you, right?' he said softly.

She recovered at that declaration and smiled at him.

'What would I do with a husband who had a more social hobby, like Barry down the road with his cycling group, or even my dad with his golf?' she said.

'Really? Could you see me getting into all that Lycra? And, please, I would rather pull out my fingernails than play golf. Give me the beautiful, wild Irish countryside any day.'

'Well, text me or call when you get in, so I know you got there safely.'

'I always do.'

'And, Daniel, don't forget my present,' Amy said coyly as she turned back to making the girls' dinner.

The traffic was light on the M7 heading to Kerry. It was just the monotony of endless road on his four-hour journey. He loved this solitude. He could run through his game plan for the hike. He hoped he would arrive in late enough to avoid any of the forced social interactions that happened in the hostels. During the summer, everyone wanted to talk about what hill they had climbed or sight they had seen. The combination of longer daylight hours, fresh air and exercise made every hiker want to show off what they had accomplished in their experience.

'We did Torc Mountain yesterday and drove up here last night. It was the perfect day to do Brandon. The view from the top was crazy amazing!' some twenty-something American was spouting off to a few lone hikers who sat at a picnic table outside the hostel. Daniel couldn't help hearing the bragging when he got out of his car and started to take his gear from the boot.

'We are going to stay here tonight and head back down to Carrauntoohil early in the morning.'

Oh God, no, he thought. *Please don't let this place be full of Americans.* He hated their overachieving attitude. All they wanted to do was master the mountain. It was all so easy for them. They were bragging to another table—an Irish hiking club—about a trip they had taken last year to Canada. They had hiked in Banff and Jasper covering an average of 15 miles every day. Canada still had mountain lions that would stalk you for hours before attacking. Daniel wondered how these two lucky men managed to miss such an encounter in all the ground they had covered. The other hikers looked impressed, and he thought they were pathetic.

The hostel was a quirky place. He was well versed in the ways of the Irish hostel and liked to think he knew the best places to stay in most of the areas known for hillwalking. He chose it because there were only a few family rooms—so no crying babies or kids arguing. They had a few single and double rooms. Most of the guests stayed in dorms. They had an all-female dormitory and a mixed dormitory. He wondered why there was no all-male dormitory. It seemed unfair that women had the luxury to sleep without men, and yet men had no choice but to sleep in the same room as women. And why would a woman want to stay in a dormitory with men? Didn't they realise that so many men were pigs?

There were a few buildings making up the hostel. They sprouted on top of a hill like mushrooms: two long dormitory buildings, a larger main house, two smaller buildings and a couple of sheds. The main house seemed clean enough inside with its varnished yellow pine floors, unremarkable rugs and furniture all the same mustard yellow, cornflower blue and deep blood-red colour combination that every countryside hostel seemed to have. The magic of this place was in the abundance of outdoor patios and picnic tables overlooking deep green fields that swayed out from the buildings like a full skirt.

Most of the guests appeared to be outside appreciating these spaces in the cooling evening, clumped in groups of varying sizes. Some had their equipment outside with them and were going through their packs or cleaning up their boots. Others had already showered and were nursing drinks, mostly beer, on the wooden picnic tables.

Luckily, there were only the two Americans. The braggart was joined by his brother with an equally loud and obnoxious voice. Then there was an Australian family who stayed to themselves. Daniel imagined that they were relieved to be hiking in Ireland. Australia, where he never wanted to go due to a healthy fear of snakes, was home to twenty-one of the top twenty-five most poisonous snakes. Who knew what one might step on when scrambling through the outback?

Daniel thought he would slip into his room—one of the few single rooms available—and go through his bag again. He wanted to avoid his fellow travellers. The Americans already annoyed him, and he wasn't in the mood to deal with friendliness. It took too much effort, and he would never see these people again, so Daniel wouldn't pretend to enjoy their company. He wanted to double-check his supplies. Amy had made him sandwiches from the girls' dinner last night: bacon loin. It was cold, salty and a little slimy between two pieces of buttered white batch bread. He had it with his flask of tea. He would try to get a refill on the tea in the morning. There were also a few chocolate Hobnobs, satisfying his sweet tooth. The perfect last supper before an expedition.

He carefully laid out his items on the bed. He added a brightly coloured shopping bag onto the bed with his gear. He had started to carry some extra things just in case. He took these out of the bag and added them to the collection of items—a hunting knife, some duct tape, a couple of metres of orange vinyl rope, wet wipes, rubbing alcohol, a handkerchief, a large Ziploc bag, some black refuse bags, and waterproof matches. He liked to be prepared for any eventuality. There were so many people who were not prepared for what they might encounter in nature.

Daniel was the sort of person who did his research. He looked up the weather conditions. He reviewed the trail notes, trying to get an understanding of the terrain before each trip. He planned. He analysed what gear he would need. He made sure he had the right socks and enough snacks.

Daniel sometimes saw people on the trail who dressed as though they were heading to the gym, in completely inappropriate attire—Lycra and hoodies—for a six-hour hike, taking selfies, and with just a small bottle of water in their hand. They clearly did not know the equation to determine how much water to bring. The answer was one litre of water for every two hours of hiking. As Ireland was not too hot, and didn't have unreasonable humidity, there was no need for more than that. On a long hike, obviously, a small bottle of water was not going to cut it.

It also annoyed Daniel when he ran into people on the trail on his way back who would ask questions like: 'Is it much further to the top?' Or, 'How steep is it up there?' They should have a map or an app on their phone to tell them what to expect.

Sometimes Daniel saw people just starting the walk as he finished up a full-day trek. They didn't carry packs or raingear. They did not check the weather conditions to know that rain was coming or the daylight hours to understand once they reach the summit, the darkness would start to settle. More than likely, they had not shared their plans with anyone, which they should do, in case they got into trouble. They were completely ignorant and unprepared. It was troubling that women especially didn't take it more seriously.

Then, again, maybe he was just a little tired and a little grumpy from the previous evening.

* * *

Last night, Daniel had had to endure a dinner party with some of Amy's friends. The hangover he felt was not from the drink but from the stupidity exhibited by their hosts, Sandra and her husband, Jonathan. Sandra was a fat busybody; one of Amy's oldest friends from school and Daniel's arch-nemesis. He had originally tried to like her, but she thwarted his efforts at every turn, making it impossible to show much more than a faint acceptance. He just could not understand why Amy stayed friends with her. But friends they were, and so he was subjected to yet another dinner party where he had to feign interest.

The other guests were new neighbours—an ingratiating couple, Seamus and Aoife. They were almost decent but too insipid to be more than that. Like Sandra, they were the flavour of people who talked about superficial things—what their old school friends were doing, and who was planning a house extension or upgrade.

Sandra started the pre-dinner drinks with the important discussion of where everyone was going on their summer holidays.

'We're off to this lovely camp in France this year. Yvonne—you remember Yvonne from school, don't you, Amy? She said it is just amazing, and the wine from the area is fabulous. They brought four crates back in the car on the ferry. She reckons the holiday paid for itself in what they would pay for the wine here.'

'How economical,' Daniel commented dryly.

'Well, Daniel, has Amy convinced you to take her and the girls outside of Ireland this summer or is it another year in West Cork?'

Sandra had caught his snide comment and wanted him to pay. Amy did her nervous laugh, quickly glanced at him and sipped her wine.

'Haven't you heard? It's all the rage now to have a staycation. The girls love the beach in West Cork. I don't know why anyone would want to spend their holidays someplace else, right Amy?'

'We do love the beach and the restaurants are really great,' she conceded. 'I don't need a fancy foreign holiday with heat rash and silly souvenirs.'

By the time the starter was finished, Jonathan, was well pissed. The more he drank, the more Sandra glared. He was completely ignoring her while topping up his drink, which now occupied the space in his water glass as well as his wine glass.

'Jonathan, can you help me get these plates into the kitchen so we can serve the main course?' Sandra managed to force out through gritted teeth. Her lips formed what might pass as a smile pasted to her face. She punctuated her request with raised eyebrows and a quirk of her head toward the door to the kitchen.

Jonathan shrugged and lumbered out of his seat, noisily grabbing plates filled with remnants of the starter—a rocket, goat cheese and pomegranate salad. Before the door had fully closed, Sandra's disgruntled hissing started. As her whispered disgust flew at such a velocity, it was unclear to the guests exactly what she disapproved of. There could be so many reasons for it, Daniel thought. Starting with the fact that Jonathan was a pompous git.

Shell-shocked, Seamus and Aoife looked as awkward and uncomfortable as Daniel and Amy. Daniel almost felt sorry for them, as they did not have the tenure he and Amy had with Sandra and Jonathan. They struggled gracelessly with conversation that might cover up the row coming from the kitchen. But the weather was only so interesting.

'What the fuck is the matter with you?'

'Me? Don't lean in too close to the candles on the table, you might cause an explosion!'

'What is your problem?'

'Other than the fact that you might need a straw for the bottle of wine you have sucked down ... nothing. Nothing at all.'

'Why must you be such a bitch?'

'Why must you be such a drunk? Do you think you are sober enough to carry out these plates?'

'Have you cooked this meat yet? It is bleeding on the plate.'

'I followed the recipe exactly, including the cook times for the fillet.'

'Well, it's bloody raw. Why did you insist that I buy you a €1,000-oven if you can't even cook a piece of steak?'

'It is medium, pink on the inside, just like is supposed to be.'

'I'm going to put mine back in the oven.'

'Why do you have to ruin everything?'

Jonathan demonstrated her premise as correct because there followed the sound of porcelain hitting the floor—an expensive Italian limestone floor, as a previous dinner party had revealed. No matter how repulsive he found Sandra, Daniel had to agree with her on this occasion.

'Now look what you have done! I only had six fillets. Just go back and entertain our guests.'

Jonathan stumbled back through the door, asking if everyone was ready to move to red wine. There were the sounds of the broken plate being picked up and a slow stream of curses, which everyone at the dining table,

Jonathan included, ignored while the weather once again became the topic of discussion. Then Sandra entered the dining room, a plate in either hand, and the same unnatural smile she had plastered on her face when she left. She blinked forcefully a few times, trying unsuccessfully to detach her upper eyelashes from the lower ones, a mishap most probably caused from her mascara's overexposure to an excellent, albeit hot, oven.

'Here's the main course. I have decided to go vegetarian tonight. It's becoming quite the health craze. Mind you, not vegan, that seems unnatural.'

Amy shared a look with Daniel. He was so glad their relationship did not work this way. But he was going to put his foot down about these dinner parties with Sandra and Jonathan. He knew everyone else would drink too much to remember all the embarrassment. He had his hike to do on Sunday, and Daniel didn't want to be dehydrated, so his sobriety was an unfortunate necessity. Amy's look reflected her knowledge that this experience would not be without repercussions. Sandra's hold on Amy would eventually have to be released.

On the drive home, Amy talked about how awful Jonathan was and how poor Sandra was a saint to put up with him. Daniel didn't really like the drunk version of Amy, especially when she prattled on unnecessarily. He knew she would feel awful in the morning when he woke her to make breakfast for himself and the girls. While Amy babbled, he tuned out and planned the ritual of his hike. He barely heard her and just said 'Uh huh' every time there was a long pause. Experience had taught him that it was best not to get into a conversation with drunk Amy, as they would only disagree, and she would become emotional.

'You aren't listening to me, are you?' Amy's voice finally found purchase in his head.

'What? Of course I am! Poor Sandra,' Daniel placated. Arguments worked in this manner with them.

Amy got upset and Daniel calmed her down.

'Yes, poor Sandra. I'll have to call her in the morning.'

'You do that.'

He would deal with the Sandra issue when he got back from his trip to Kerry. He needed this Sunday to happen first. There would be leverage to work with after he got back.

When he pulled into their spot outside the house, Amy reached down to grab her clutch bag before getting out of the car. Her eyes closed as if the exertion of talking so much, so emphatically, had exhausted her. Daniel was simply thankful that she didn't pass out or get sick in the car. She opened her eyes as she fished up a spanner on the floor of the car instead of her purse.

'What is this?' she asked as she stared at the wrench, her wine-infused brain trying to figure out why she was holding it instead of her purse.

'It's a wrench.'

'I know it's a wrench. Why is it here? Shouldn't it be in your toolbox? Do you want me to put it away?'

She tried to look at him questioningly, but she was a bit too tipsy. Instead, she looked like a bobbly-head doll, her head rocking back and forth, unable to remain steady.

'No. That's OK. I just bought it the other day in Woodies. I don't have a proper wrench in my toolbox.'

'Well, I won't give out to you the way Sandra does to Jonathan. I know you'll take care of it. I need to go straight to bed. You do too. You have a big day ahead of you on Sunday.'

* * *

In the morning, the hostel smells of old fried food when he gets to the dining area. There are a few people sitting down, digging into their plates with vigour. The food is typical of country hostels, and there is comfort in it: the melange of gelatinous baked beans, runny fried eggs, sausages and white toast. The other guests look up and nod to him. In the corner, one woman sits alone. He had noticed her as one of the people at the table with the American boys. Daniel had overheard her saying to the Americans that she had just finished up working for six months as an au pair. She was taking a week to hike in Kerry before she went back to Sweden to start her master's in urban development.

She is tall and lean, not pretty but certainly not ugly. She is drinking a cup of coffee from one of the thick off-white mugs offered at the coffee and tea area. Instead of the plate of full Irish, she eats a granola bar and a banana that looks like it may have been in her bag a few days. The skin is more shades of brown than yellow. She glances up at him and offers a small smile before looking back down at her travel guidebook, which is not in English.

Daniel takes some toast and a cup of tea at a table across the room from the foreign girl. Once he finishes his breakfast, he fills his flask with tea and a bit of milk. He then heads out to the parking lot with his pack and overnight bag in either hand. On his way to the car, he looks up at the skyline. The sun dangles at a height even at 8 a.m. There are fluffy, cotton-wool clouds. It doesn't look like it will rain, but on the Kerry coast the weather is changeable, and hikers have been known to get into trouble if they are not prepared for the sudden rain or fog. In Scotland a few years ago, an entire scout troop had to be airlifted off of a mountain due to bad weather. He doesn't remember hearing if anything like that has happened in Kerry. More than likely, you would just get soaked through and catch a cold.

Daniel arrives in the Faha car park outside of Cloghane. He gets kitted out and takes off through the wooden gate into the fields that are home to the sheep, that share this first part of his walk. The beginning of the walk is an easy ramble, mostly green grass and sheep droppings along the dirt path which is clearly marked with yellow arrows or sticks tipped with yellow. The rocky rubble of Mount Brandon can be seen in the distance. Even at the end of summer, the air still carries the bite of the ocean winds blowing in from the west. Daniel walks on the increasingly rocky paths, through stony terrain that has been carved out by ancient glaciers. The path is now almost entirely rock. At times, the rocks overhead form a ceiling of sorts. The only company on the walk are the sheep he passed below and the crosses that mark the way. It is not clear enough to see the peak, but Daniel can see the closest wooden crosses. He makes it through the scramble and, in just under three hours, he reaches the summit ridge.

He gazes over at the western side of the mountain. The contrast is striking. Instead of rocks and rubble, there are sheets of fertile, green fields and, in the distance, the Wild Atlantic Way. The wind has picked up, and the sun shines in his eyes. He tries to make out any figures walking up the west side of the mountain. Nobody. Daniel finds that in the late summer there are fewer people doing longer hikes on a Sunday—just the tourists, and rarely the natives, who want to be home for their Sunday dinner.

One mountain, two landscapes. Daniel has an affinity to this spot. It is holy to him but not because of the station crosses on its summit. He feels a kinship with this place where two completely different personalities can take up the same space, and that is what makes it so beautiful. Like complementary colours, the contrast in the hues and terrain only enhance the beauty of each side.

He eats lunch in the shadow of one of the crosses, sitting on the rubble of rock that holds up the marker. The breeze is strong. As he is finishing, a fog rolls in from the Atlantic, blanketing the agreeable side of the mountain before creeping slowly up to cover the peak and then roll down the challenging side to find a resting place outside his diminished line of vision. And in the distance coming up to him, he spots the slow trudge of another figure. A woman. Daniel recognises her shape. It is the woman from the hostel. He looks up at the station of the cross and realises that it is a sign. Mount Brandon has given him a gift. Number Five.

He did not bring the wrench after all. That was the tool Daniel had used on the fourth woman. He had bought one for Number Three and threw it out the window as he drove home through the twisted narrow roads in the Dublin mountains. A few weeks later he regretted it, as it meant he needed to buy another one for Number Four.

By Number Four, he found he needed to plan his opportunities with both precision and a certain degree of spontaneity. It had been a few months since Number Three, and he was getting short-tempered and antsy. The circumstances surrounding the first two women had felt right. The variables had all lined up in perfect order giving him a satisfying sense of purpose.

The first time, the first one—well, she had practically killed herself. Daniel had tried to feel sorry for her after he did it. Then he thought, *what kind of idiot comes up into the Wicklow mountains on her own to go hillwalking?* Weren't there enough crime shows on TV to put a little fear into people? Surely, she had a friend who would have accompanied her, or a club she could have joined if none of her friends liked doing outdoor trekking.

The hike was not technically difficult nor was it poorly marked. He had been on so many other treks where just the smallest mistake could kill you. When he travelled through the US, there were so many national parks where the heat could kill you if you didn't pack out enough water in the summer, or you could come across a bear foraging for food or protecting her young. Last year, there had even been a spate of forest fires on the West Coast that had killed a few hikers.

But here in Ireland, it was just a simple stroll on simple ground—no spiders, snakes or large animals to be afraid of. There were hills rather than mountains. Carrauntoohil in Kerry was the highest mountain at just above 1,000 metres. For most hikes, the only thing one had to worry about was the mud and nettles. During the spring, the trails held an abundance of overgrowth and an obvious absence of people. Miserable weather and muddy paths meant only the truly avid hillwalker would take on a long hike.

Daniel had found his first victim sitting on the ground groaning in agony over a twisted ankle, in an isolated spot halfway through a six-hour hike. He liked the spongy feeling of the wet ground and the cool damp ripe air filling his lungs. So when he came upon her, he was annoyed. Daniel had made a list of the hikes he wanted to complete this summer. Sundays were his hillwalking days. Amy could head over to her parents' house for Sunday lunch with the kids. It was a win-win situation for everyone. He didn't particularly like his in-laws, and they actively did not like him. Amy spent most of the time trying to keep the peace between her parents and Daniel. The girls, sensing their mother's lack of attention, tended to whine and behave badly in an effort to garner a greater share of their mother's affection. It was undeniable that the situation was toxic. He had planned a hike for each Sunday until October.

The solitude of the hills and strain of the exertion gave Daniel a sense of peace that helped him through the week. So when he found the lady—a German in her sixties, named Anya—he tried to catalogue in his head how to get away as quickly as possible.

She was slim and sturdy. Khaki convertible hiking trousers with enough wear in them to show she was not new to her hobby. She was wearing some kind of long-sleeve purple thermal under a turquoise fleece and a blue neck scarf. On her feet were a pair of well-worn brown leather Swiss hiking boots and woolly grey socks. Her backpack and hiking poles lay beside her on the rocky outcrop beside the trail. Her longish hair was a mix between dark brown and grey, but mostly favouring grey. It was stringy and tied in a ridiculous plait at the back of her head.

She did not see him at first. She was trying to unlace her left boot, alternating between soft groans and foreign curses. Daniel thought he might try and back away slowly and take the long way around her. Unfortunately, when he stepped back his foot landed on a moss-covered rock wet from the spring rain which made him slip. His boots landed heavily in the mud making squelching sounds as he tried to keep from falling, and this caught her attention.

'Ah, can you help?' she asked in a way that sounded arrogant.

'Uh, yes, sure. What do you need?'

Daniel could feel the pressure building in his head as he did the sums on this chance encounter. The woman did look fit but was not young so would not be very fast hopping back to the parking area at the entrance to the walk. They were two hours into the hike, and it would be at least another hour to get to the vista where the trail looped around. It would be another three hours to hike back. If they left now, at ten o'clock, it would be at least three if not four hours back. That would mean that he would not be able to restart the hike until two o'clock, and even if he ran and did not stop to eat, he wouldn't be finished until eight o'clock at night, and it would be too dark to get back safely. He was much smarter than this woman. He knew that the ground would be too much of a liability with its muddy, slippery surface, tree roots and outcroppings of granite.

He seethed at the thought of this. She had

probably slipped because she started out too early and could not see the ground clearly in the morning haze. The damp, still-cold air was hanging heavy even now like the gauzy sheet of an ancient mummy, with the smell of mildew and rot weighing it down.

'I will need help to stand up. My ankle is twisted. I think it is broken. My rental car is in the parking lot at the entrance of the trail. I will need help getting back there. My phone fell out of my pocket when I fell. It is covered in mud and water, so it doesn't work.'

'There is no service up here, anyway.'

'Can you lift me? I should be able to get back with your assistance.'

Daniel looked both ways, up and down the trail. There was nobody else. He had only seen one other car in the parking lot. It must have been hers. He was going to have to do it. All he could think of was why had he not chosen a different hike on his list to do today? Why must the woman inconvenience his training schedule? He tasted the disappointment. It was like he had expected a fillet of steak and had bitten into a piece of overcooked liver.

'Yes. Of course. It's slippery, so I'll lift you from behind where the rocks are dry,' Daniel said as he steadied himself on the rocky outcrop behind her and bent down to put his hands under her armpits to hoist her up.

'OK. I am Anya, by the way.'

'Well, Anya, aren't you lucky I was doing this hike today? It doesn't look like anyone else was up to it.'

She looked at him expectantly waiting for him to tell her his name. Daniel didn't say anything else. He pretended that he was concentrating on making sure his foothold was stable. His frowned in an effort to feign attentiveness. His real thoughts were not on getting Anya up without slipping. His real thoughts were on the sharp jagged outcrop of granite, grey and wet. They were weapons, and they would be his salvation.

His mind was moving at twice the speed of his actions, assessing the height and the force he would need to use. Too little would be a disaster, and it would get messy and it would ruin the rest of the hike.

He looked down at her—he was poised for the lift, his eyes in line with her chin. He didn't want to look in her eyes in case she suspected his plan.

'OK, Anya. Are you ready?'

She gave an abbreviated nod and said, '*Ja.*'

He lifted her half a metre so gently and used all of his strength to support her. She was lulled into a sense of security, allowing him to bear her full weight using only her good leg to act as a balance. Once he felt all of her bulk, which was no more than 60 kilos, he tensed his stance, shifted his hold and threw her with full force onto the most serrated of granite rock in the outcrop.

Her eyebrow shot up in shock, her eyes widening with the realisation that this was no accident, and her mouth opened to cry out. Before she could scream, the back of her skull made contact with the hard surface. The sound was sharp and fast and sickening. The air that was to be used to scream just puffed out of her mouth like a balloon deflating with a soft groan. And then there was silence.

Daniel assessed the scene. He was wearing his lightweight hiking gloves when he picked her up so there would be no proof of his hands on her. His boot prints were on the muddy path, but they only went one way as he had stepped in the mossy ground around the trail when he came across her. If anyone came upon her now, they would think she just slipped, and her head hit the rock.

He put his boot into the last print that he had made on the trail and continued his hike, stepping over the woman but not making his steps any bigger. If someone saw the prints, they would think he had been ahead of the woman on the trail. It started to drizzle, and he had to eat his lunch while walking instead of taking a picnic at the vista. The damp had moved from a drizzle to soft rain and his ham sandwich had never tasted more satisfying. He savoured the flavour for a long time after he finished.

On his way back he did not encounter any other hikers. The weather and the length of the hike had probably deterred anyone from attempting it that day. As he completed the loop, he debated trying to go off-trail to avoid the scene. But Daniel really wanted to see her; make sure she was not just something he had daydreamed about. He just wanted a look. He came across Anya, still in the same position. Her clothes were soaked and the mud from the ground was permeating into the fabric that rested on the ground. The granite rock was pink with blood and rain, a watered-down version of her lifeforce. The ground beneath the rock was a gloopy mixture of blood and mud. His footprints were erased by the slow and steady flow of rain, leaving no trace of his action. As he passed her, he had a strange feeling, heady with the rush of empowerment. There was a sense of accomplishment. He had purpose. Daniel had never felt so good.

When they found her body a few days later, the TV news said a lone hiker had a fall. He knew better. She had made a bad choice. She should have never been on the trail on her own. As Amy clucked at the TV, watching the 9 p.m. news while folding laundry, and said, 'Imagine dying like that on your holidays.'

Daniel could not bring himself to speak and only nodded. The only thing that really registered was the aftermath of euphoria. He had done it. His first kill, and nobody was the wiser. He found himself online searching for any news on the case, but it was quickly passed over by other more exciting news of shootings in Europe.

The second one was even more simple. She was a bonus. It was his responsibility to show the world that even without predators, Ireland was not always a safe place. There were so many little things that could befall an unsuspecting tourist or an avid hillwalker. It was really quite easy to blame an accident on the wind or a wrong step in the name of a good picture. He realised after Anya that a woman disappearing was easily explained away. If a woman decided to do something stupid while she was alone, who knew what could happen?

Number Two was simply stupid. She was young, in her very early twenties, and as he later found out, Filipino. She was by herself, taking a selfie. Her backpack was some 20 metres away from the cliff's edge. He followed the scattered remains of her lunch in disgust—a bunched up empty crisp bag, a lost serviette, some rice carelessly scattered on the ground—all the rubbish led him to her. Standing at the very edge cliff, he found her absorbed in fixing her hair and pouting into her outstretched hand that held her phone. The wind was something else that day. It screeched as if giving out to the young girl who was disregarding the beauty of nature by leaving her waste behind. She didn't hear him as he slowly made his way to the place where she stood. It was only in the very last second that she saw him. Then he pushed her down to the dark grey sea below with its white caps like the ridges of a shark's mouth ready to swallow her whole. Her scream was lost in the wind, the two noises mixing together in perfect harmony. Once her body hit the rocks close to the water the scream stopped. He barely heard the splash as her lifeless body was swallowed by the angry white caps. It was only when he started back down the hill that he realised she had been with a group. He came upon five students 200 metres down the path.

'Sylvia, come on!' one of the girls was yelling. She stopped shouting when she saw him and nodded a hello.

'Did you see a girl up there?' a young man asked him. 'Has she started walking this way?'

'No, I didn't see anyone up there,' he told the

group. 'Someone left their backpack up there, though.'

'Come on, Ricky,' the shouting girl said. 'Let's go find her.'

He made his way down the trail quickly, avoiding the sheep's dung, staying on the driest part of the path and admiring an orchid and saxifrage along the way. He hurried in case the group found the girl too quickly. He did not want to get dragged back to help find her or go get help. He needed to get home. He had promised the girls he would read to them that night before they went to bed.

After the first two, he was obsessed. He wondered about them. Weeks after Anya and Sylvia, he would suddenly think about them. What was their last thought? What were their bodies like now? What part of their body had already decomposed? The true thrill came from another thought entirely. He had gotten away with it. Nobody suspected him. As long as he was careful, he could do this forever. He began to feel this need to find others: women who were alone in the wilds of Ireland. Tourists who really had no right to be on Irish soil, denigrating the sacred spots with Instagram shots, rubbish and foreign tongues. They were the perfect target. It would be days before anyone would notice that they were missing.

Daniel loved the high he got from the kill. His mind sharpened, honed in its awareness to get the job done without getting caught. The problem came when it was over. The endorphin rush after Anya carried him through weeks of office small talk and family dinners. With Sylvia, it was half as long. And the desire to feel it again was ferocious. Daniel imagined that this must be what heroin addiction was like.

A few weeks later Daniel bought the wrench on a routine visit to Woodies to get some lawn fertilizer. In the four Sundays after the selfie incident, there was nothing. No women in a compromising situation of which he could take advantage. He had not searched the first two women out: they made themselves known to him. At the same time, he got a certain sense of satisfaction, knowing they got what they deserved. Now Daniel felt desperate to see if he could do it again.

He was smart enough to realise that not every situation would be so easy. Murder was, in fact, quite simple. It didn't take a lot of preplanning. Daniel just had to be prepared, and he would need to respond quickly to opportunity. He would need some tools and anticipate situations once he found his next prospect. There was always going to be another unworthy person, unprepared. People always thought it couldn't happen to them. It couldn't happen in such a safe country. It was on dirty streets, in a bad part of town, in a foreign country. They just never learned. He was the perfect person to do it. He was good-looking, not a model but he knew he looked OK. He appeared to be a dependable, middle-class, young dad because that was what he was. Other than Amy's bitch friend, Sandra, most women found him rather charming. Nobody would suspect the monster that was inside Daniel.

Number Three proved a bit trickier but perhaps more rewarding. Daniel finished his hike late on purpose. It was almost dusk, the sky heavy and the air still warm enough to carry the notes of the pine trees. There were no other cars in the parking area. The last person to come down the trail was a lone girl. She was petite and looked even smaller because of the large pack on her back. The features on her face were also small with the exception of her nose. Her nose should have been on a much larger face.

Daniel had dawdled on this hike which he never did. There was a reason. On this particular day, it was not about the hike. It was about the kill. He had started to feel desperate. As he hiked, he assessed the people on the trail. The big-nosed girl was ideal for the his most chancy game yet.

It happened exactly as he had orchestrated it. Daniel had laid his pack a few feet from the boot of his car. He had taken off one of his boots and was standing at the back of his car with the boot open. When she was at just the right spot, he called out to her.

'Hey! I'm sorry, but could you do me a favour?'

She looked at him with curiosity and wariness in equal measure.

'It's just I twisted my ankle up there where you are. Just my luck, huh? I took my boot off because I thought it would feel better, but it doesn't. I just need to get my pack. Would you mind? Could you just hand it to me?'

The explanation put the girl at ease.

'Oh, yeah. Sure. No problem.'

'Thanks. I suppose I should be grateful that it happened at the end of the day and not halfway up there,' he motioned to the pine copse just beyond the parking area.

'Yeah. It still kind of sucks.'

She reached the pack and picked it up with one hand. She took the remaining dozen steps to get to him.

'Are you American?' he asked.

'Yep. Just over for a few weeks before heading back to school.'

'By yourself? Sorry, none of my business.'

'Yeah. No. It's cool. My boyfriend was supposed to come with me, but we broke up.'

'It's brave of you. Coming out here on your own. I don't think I'd have been able to do that when I was your age.'

She smiled at him, and she started to feel brave just because he said it. She went to give him the backpack. Because she was looking at his face and feeling safe, she didn't see Daniel take his hand out of the boot. He swung the wrench around, smashing it against the back of her head. She grunted as her eyes closed, dropping the bag between them and falling to the ground.

She was alive when he brought her to the forest of pine trees. The shade of the trees made the ground soft and giving. He had duct-taped her hands and feet together. When she woke up her eyes tried to focus on him but could not. She did realise that she was in danger. She just did not know how much.

'Please don't do this. I won't tell.'

'I know you won't tell. How could you be so stupid to be the last person on the trail?'

The girl started to say the strangest things in her last minutes of life.

'I need to collect my earbuds from the hostel. I left them there this morning. Can you drop me off there to pick them up? I need to get to the next hostel by eight p.m. tonight.'

It was like she didn't realise that he wasn't the good guy. He was disgusted with her stupidity. And so he hit her with a rock, smashing the front of her skull, three times. She was unconscious, and he wished she would open her eyes. Her breath was very shallow, irregular gasps of air. He waited until there were no more attempts to breathe before he removed the duct tape, took off the simple silver bracelet on her left wrist and covered the body with some clumps of moss and loose decomposing branches.

Daniel started to worry on the drive home. He had her pack in the passenger seat beside him, along with the wrench. He got rid of the pack, opening it as he drove, throwing the contents out onto the side of the road sporadically as traffic allowed. Finally, the pack went out the window too. Then it was just the wrench. He thought he better get rid of the weapon. He pulled into a lay-by, got out of his car, and threw the wrench as far as he could.

The Gardaí found the body twelve days later. The news said Natalie Beckett, a 21-year-old college student visiting Ireland from Michigan, was found dead. Foul play was suspected based on the injuries she sustained, and Gardaí were seeking information from anyone who had been in the area over the weekend. They were questioning the hostel owners where Natalie spent her last night and trying to get in touch with persons of interest who were seen with her that night. And then nothing. No further news on Natalie. She was just a statistic—an unsolved case.

Number Four was even more complicated. He liked the challenge. It required more brain space to think through the steps in real time. By this time the wrench and duct tape had been joined by a few other items in the boot of the car—the black refuse sacks, a balaclava, the hunting knife, wet wipes, the vinyl rope. After Natalie, it seemed people were a little more careful on the trails but, surprisingly, not careful enough. Nobody had realised the pattern. Yet Daniel's hunger to watch another woman realise too late that she had seen her last day was becoming unbearable. When he found a lone woman setting off on the Coumshingaun Loop walk in Waterford four Sundays later, he trailed her.

He followed her directly to the Coumshingaun clifftop, which would have been the perfect opportunity to make a move. It was August and, unfortunately, the trail was busy. A hiking club was appreciating the view at the vista. She stayed close to the group as they moved north and then east along the corrie rim. It was here she sat along the clumps of purple sage grass to have a snack, looking on to the fine vista over the dramatic north-facing cliffs. He properly caught up with her on the descent from Stookangarriff Ridge. The other hikers were way ahead by now and seemed to be moving quickly. He walked past her and just nodded his head.

'Fine day for this, isn't it?' he said and kept walking. He didn't want to make her nervous.

'Yes. It is beautiful,' she replied. When he first saw

her, he thought she didn't look Irish and her voice confirmed it. She was Australian or perhaps a Kiwi.

The next part of the walk wasn't difficult, just boring, and Daniel thought it could be considered a little deadly. The track was heathery, making it uneven and knee-jarring. In Peru, where Daniel had dreamed of going, altitude sickness could make you dizzy; you could lose your step and plummet over the mountain hundreds of metres below, or it could make you confused and you could go wandering off in the wrong direction. In Waterford on a fine day you could slip on the uneven ground, twist an ankle. If there was nobody on the trail, you could be in trouble as it was a good enough distance to easier terrain near the lake. However, you had to make it through the moraines at the mouth of Coumshingaun before the pleasant ramble down to Kilclooney.

Before it became easy, Daniel ascended on a path diagonally to the large boulder he had encountered earlier. He sat in wait with his pack on the ground and rubbed dirt on the back of his hiking trousers. He imagined what it would look like if he slipped and strained his knee.

He heard the woman coming down the path, humming a tune he didn't recognise. When she rounded the corner, she looked up and saw him, she stopped humming and slowed to a stop.

'Sorry, I didn't mean to scare you. I just slipped on some of the loose dirt coming down and twisted my knee. It hurts like hell. Just taking a breather.'

Daniel pretended to delicately put weight on the alleged injured leg and then gasped and came back. The girl softened her stance. He was counting on her to be a Good Samaritan and he wasn't disappointed. It was refreshing that people still want to help those less fortunate.

'Here, let me try help.'

She got close to him and offered him a shoulder to lean on.

'No, don't worry. I don't want to hold you up. I'll just take my time.'

'Honestly, I don't mind. We have finished most of the hike. Let's see how you get on.'

'OK. If you really don't mind. It's awfully nice of you.'

As she helped a limping Daniel, he learned that Beth was in fact from New Zealand. Much later, he would learn how soft her skin was when struck with metal, how easily pierced and how heavy she was even though she looked quite lean. In the meantime, he gleaned that she had taken a year off work as an accountant to travel. She missed her family in Christchurch but was working on a travel blog that might eventually become profitable. She had been in Ireland for two months and really loved it. It reminded her of home more than any other country. When Daniel noticed that there were no other hikers from any angle, he decided to make his move. They were on the easy path with enough trees to provide cover and the parking area was not yet in view.

Daniel said he needed to stop and get out a second water bottle. He turned slightly away from Beth and then took the wrench out of his backpack. He clobbered her on the side of her head. Unlike Number Three, she was not knocked unconscious the first time, and she started to struggle so he delivered a second blow. She wasn't dead, but he couldn't sit with her like he had with Number Three. He quickly dragged her off the path where they were hidden behind some brush and trees. He got the orange rope from his bag and wrapped it around her neck. It was harder work than he thought. She opened her eyes. They bugged out as she weakly tried to grasp at the rope around her neck. He was beginning to get worried when she finally she stopped breathing, the two of them staring at one another. He dropped her and tried to cover up as best as possible, and then jogged the rest of the path back to his car.

Beth Simpson was found three days later. There was an appeal for anyone in the area on the day to come forward with information. Had she been talking to anyone? Was there any suspicious activity in the car park? In the end, the Gardaí charged a local man in his twenties who had been seen having drinks with her in the local pub the night before. Apparently, Beth had been seen leaving with him, and he admitted to having sex with her in the local park on the way back to the hostel. His former girlfriend said he had stalked her when they split up. He was insisting he was innocent. The trial date was set, and it appeared he would go down for her murder. His mother had been hospitalised due to the stress.

* * *

Daniel was now back at the car in Faha. He unlocked it, popped the boot. The backpack was unloaded. Then he changed his hiking boots for a pair of old runners. His thick socks were hot from the walking, and they smelled of sweat and dirt. He grabbed a wet wipe and cleaned his hands. There was no blood. He grabbed his phone, keys and wallet, slammed the boot and got into the car. Daniel still felt the euphoria of a day well spent and the slight ache of his muscles. He was elated. Everything fell into place, and he wondered what was happening on mountain. Had the mist turned into rain higher up? Had the sheep found Number Five's backpack beside the corrie? Was her body floating, cold and lifeless in the water or had it sunk to the bottom, waterlogged and bloated to be found weeks later? He hoped he did not have to wait too long to hear about Hanna Nyberg and what the coroner expected had happened. He wondered who will be blamed. Maybe those arrogant Americans will be called in to be interviewed.

He is halfway back to Dublin when his mobile rings. He glances down briefly. It's Amy. She must have put a DVD in for the girls before bed. She can be lazy when he is not around to dictate the bedtime schedule of activities. He can't be too angry with her, though. She is weak without him. And it was a good day. He answers the call and puts her on Bluetooth. He wouldn't want to get caught by the Guards for using his handset.

'Hi honey. How are you? How are the girls?'

'Good. We're good. I just wanted to check to make sure you are on the road.'

'Yeah. I am halfway home. I should be there by nine thirty. What did you do today?'

'Just the usual. Went to Mum and Dad's for lunch. The girls and I went grocery shopping, and I told them if they were good, they could watch *Frozen* before they go to bed.'

'That sounds nice. I hope you are still going to read to them. Try to do it with a little enthusiasm. Emma likes that I give each of the characters voices,' Daniel tells her smugly.

'Sure.' Amy is amused. 'How about you? How was your day?'

'It was brilliant. I made it to the summit in three hours, which is a pretty good time and the weather held out.'

'And?' she prods.

'Swedish,' he concedes.

'Swedish? We don't have something from Sweden. And here I was expecting another American or a Canadian. I think Kerry is overrun with them in the summertime. Swedish is unexpected.'

'I told you I'd bring you home a special present.'

'And so you have. OK. Drive safely. I'll see you when you get home. You can tell me all about Number Five, then.'

Tainted Love

Adrian Taheny

Mammy was sick for only a few weeks. Three or four. She said she was going into hospital for a procedure and told me to be good and look after Daddy. The doctor said she would be home in a couple of days, but she never came home. I didn't get a chance to say goodbye. I never got to say how much I loved her. How much I needed her. My sister had just started in college, and I was left alone with Daddy. I tried to talk to him but he just ignored me. He looked on me as some sort of home help. The pub was where he spent most of his time. It was his way of coping. And I didn't matter. I was only thirteen.

School was a nightmare too after she died. Everyone looking at me and wanting to say the right thing but not knowing what to say,

'I'm really sorry about your Mum. If there's anything …'

* * *

When I was sixteen, I had sex in my house with a boy from school. There was never anyone home anymore. It was meant to be a bit of fun. Everyone else at school was doing it. Or, at least, they were talking about doing it. I didn't even like him. He said he was being careful, but he wasn't. When I did the test two months later, two coloured lines appeared on the strip. I was scared at first, but as the weeks passed, I grew more determined to have my baby. I told my sister because she would have guessed soon enough. She promised not to tell anyone as long as I went to the doctor.

He was nearly twenty-three weeks when I miscarried. The bleeding came first and then the pains. Terrible pains. I was in the kitchen. He was born before I could call for help. There was no one at home. I eventually managed to reach the telephone and call my doctor. He sent for an ambulance. I sat on the floor with my dead baby in my arms. All the hopes and dreams I had for him died too.

The Guards arrived at the same time as the ambulance, and then a priest.

'It's God's will', he said. 'Always remember the words of the Bible: "For the sins of the father shall be visited upon the sons for generations."' He was telling me that God killed my baby and I should count myself lucky!

An undertaker took my baby from me and promised to take care of him. I was taken away in the ambulance before my father arrived back from the pub. The Guards had called him and told him to get home as soon as possible. He didn't even know I was pregnant. My sister was in college in Dublin. She came home that night and stayed with me in hospital.

The priest came the following morning. 'We can't baptise him,' he said.

'Why not?'

'It's a church rule. We can only baptise the living. We can do a blessing and naming ceremony.'

We buried Josh three days later. I couldn't stop crying. The priest spoke, but I didn't hear what he was saying. I didn't want to hear. I hated God. Why would he do this to me? To my son. As they lowered his small white coffin into the ground, I made a promise to my little boy. I would be in control of my life, and would never let any man hurt me again the way these men did.

'My life, my rules, my way.'

* * *

The years in school after Josh died are still a blur, but I made it through with the help of medication, counselling and sheer determination. I knew that I needed to get away from home; from my father.

'So what are you going to do with yourself?'

'I just want to get away from here.'

'I'm your sister. I care about you. I want you to be happy.'

'I'm going to DCU. I want to be a journalist.'

'OK. Didn't see that coming. Why journalism?'

'Because it's now all about the truth. I've been lied to and exploited by men for long enough. At school. At home. By a Priest. Even God had a go. It's my time to turn the tables.'

Becoming an investigative journalist was attractive because you do most of it on your own. You take time to build a picture. You build relationships—but only to get the story. Find out their secrets. Expose their wrongdoings. And when you nail your man, it's all worthwhile. You get to expose them for what they really are. Bastards.

'You're like a misogynist … only the opposite.'

'The word is "misandrist". Look it up, sis.'

* *

Nowadays, I go to sleep with the light on and a book lying open in front of me. That's the new routine. No phone or iPad for an hour before bed. It's bad for the brain. Affects sleeping. So my editor told me. 'Read a book instead.' After days spent chasing the business news on Twitter, in between phone calls and interviews, he's probably right. I hardly have time to file copy for the next day's paper.

My mobile is on charge in the hall. It starts to ring with a familiar tone. I quickly realise it is one of my key contacts calling me. I had the ringtones set up that way. I jump out of bed and retrieve it. Peter Kane's name is lighting up my screen. It is almost midnight. What did the Chief Executive-designate of one of Irelands leading banks want to talk to me about at this hour of the night? We hadn't spoken since I dumped him four years ago. I press Accept.

'Laura, it's Peter. I need your help'.

* * *

I was a young reporter back in 2008 when the Irish banks were about to collapse, and the Minister for Finance stepped in and issued a state guarantee. It was mayhem at the time. That's when I first came across Peter. He was assistant to the Chief Financial Officer of one of the leading banks and would attend the meetings with government ministers, committees and press briefings. He was the man with all the files. A support role. He was there to provide answers to his CFO or the Chief Executive when required. And he was often required. I noticed him back in those early days. He always came across as composed and confident. Never flustered like the other two from his bank. I got talking to him by accident. Well sort of. The other two wouldn't talk to anyone. And everyone wanted to talk to them. All the big players from the national media were pushing for interviews or even a comment. Very little was forthcoming. I decided to try the 'back door'. I knew when and where Peter's group would be leaving the meeting. So I positioned myself on a corridor along the route. He was always a few paces behind the other two, and when I dropped my satchel and spilled my papers onto the floor, he did the gentlemanly thing and stopped to help.

'Laura Noone,' I said. 'Thanks'.

'Peter Kane,' he said. 'You're welcome'.

I wanted to say something else to him, ask him a question—loads of questions—but now wasn't the time.

A week later, and we were back again at Government Buildings. Another committee meeting.

'It's Laura, isn't it?'

'Hi, Mr Kane.'

'Call me Peter.'

And he was gone. Trailing after the other two into the committee room. He remembered me. Knew my name. Now I was in with a chance. A few words. Maybe an interview? No, that's not going to happen. Take it slowly. Let's see what happens on his way out, later. And stay composed. He's not bad-looking. Very well dressed. Better than the other two. Looks like they got dressed in the dark. *Easy tiger. Concentrate on the job. The story. Get the story.*

* * *

'What's up, Peter? Why are you calling me at this hour? Why are you calling me at all?'

'I need to see you right away. I'll come over. Are you still in the same place?'

Same place. Where we spent so many nights together before he showed himself for what he really was. Just like the rest of them.

'Yes, the same place. But not here. I'll meet you in the hotel around the corner.'

'Twenty minutes.'

He hangs up. He doesn't say what is so urgent. But I'd better meet him. He sounded worried. Luckily, my sister is staying with me for a few days and she can keep an eye on my son, while I'm out. Troy is only four.

* * *

He passed me his business card in Government Buildings. Discreetly.

'Call me.'

I did. The next day. He couldn't speak. He would call me back later. He had my number now. And he did call me. Later that day. Sounded like he was outside. Noisy. Would I like to meet? Somewhere quiet?

We met on a bench along the canal. Two strangers sharing the same seat. Sitting a little apart. Him with his *Irish Times* and me with my iPhone.

'We need to be careful.'

'I understand. Why did you want to meet me?'

'You're looking for a story?'

'I'm following the collapse of the banks, yes.'

'I may be able to help you.'

'How?'

207

'I can give you the inside track on what's really going on.'

'Where's the catch?'

'There is no catch. These assholes thought they were infallible. They could do no wrong. It's payback time.'

'What's in this for you?'

'Immunity of sorts. I want the truth to come out, and when it does, I want to be in the clear.'

'Have you nothing to hide, Mr Kane?'

'I was a junior doing what I was told, while these guys were doling out money to developers like there was no tomorrow.'

'Why do you think I can help you?'

'The committees and inquiries will never get to the bottom of this on their own. They're out of their league. They don't know the right questions to ask.'

'And you do?'

'Yes, and I am prepared to share them with you. You use your paper and your contacts to highlight them, and the truth will emerge, eventually. Do we have a deal?'

This was too good an opportunity to miss. I nodded.

'Good, you can start with these', he said, sliding a folded sheet of paper across the seat to me.

As I motioned to open the page, he stopped me.

'Not here. Not now. Read them later. And remember to include the follow-ups.'

'Follow-ups. What are they?'

'These boys will have an answer prepared for the likely questions that may be asked at committee but not for these follow-up questions. They believe they can say anything they want, basically because the politicians don't understand their business. That's their Achilles'. The follow-ups will rattle them and eventually expose their cover-ups.'

I wanted to know more, but he had to go.

'I'll meet you here in a week. Same time?'

I agreed. Walking back to my office, I had to check myself from smiling. He really was very good-looking. And he was going to help me get my story.

* * *

The editor wasn't convinced about my proposal to do a feature article on the committee meetings. When I told him I had information that would help bring these bankers to justice and a great deal of attention to our paper, he became a little more interested. I explained what I had but refused to reveal my source.

'OK, let's run with it. You're a one-woman wrecking ball.'

'They're only getting what they deserve.'

I knew a couple of politicians on the committee: one socialist and one independent. I made a couple of calls and, within hours, I was briefing them on particular questions to ask. It suited them to keep their source confidential. They realised they would grab the news headlines when they backed their prey into a corner during the sessions. To be honest, the first few efforts were almost embarrassing because they were asking questions they did not fully understand, but they had the likely answers they would get, and they also had the 'follow-up' questions. The first week was lively, and it became clear that the bankers were rattled by the end of the sessions. They had to take time out to confer. They put hands over microphones while they whispered to each other. And there, behind them, doing his best to advise them on the answers was Peter Kane.

* * *

Troy is fast asleep. My sister's door is open, and I can see she's reading.

'I'm going out for a few hours. He's asleep. See you in the morning.'

* * *

We had met a few times on the bench by the canal and exchanged pleasantries, among other stuff. The plan was working well. Our paper was fast becoming the point of reference for the media and public alike. We were quoted regularly on *It Says In The Papers*. Invitations came in from other radio and TV shows, but I always declined. I was in control of the situation. Feeding just enough information through my articles to move the process forward. My editor always wanted more, but it was going to be my way and at my pace. These boys were going down. The committee sessions had become compulsive viewing as the top bankers were showing signs of crumbling under the weight of questioning. There were calls for a judicial inquiry and for heads to roll. Peter's face was becoming well known from TV and, eventually, he suggested we could no longer meet in public. It was too dangerous.

I cooked supper that first time. A fancy supper. He would call to my place after work, around seven. I bought a bottle of wine, just in case. It was when I was checking my make-up in the mirror that it finally hit me. *Could I fancy this guy?* But he's married. Probably has kids. *Don't let my guard down. Keep it strictly business. Get the story.* A bit of lipstick wouldn't go astray.

'Jesus, you look different.'

'What do you mean, different?'

'Nice different. Can I come in?'

'I just threw something in the oven. Are you hungry?'

He was, and yes, he would have a glass of wine.

'White is fine.'

We talked about the committee meetings and how the plan was progressing. Our circulation was doing well, and his bosses were struggling to cope with the pressure from the politicians and the press. And he told me about his own family. He was married to Sue. Their son, Dylan, died when he was just ten.

'I'm sorry.'

'Losing a child is the worst thing that can happen to anyone.'

'I can only imagine.'

'It was cancer. His death nearly split us up.'

A long silence, and then he changed the subject.

'What about you?'

'My job keeps me busy. Don't have much time for anything else.'

'I better go. It's getting late. I need to be in early in the morning.'

'Aren't you forgetting something?'

'Yes, of course.'

In the doorway, he handed me the folded sheet of paper. Then he kissed me on the cheek and left. It all happened so fast. I stood on the spot for some time after he left. Trying to understand what had just happened. Or, more importantly, how I felt about it. I worked with men on a daily basis, but it was always strictly business. I avoided situations that might lead to any form of intimacy. My social life was at best solitary and, at worst, non-existent. It was just a kiss.

* * *

His visits became routine, with him stopping by for supper once a week. He would update me on what was happening at the bank and feed me the questions that needed to be asked to keep the pressure on. I felt myself getting to like him more and more. I trusted him, and I enjoyed his company. Maybe he was different to all the others. I began to think that if my son, Josh, had lived, he would have grown into someone like Peter Kane.

'I brought a little something to celebrate. Champagne.'

'What's the big occasion?'

He told me the end was in sight for his bosses. The media pressure had gotten to the board, and he was confident that their resignations would be tabled at the board meeting during the following week. I could use this information to make some very startling predictions in Friday's paper.

We toasted his bank, my paper, and then we toasted each other.

'It's getting late. I should go.'

'What's the hurry?'

'Let me help you with the dishes.'

I dropped a fork on the floor as we loaded up the dishwasher.

'You make a habit of dropping stuff.'

We banged heads as we both tried to pick it up.

'I'm sorry. My fault.'

'No, mine.'

We were on our knees looking into each other's eyes. He placed his hands gently around my neck and pulled me even closer. Then he kissed me. This time there was no mistake. It wasn't a 'thank you' kind of kiss. Much more than that. It was deliberate and sensuous. I tried to pull away.

'We shouldn't do this.'

But it was too late. I felt different inside. I wanted him. I pulled him towards me. I held him. I kissed him. All the time telling myself he was married, and this was wrong; but the kissing continued, and my self-righteousness got lost somewhere in an unfamiliar moment. I led him into my bedroom, and we undressed each other in a mad frenzy. His usual calm temperament disappeared as he turned into some kind of wild animal, and I became his willing prey. He hunted me with an appetite that seemed insatiable. Some two hours later, we lay side by side on our backs in silence. Exhausted.

* * *

It's not far to the hotel now. I haven't seen or heard from Peter for the last four years. I saw him in the papers and on

TV, but we never met.

* * *

At first it was business. Me getting the story. Him getting the job he wanted. It became more than that. This was the first man I had put my trust in for a long time. I believed he was different from all the others. But now he was cheating on his wife—with me. I allowed myself ignore that because I lived for the evenings when he would come over and have dinner with me. I loved lying beside him in bed, exhausted from our crazy lovemaking. We couldn't be seen out in Dublin, so he arranged trips to London, and I would rendezvous with him there. There we could be out in public together like a normal couple.

* * *

'Thanks for coming. How are you?'

'I'm OK. What's up? You look bothered.'

'I'm getting a drink. Do you want one?'

He calls the night porter and orders a whiskey and a glass of wine for me. He's visibly distraught.

He always liked to be in control. He carefully planned everything. How to get rid of his two bosses and put himself in position for the top job. Those plans got held up after the bailout when the government put a cap on the salary and opened up the role. An Englishman called Elliot Percival got the job. That really pissed Peter off. He was given the Chief Financial Officer role, but he knew if he bided his time his turn would come. And it was coming in a couple of weeks. It was all over the papers. The board would appoint him Chief Executive following the premature departure of his boss. (I remember wondering at the time if he could have had something to do with that.)

'I had a call earlier today from someone I used to know.'

'And?'

'He's getting back in business. The building game.

Offices, apartments, shops, the lot. He needs finance.'

'Should be no problem to you when you land the top job at the bank.'

'He's looking for guaranteed funding for his projects in advance or …'

'Or what?'

'He's threatening to go public on the €250k bribe I took from him years back.'

I did know about his dealings with this developer. He told me late one night after a few drinks. We had just run a story about bribery and corruption among politicians and property developers. He had read it. Thought it was a strong piece.

'Thanks. I had a good source.'

'Are you two-timing me?'

'Very funny. He's an ex-minister. He lost out in the government re-shuffle. His sort can be very helpful at times like that.'

'Did he never take a bribe himself?'

'Maybe, but he was a small player. I was more interested in the bigger fish.'

'The politicians or the developers?'

'The politicians. I don't bother much with the developers. They're just playing by the rules set by the politicians. And politicians are elected to serve the people. Not themselves.'

That's when he let it slip.

'So I'm safe.'

'What do you mean?'

'Nothing. Let's have another glass of wine.'

'Then you'll tell me?'

'There's nothing to tell. Honestly.'

He was lying to me. I poured him another drink and then another.

'Let's go to bed.'

'First, you tell me what you meant about you being

safe.'

He made me swear I wouldn't tell anyone. 'It will be our secret.'

He told me he had gotten friendly with a number of developers in the good old days. Every bank wanted their business, but he was able to prioritise their loan applications, and they passed through his bank's credit committee very quickly. They started to give him small gifts in the beginning. The tent at the Galway Races. Weekends away and corporate hospitality at soccer matches in the UK. When the banks and the economy crashed, they needed him even more. One in particular.

'He owed close to ninety million between all the borrowings his companies had from the bank.'

'And you got him off the hook. How?'

'This guy had done it all. Forged documents. Borrowed more than once on the same assets. Most of them non-existent. The checks and balances were pretty lax in the good old days.'

'So what did you do?'

'I had access to all the non-performing loan files. It was just a case of removing the original personal guarantee he had signed to cover his company loans. He was in the clear.'

'Did no one ask questions as to what happened to it?'

'Of course, but the bank was in chaos and missing documents were a regular occurrence.'

'And?'

'He paid me €250k in cash. Now are you coming to bed?'

I should have known he was too good to be true. He was just as bad as all the rest. A bastard. Cheating on his wife and up to his neck in corruption.

'I'll follow you in a minute.'

I knew by now that I needed someone in my life.

Being with him had convinced me of that. It wasn't going to be Peter Kane, but he was going to help me. I stopped taking the pill. It took a while, but as soon as I knew I was pregnant, I dumped him.

'We need to talk.'

'That sounds ominous.'

'It's time to end this.'

'Why?'

'Because I want to.'

'But I thought we were doing OK?'

'Time to move on.'

He pleaded with me to reconsider. Started making all sort of promises. His relationship with his wife was non-existent. He could move out. We could make a go of it together.

I told him it was over.

* * *

I hadn't heard from him again until tonight.

The night porter arrives with the drinks. He throws back his whiskey in one large gulp.

'What do you want from me?'

'I want you to do what you do best. Destroy him before he destroys me.'

'And just how am I supposed to do that?'

'I'll give you all the details of his sordid past. Everyone knows he went bankrupt, but there's a lot more to tell. How he got his planning approvals. Who else he paid for favours along the way. Councillors, politicians, even a government minister or two. I can give you the details, anonymously. You do the rest.'

'What's in this for me?'

'Another exclusive exposure of a disreputable businessman. Maybe another tribunal of enquiry.'

'And for you?'

'A second chance. I made a mistake doing what I did. I realise that now. But I did it for my son. He was dying, and I had to try and save him. We needed the money to get him to the Mayo Clinic. They did their best to save him.'

This is all too much for me to take in. I need to get out of here.

'OK, stop.'

'Will you help me?'

'I need to think about that.'

'Please, Laura?'

'I'll meet you back here tomorrow.'

Why did I ever get involved with him? It should have been about getting the story. Just that. But I let my guard down. Left myself vulnerable. Broke my own rules. I thought he was different to all the rest. I loved being with him. I even managed to ignore the fact that he was married. How was I so stupid? I should have seen through him from the start. That day on the bench by the canal.

'Have you nothing to hide, Mr Kane?'

He lied to me then. I need to get home.

* * *

'Hey, sis, where were you?'

'I was meeting someone at the hotel.'

'Meeting who?'

'Troy's father. Peter Kane.'

'I thought you were never going to see him again.'

'I wasn't.'

'So why did you meet him?'

'He called me. Needs my help with something.'

'Are you going to help him?'

'I'm not sure.'

She doesn't need to know the details. I have an opportunity to break a big story. It would be an exclusive and could run for weeks. Longer if they set up a tribunal. I don't reveal the source of the information and the focus will fall on the politicians and some government ministers.

'Troy will want to know about his father at some

point in his life. What will you tell him?'

'I'll deal with that when it happens.'

* * *

I made a promise when Troy was born. He was going to be different from all the rest.

'Is this your first baby?'

The nurse was telling me to take deep breaths and push. Had I given birth before? Can you give birth to a dead baby?

'Nearly there. Push harder. Deep breaths.'

Then nothing but silence. Like back in the kitchen when Josh came out.

'Please tell me he's all right.'

And then the beautiful sound of my baby crying.

'Congratulations. You have a son.'

'The nurse placed him gently in my arms. I could smell him. I held him even closer to me. I could feel him breathing; his tiny body touching mine. My son. My beautiful little boy.

'I will look after you. I will always be there for you.'

* * *

'I need to go out this morning, sis. Can you keep an eye on him? There is something I need to do.'

It could have been so different. If he wasn't married. If I had met him sooner. He took the money to try and save his son. He doesn't even know we have a son. I'm meeting him back at the hotel. I can see him pacing up and down in the lobby. Not his usual calm self.

'Where were you? I was afraid you weren't coming back.'

'Nice to see you too. You look shite. Did you get any sleep last night?'

'I got a room here, but I couldn't sleep. Are you going to help me?'

'Does your wife know about all this?'

'No, and she doesn't need to. She's not well. She hasn't been well since Dylan died. She blamed me for it.'

'That's a bit unfair. You did everything you could to try and save him.'

'She's been in and out of care since it happened. We separated a couple of years ago. She has the house. It's how she wanted it.'

Maybe he does deserve a second chance.

'It would have to be done in secret. We couldn't continue to be seen together in public. Meet in private. No text messages, no emails. All verbal. I make my notes.'

'It could be like old times.'

'No, it couldn't Peter. That's over.'

'I'm a free man now.'

'And I'm a free woman. Let's get this straight from the get-go. Our personal lives are separate. It's a business arrangement. No funny stuff. Agreed.'

'If you say so.'

* * *

I ask him to meet me in a small pub not far from Dublin, but far enough.

'Is that you, Laura?'

'Of course its me.'

'What's with all the headgear and the sunglasses? You look like one of those suicide bombers from the TV news.'

'We need to be careful.'

'I know that, but the Naul in Meath? Are you not overdoing it just a bit? Are we going to eat?'

'Just coffee for me.'

'OK, if that's what you want.'

'Let's not waste time. Tell me all about your old friend, the builder. I'll take notes.'

We spend a couple of hours together. He does most of the talking while I take notes. I start to feel some sympathy for him. Losing his son then his wife. Maybe things could be different.

'Have you everything you need?'

'Sorry?'

'For the story?'

'The story … Yes, I have.'

'What did you think I was talking about?'

'Nothing. I was just finishing my notes.'

'Will you run it?'

'I'll write it up and, after that, it's up to my editor.'

'I really appreciate what you're doing for me. I can't thank you enough.'

'I'm doing it for us.'

'Us? I thought there was no more "us".'

'You get the big job, and I get the story and the glory. Remember?'

I can't tell him that I'm doing it for our son too. Not yet. Once the story runs, and he gets the bank job, he's in the clear. He did try to save his son. He could be a good father for Troy.

'I need to go and write this up. See what the editor thinks.'

'You sure you have everything you need … for the story?'

'Yes, I do.'

'I'll call you as soon as it's all over.'

Now's not the time to tell him. I need to concentrate on getting the story right. *Nail these bastards.*

* * *

'Congrats, Laura. You did a great job on the builder story. Two ministerial resignations already and a judicial enquiry to follow.'

'Thanks, boss.'

I went ahead and did the story. All of it. The builder, the politicians, the Galway Races tent, his generosity to his friends in high places. I named names. Once the legal boys were happy—and that took some convincing—the story ran front page.

'They'll be after your source. This could get nasty.'

'Can't happen. Journalistic privilege. I'll need your support.'

'You'll have it.'

He hasn't called me since the story appeared and all hell broke loose. And he got the top job. Chief Executive of one of Ireland's leading banks. That was four months ago. Looks like he's in the clear.

He's the new face of banking in Ireland. The 'go-to' man for anything to do with money or the economy. He's all over the media. He made it to the cover of *Finance & Business*. Their Man of the Year. I cut out his photo and put it in a frame. I keep it in the locker beside my bed.

'I am sorry, but unfortunately Mr Kane is away on business this week. Do you wish to leave a message?'

He has a personal assistant. I tried calling him on his mobile but he's not answering. I sent him a couple of text messages too, but he hasn't replied. So I write to him. I tell him I know what it's like to lose a son. That I understand the pain he went through. I ask him to call me.

'Do I have a daddy?

'Of course you do, Troy.'

He still hasn't replied. No letter. No texts. No calls. He's ignoring me. I want to tell him about Troy. Our son. That he has a son. That we can be together as a family.

'Is Daddy coming home soon?'

Why won't he contact me? Is he hiding something? Is there something he didn't tell me? Did he tell me the truth about his wife leaving him? About his son dying? Dylan. Cancer, he said; when he was ten. It will have been in the death notices. Here it is …

After a long illness … bravely borne … Dylan … aged ten … devoted mother, Sue, adoring father, Peter … Thanks to staff at

**Our Lady's Children's Hospital, Crumlin
and Mayo Clinic. Donations in lieu of
flowers to the LFS Association.**

What's LSF? I need to google it. He died of cancer,
and his wife blamed him. That's what Peter said. Found it.
Li-Fraumeni syndrome.

**Li-Fraumeni syndrome is a rare inherited
syndrome that can lead to the development
of a number of cancers, including sarcoma.
This syndrome is most often caused by
inherited mutations in the TP53 gene . If
someone has Li-Fraumeni syndrome, their
close relatives (especially children) have an
increased chance of having the mutation too.
Since inherited mutations affect all cells of a
person's body, they can often be found by
genetic testing done on blood or saliva (spit)
samples.**

'Just a moment. I will check and see if Mr Kane is
available to take your call. Your name is …?'

'Just tell him it's Laura, and that I need to speak
with him urgently.'

You better take my call, you bastard.

'Putting you through now.'

'This is a surprise. I meant to ring you to say
than—'

'You told me your son died from cancer.'

'Yes, he did.'

'Did he have Li-Fraumeni syndrome?'

'He did. But what has this got to do with
anything?'

'Is that why your wife blamed you for his death?'

'I only discovered I was a carrier when Dylan got
sick. It was too late. Are you still there? Laur—?'

* * *

The doctor said he could do a test, but he would need to know if there was there a family history or diagnosis. I told him the father was a carrier. The results will be back in a couple of days.

I have to go and meet a consultant at the hospital. They wouldn't tell me the result over the phone. My beautiful little boy. This can't be happening to me again.

'He has tested positive for the TP53 mutation.'

'You mean he has Li- Fraumeni syndrome?'

'Yes, he does, but that does not mean he has cancer, or that he will get it. It just means he is more likely to than other people.'

'And he can pass it on to his own children?'

'Yes, that is a real probability. But it's a long way off. He's only four. Can I arrange for you to meet one of our genetic counsellors here at the clinic? She can explain in more detail and help you deal with the condition.'

'I don't need counselling. I've been through this shit before.'

His son died from cancer when he was ten. He was in the Mayo Clinic for nearly two years. He must have been eight when they took him there. So he must have been six or seven when he got sick. Maybe even five. I read there is a 90 per cent chance of Troy developing cancer at some point, and it is more likely to happen sooner rather than later.

When Troy was born, I promised to look after my little boy. That I would always be there for him.

I made a promise when Josh was buried that no one would ever do this to me again.

Peter Kane is not getting away with this.

* * *

His wife, Sue, has agreed to meet me. I tell her I'm doing a profile on her husband for my paper. She is reluctant at first to get involved until she hears it is going to be a 'warts and all' piece. She invites me over to her house.

'I want the truth to come out, but he can never know that I spoke to you about him.'

'Sounds to me like you are afraid of him.'

'You have no idea what he is capable of.'

Either this woman is nuts, or there is another side to Peter Kane.

'You have my word that he will never know you spoke to me. Let's start from the beginning.'

She is not holding back.

'And you say he was always ruthless?'

'He only cares about himself. He does whatever it takes to get his own way.'

'He comes across as a charming, handsome and smart individual.'

'Have you met him? Talked to him?'

'A couple of times. Business briefings mostly.'

'He loves to be the centre of attention. Getting his picture in the paper. Appearing on TV.'

'Getting the top job in the bank was important to him?'

'There's nothing he wouldn't have done to get that job. He told me he was going to get rid of the other two "wankers" after the bank collapse.'

'Did he tell you how he was going to do that?'

'All he said was that he had some young journalist wrapped around his little finger, and she was going to end up doing his dirty work for him.'

The fucking bastard used me. And I fell for it.

'Can I ask you why you split up?'

'We had a little boy. Dylan. He died when he was just ten.'

'I'm really sorry.'

'He was sick for nearly four years. We did everything we could, but it was all in vain.'

I can't ask her about TP53.

'And his death was the cause of you two splitting

up?'

'He blamed everyone for his son's death. The doctors, the drug companies. God. He even blamed me.'

'How could he possibly blame you?'

'That's what he does. If it goes wrong it's always someone else's fault. He only cares about himself, and he will twist the truth around to prove he's right.'

'It must have been a very difficult time for you?'

'It was. But I got through it.'

'And, Peter?'

'He acted as if nothing had happened. Never spoke about it again. Started to spend more and more time away from home. From me. There were other women.'

'Other women?'

'He told me all when he was leaving me.'

Jesus, did he tell her about me?

'He said he didn't need me anymore. He could have anyone he wanted, anywhere, anytime. And he walked out on me.'

'You said you're afraid of him. Why?'

'Because I know what he's capable of. Nothing and nobody gets in his way.'

'Have you heard from him recently?'

'He rang me to tell me the good news about him landing the top job at the bank after he got rid of the English "wanker".'

'Elliot Percival, the Chief Executive?'

'He expected me to congratulate him!'

I need to end this.

'Sue, thank you for being so honest and upfront with me. And I'm really sorry about your son.'

'He must never know I spoke to you.'

'You have my word.'

* * *

Elliot Percival agrees to meet me in London. I tell him I am doing a piece on Peter Kane. He says he isn't interested. I tell him that I know Peter was involved in his decision to resign early from his position at the bank, and that I want to hear his side of the story—in confidence.

'He resented me from the day my appointment was announced, and he made no secret of that in private.'

'And in public?'

'He continued to be Mr Charming and supportive of everything I said or did.'

'How would you describe him?'

'He was arrogant beyond belief. His point of view on any and every subject was the right one. He never listened to what anyone else had to say.'

'How could he get away with that?'

'The media loved him. The investors too. He played them all to get what he wanted.'

'And you? What did he do to you?'

So now I can't take notes. No recording either. This is between the two of us, and he will deny he ever said it if anything comes out. He's a retired man with a wife, three children and two grandchildren. His family can never know what happened, but if it helps me to expose Peter Kane for the selfish, manipulative individual he is, then he is prepared to take the risk.

'We were in the US for three days meeting investors. Briefing them on our annual results. New York, Chicago and Boston.'

'Just the two of you?'

'As Chief Financial Officer, I had to bring him along.'

'What happened?'

'I made a terrible mistake, and he found out.'

'Mistake? How? What kind of mistake?'

'I invited a prostitute to my room at the hotel in Chicago. It was late, and I assumed he had gone to bed.'

'But he hadn't?'

'She stayed about an hour, and as I opened the

door to let her out of my room, he was standing there in the corridor.'

'Peter.'

'Yes. Almost like he was waiting.'

'And?'

'He smiled at her as she left, then continued to stare at me until I eventually shut my door.'

'He said nothing?'

'Not then. Nor the next day. Not until we were on the plane home.'

Peter Kane told him that he had two weeks to hand in his resignation to the board of the bank. If not, his wife and family would get to know of his nocturnal activities in Chicago.

'He blackmailed you?'

'I submitted my letter of resignation two weeks later to the day.'

'And you haven't told anyone else about this?'

'No, and nobody must ever know. It may seem harmless enough to someone like you, but my career, my family, my whole life would be destroyed if it ever came out.'

'You have my word.'

* * *

Finally, a call. He wants to see me in his office at the bank's headquarters. His PA rang me. Said something about a private briefing on year-to-date company performance. *My arse!*

'Please take the lift to the seventh floor. Mr Kane's PA will meet you there.'

His wife said she was afraid of him. He is capable of anything.

'Follow me, Ms Noone. Mr Kane is ready for you now.'

Ready for me now. Let's see about that.

'Come in, Laura. Sit down. That will be all, Tara.

Hold all my calls for the next fifteen minutes.'

I'm getting a quarter of an hour of his precious time. I should be grateful.

'It's lovely to see you. Great you could call in here. To headquarters.'

He looks very much at home sitting there behind that enormous desk.

'I think there may have been a misunderstanding when we last spoke on the phone.'

'Why would you think that?'

'You hung up, or we got cut off all of a sudden. You were asking me about my son's illness.'

'Ah, yes. I remember now.'

'What was all that about?'

'I am planning to do a profile piece on *Finance & Business*'s Man of the Year. Just wanted to get my facts correct on your son's illness.'

'What has that got to do with an article about me? It's not relevant.'

'Maybe you're right, but as you know, I'm always very thorough with my research. I like to do a good job.'

'And you always do. When were you planning to run with my profile piece? If you need any photos, my PR company can supply them. And charts or graphs. I can get my accounts people to send them on to you.'

He's off again. As soon as he sees an opportunity to be the centre of attention, he grabs it with both hands.

'That won't be necessary. On second thoughts, maybe a photo might be useful. Would you have one with your wife and son?'

'My ex-wife. My dead son. No, I do not. Why would you want something like that?'

'Our readers like to get an insight into the real people behind the big titles. What's the Chief Executive really like? What make him tick?'

'You're wrong there. They don't. They want to

read about how he got to the top. What makes him successful.'

'I think I know what my readers want.'

'You're wrong.'

I think he really believes that shit.

'What about all the stuff I wrote about your builder buddy and the politicians he bribed? They lapped that up.'

'That was different. People love to read about politicians in trouble.'

'And the "wanker" bankers. Your two bosses that I helped you shift.'

'They got what they deserved. Clueless and no backbone. They needed to go.'

'Tell me something. Do you ever feel a smidgen of sympathy for any of the people you shafted along the way?'

'No. I did them and the rest of the world a favour. You did too. We're very alike, you and me.'

'No, we are not. How can you even suggest such a thing?'

'You're known as the "Wrecking Ball" because of the reputations you destroyed. All men.'

'There's one big difference. I do it because they deserve it. You do it because you think you deserve it. And, of course, you always benefit from their loss.'

'You're wrong again. To succeed in this life, others must fail. It's as simple as that.'

He's on a roll here. Let's see how far I can take this.

'Is that what happened to Elliot Percival?'

'A loser.'

'He failed. You succeeded. Literally.'

'What has he got to do with all this?'

'He got in your way and you got rid of him. That's how you get things done, right?'

'That little man is irrelevant. He should never have been there in the first place. The job was mine. He got in the way.'

'And you got rid of him?'

'I didn't say that. In a way, he managed that all by himself.'

'So you didn't need me to do your dirty work for you on this occasion?'

'Where do you think you're going with all this?'

'You pushed him out, didn't you?'

'It's none of your business but, yes, I got rid of him. He made one mistake too many, and I left him with no alternative.'

He's actually enjoying all this. Revelling in his destruction of others. He doesn't care about anyone else.

'Do you have any regrets?'

'None.'

'The loss of your son. Then your marriage breaking up. Surely that hurts?'

At least that got him up from behind his fancy desk. Maybe he's going to throw me out?

'My son died from cancer. He got it because he inherited a mutated gene that was passed through me from his grandfather or great-grandfather or both. Who knows where it started?'

'You told me that your wife blamed you. Did that hurt?'

'She was wrong. It wasn't my fault. She's a crazy woman.'

'Is that why you left her?'

'Yes, it is.'

'So you did leave her?'

'I told you. There was nothing more I could do for her.'

Time for me to get out of here.

'I have more than enough now for my story. We should leave it at that.'

'But we haven't talked about me. The job. The results.'

'I have all I need.'

'I'll get my people to forward the graphs and charts and my photo.'

'Whatever.'

'Laura, why can't we remain friends? We're a good team, you and me.'

He's unbelievable. He's trying to twist me around his little finger again. Fool me once, shame on you. Fool me twice, shame on me.

'Laura, Laura. I didn't invite you here to troll over the past. You know me for a long time now. We did some good things together. We're very alike, you and me.'

'Stop. Let go of my arm. You're hurting me.'

'I don't want you making a fool of yourself, that's all.'

'That's very considerate of you, but I don't need your help or advice.'

'I'm sorry you feel that way.'

'Goodbye, Mr Kane. I've wasted enough of your valuable time already. I'll find my own way out.'

'I'm always here if you need me.'

* * *

My editor took some convincing, but he agreed to run the story.

'This is sensational. You certain about all your facts?'

'One hundred per cent.'

'And your sources? Are you happy you can keep your promise to them?'

'He confirmed everything to me himself. Boasted about it.'

'You may not come out of this too well yourself.'

'He used me. And I let him. That was my mistake.'

'You could just let it go? Move on.'

'No way. He is a manipulative, self-centred, arrogant bastard who believes he's somebody. That's his mistake.

    'OK, Laura. If you're sure. We run the full story on the front page tomorrow, under the headline: **REMORSELESS BANKER EXPOSED**.

* * *

Ten years for corruption and blackmail. That's what he got. Not nearly enough, but it will feel like an eternity for him.

    I see him in my son's face all the time. I try to block it out but it's impossible. He looks just like his father. But that's where it ends. He's not going to be anything like him.

    I bring Troy to the hospital every six months for a check on his health. He's nearly seven now.

    And I still go to sleep with the light on and the mobile charging in the hall.

All That Glisters

Jenny Wright

The thumping in his chest gets stronger as he approaches the apartment. He takes out his key and turns it in the lock. The moment he opens the door into the hallway, he notices the special quality of quiet that meets him. After years of use, his emotional antennae are on constant vigilance against the slightest change in vibrations, and he knows this is going to be bad.

* * *

At a very early age, Rob and his sisters learned how to sense moods in the air. First home from school would know within a split second whether it was safe to be noisy, or if it would be better to tiptoe around. A code warned the others: 'good' tidings of comfort and joy, or 'bad' tidings of something else entirely. 'Good' meant make as much noise as they liked, playing with the dogs and generally being riotous and rowdy. They never quite relaxed, though—it could turn bad in a heart's turn. When it was 'bad', they had to creep around whispering and closing doors quietly. Their mother's rages were sudden and terrifying. Jess and Frankie grew up to be fierce and brave, fighting every injustice perpetrated on them by their mother. Rob never learned his sisters' skills. He was in awe of them, though he wished they would not fight back; it took so much longer for things to calm down again. All he wanted was for the fighting to stop and peace to prevail, but his attempts at appeasement—which history might have told him—never worked out well. When the fighting got loud at night, the three of them would creep from their rooms to sit huddled on the top stair, comparing notes, trying to work out a pattern, some way of controlling it. They only ever heard their mother's side of the

233

argument—their father spoke so softly—and once, the shocking sound of breaking glass. They were terrified of divorce; along with cancer, it was what nobody spoke about and the very word was dreadful.

* * *

Rob closes the inside door quietly.

The apartment is starkly furnished, sharp edges everywhere, shiny wooden floor, straight-back chairs, a single square vase with one white flower. Early evening sun. Blinds, no curtains, no cushions, no sofa. Nowhere soft to sit. A design magazine apartment that looked perfect until human detritus cluttered it up. No toys.

Olivia is sitting in the swing chair by the window at the steel and glass table, which cost more than Rob's car—as she likes to mention from time to time. She is holding in one hand a glass of wine, a mist of condensation on the outside and, in the other, a just-lit cigarette—her props. To the untrained eye, she's sitting, smiling peaceably, welcoming her husband home from his day at work. The smile does not spread up to her ice-blue eyes. A faint scratching noise breaks the silence. Her legs, shiny in sheer tights and pointed shoes, are crossed, one leg bouncing nervily, sunlight glinting off every bounce like a flashing strobe. His stomach gives a lurch.

'Hi,' he ventures, attempting a jaunty opener. 'Pat gone?' Pat picks up Mel from crèche and looks after her until Olivia gets in. He briefly wonders if Pat knows what is going on. He knows his casual tone does not fool Olivia for a second, but she says nothing. He sees what is going to happen and knows damn well that no matter what he does, he cannot stop it. She is well on her way to oblivion, looking forward to a brief foray into warfare with her 'pathetic little husband' on the way. His six-foot-three frame does not protect him from her insults, which always contain the word 'little'.

* * *

It began to occur to him that Olivia *allowed* herself rages—she could restrain herself if she chose. She would inevitably apologise afterwards, saying that she'd lost control, swearing that it was PMS or a bad day at Morton and Allen, that those bastards were out to get her; blaming the air if she could. She only lost control in the privacy of her own home, or with complete strangers, never with their friends or her family. That was self-control.

It shamed and pained him to admit that the very excitement he had sought when he first met Olivia was what was so very frightening and dangerous now. They always had passionate rows, but then they would have passionate make-up sex. He suspected the rows were just foreplay. He later understood that her very unpredictability was what had seduced him in the first place.

* * *

He spotted her the minute he walked into the gallery with Mark. Tall and straight-backed, with rich red hair, she was standing with the artist and a couple of people he knew, and he walked right over and joined the group.

'Hi,' he announced boldly, holding out his hand to Olivia. 'I'm Rob Thomson.' She took his hand limply for a brief second and said nothing. 'And your name?'

'Oh, sorry, Rob,' his friend piped up. 'this is Olivia Atherton.'

'Well, then, Olivia Atherton,' Rob replied, 'can I get you a glass of red?'

She shook her head and turned away to talk to someone else, ignoring Rob, not acknowledging his grin. Her indifference puzzled him at first, and he reluctantly concluded that she was not interested. Her subsequent surreptitious glances, however, suggested otherwise.

Rob liked to be liked. Inside he was a little puppy, lying on his back to have his tummy tickled. If he was nice, people would like him—simple as that, and he found it hard to make himself disagreeable. Rob, who had sailed through so many of life's complexities on unadulterated charm, set himself the task of winning over Olivia. Her silky jacket matched her lapis earrings, and when she brushed against Rob's arm as she turned away, he felt an overwhelming urge to take a handful of her thick auburn hair and kiss her. An impulse he resisted—for the moment.

He gazed after her as she wandered off to look at the sculptures and was about to sidle over, when an older man approached her, handsome and dressed entirely in black, his greying hair just visible beneath a fedora. She turned to look at him, and without a word he handed her something, after glancing around to see if anyone was looking. He missed Rob's hankering scrutiny. Olivia tucked a little bag into her pocket and also took a quick look around. After a muttered conversation, they separated, and she continued to wander through the art works on her own. Rob did not take his eyes off her until she returned to the group. Her diligent avoidance of eye contact with Rob only spurred him to renewed efforts. At one point, he spotted her in a mirror, looking at him. *I'll make her smile at me before the evening's out*, he told himself with a determination that he had not always applied to other areas of life. Olivia allowed herself a small smile at one of his remarks, and his spirits soared, way out of proportion to the achievement.

He was annoyed when the older guy came over to the group. 'This is Paulo,' Olivia said to Rob, and then whispered to him, 'He can get you anything you want.'

He eventually managed to engage her, calling on all his reserves of wit and charm. Fuelled by the wine on tap, it was not long before she smiled at him again, and turning her back on the assembled company, she looked up at him through mascaraed lashes and, with mock coyness, pulled the little bag from her pocket and waved it in his face. After a swift visit to the ladies' facilities to snort the contents, they left the gallery and went to Rob's place.

There followed a period of passionate intensity and insatiable sex, fuelled by much wine and many lines of coke. They partied hard, out every night. They were the golden couple. They were not devoting themselves wholeheartedly to their careers, although they concentrated just enough not to be fired. Strictly speaking, Rob could not be fired because he and his friend Mark had opened their own tech start-up company just over a year before. However, Mark appealed to Rob more than once over the next months. 'You're fucking up, Rob,' was what he actually said.

This period of intensity and insatiable sex differed from other such episodes in Rob's life that had eventually petered out into indifference. He remained totally hooked. Olivia possessed the kind of beauty achieved only by the truly self-assured and self-absorbed.

She got bored. She required fresh challenges constantly, and his evident dependence slowly began to turn her off, though she herself might not have realised this—self-awareness not being her strongest point. His constant attendance to her every need seemed to make him craven and pathetic. She left his calls unanswered for days, or replied with monosyllabic cruelty, leaving Rob all the more desperate. She understood this early on and instinctively knew how to keep him hanging on; because she could, and it amused her; attentive and loving, generous with her attention and her body, only to retreat when she saw he was relaxing—he was way too easy.

Once it had begun, her contempt for him was a fast-growing fire. At first, she seemed to enjoy the constant adulation and devotion; he was 'pretty hot', she told her friends. She was always on the lookout for someone new to amuse her. He, however, could not look at another woman without Olivia flying into a rage when they got home. She was jealous, but it was jealousy born of possession, not passion. She required 100 per cent devotion at the altar of Olivia. She enjoyed the fights and the sex, but, to her, Rob's charm was a thin veneer, which could be rapidly peeled off to reveal a grubby little boy underneath.

It started with verbal abuse, criticising his clothes, his hair, his friends and family—anything. She was expert at the backhanded compliment.

'You always seem to be the centre of everything. People gravitate towards you.' He would beam at such praise. 'Such a show-off.' And she would look carefully at him to see if she had hit her mark.

She began to undermine him in company.

'I married down,' she would later announce to her friends, who agreed that she was not joking. She mocked his Scottish accent, only faint by now, though she said it had charmed her at first. Her own accent spoke of hundreds of years of privilege and country houses bulging with guns and fishing rods. There were stables too, of course; and spread liberally throughout the vast house were photos of Olivia growing up with some horse or other, in riding gear and clutching cups and often, chillingly, a whip. Olivia came from a class of people who never doubted for a second that they would inherit the earth and 'bugger the bloody poor'. Rob found all of this opulence strange and new.

He kept his mouth closed when he heard Olivia's father pronounce, 'We're going to have to do something about that Labour chappie. Bloody communist!' referring to the newly elected MP for the area. The landed gentry were in shock. Rob was pleased to hear Olivia's younger sister Charlie, plainly echoing his own thoughts—out loud.

'Oh Daddy, shut up, you're worse than Attila the Hun.' He just guffawed and, throwing his head back, swigged his whisky. He clearly thought of his younger daughter as a frisky pony that needed to be reined in and would soon grow out of her silly lefty ideas.

* * *

Almost simultaneously with Rob's reluctant recognition that there could be no future for them together, came Olivia's clipped announcement one morning that she was pregnant. She was dressing as she told him, 'It's far too late for an abortion. I'm already over 20 weeks.' She tucked her hair behind her ear, grabbed her bag and, without waiting for Rob to say anything, left the apartment.

Olivia was the last person to get pregnant on purpose. Rob did not understand how she was not showing. Walking in from work that night, he gamely asked,

'Had we better get married, then?'

'I suppose we'd better.' She had obviously considered it. He could only imagine that some part of her wanted to take the conventional way. It was not as though she couldn't afford to raise a child on her own. Her parents would hire nannies and au pairs for her. A quick check on the pills by the bed explained the pregnancy: she had missed a couple this month. There were three remaining in the previous month's pack.

After she had gone to bed, her phone pinged on the table in front of him. A message from Paulo.

When?

What the hell did that mean? Rob looked for the thread of their previous conversation, but there was nothing. She must have deleted the messages. A couple of days later, he looked at her phone again, and the message was gone. Was she sleeping with Paulo or did she owe him money?

He spent the next few weeks trying to work out how their lives would be. He hoped that things might improve when the baby arrived. Sometimes, Olivia would soften, but he was never relaxed enough to enjoy it and knew it was fake.

The night before the wedding, Rob saw another

message on her phone, from Paulo again.

? it read.

He was perplexed. If Olivia ever needed money, she just had to ask her father, no questions asked. Mercifully, Rob and Olivia had kept their finances separate.

* * *

They went through with the ceremony in the grounds of her parents' pile in Gloucestershire, before a large gathering, and everyone pretended that they were love's young dream. A few of Rob's friends turned up, but not his parents, whom he did not invite. It was unthinkable to introduce his parents to this family. His sister, Frankie, was his only relation there, without husband or children. Standing waiting for Olivia's father to deliver her to him, Rob scrutinised the assembled company of guests, the men in tails, despite the heat, and the older women, of whom there were hundreds it seemed, clad in floral print and quite spectacularly huge hats.

Mark was there.

'Olivia's mother is acting like it's a funeral. What a complete dragon. I heard her say to Charlie, "I don't know why she can't just live with him; she didn't have to marry him".'

Rob laughed at Mark's attempt at a posh accent.

Charlie was sitting alone in the back, with an expression that suggested she would rather be anywhere but here. She had declined the invitation to be bridesmaid, Olivia had told him. He wondered if she had been crying.

* * *

The pregnancy and birth of their child, Melanie, passed in an agony for them both. Olivia was disgusted by all the changes in her body. By the time the baby arrived, they were barely communicating on any level. Rob got tired of hangovers and was mostly abstemious. He had worked out that all situations deteriorated if they were both drinking. Olivia laid off the coke during the pregnancy, although she did not entirely give up drink. Why should she? He was just 'a sanctimonious little prick'. The whole sordid process of pregnancy outraged her, and it was easy to blame Rob for it all. She had not been in control of herself or her body. She had shown Rob her fear and pain while expelling 'this fucking thing' from her body. For a brief few moments after the birth, she had softened, her face smooth and her expression open. But, when the midwife tried to hand over the baby, no welcoming arms stretched out from under the blanket, and she turned her head away. Rob took the swaddled baby and walked around with her, suddenly and plainly in love. By the time he looked up at Olivia again, her face had settled back into its customary hostile arrangement, yielding nothing. Her mouth was set in a downward turn, and when the nurse asked her if she was going to breastfeed, she replied, 'Certainly not!' in a tone of disgust.

* * *

The first time she hit him, he was stunned. She had taken to throwing things in his general direction. A glass was thrown against a window, breaking both and narrowly missing Rob's face. In a temper, she hurled a plate of spaghetti onto the floor just by his feet, splattering his jeans and shoes with tomato sauce. Eventually—inevitably—her aim improved. She was sitting one night at the table, drinking a glass of wine and smoking, occasionally poking at the mess on her plate and glaring at Rob, who was steadfastly eating his meal. He finished, and when he leant over to take her plate, she stubbed her cigarette out furiously in the mess and flipped the back of her other hand up to his face.

Rob had wondered if this mood would peter out or progress to another 'episode'. The hand flip answered that question.

'What happened to your face?' she asked the next morning, bleary-eyed and clutching a cup of coffee, as he came into the kitchen holding Mel. He was not going to start explaining his bruised face in front of Mel. He was furious and helpless.

'So you don't remember?' He was beginning to doubt her memory lapses.

By now, he was in a constant state of anxiety. She was screwing around and never bothered to hide it. As long as she was sometimes attentive, judiciously bestowing smiles and sex when she thought her grip might be loosening, Rob was unable to extricate himself.

He was frequently the target of her fury now. He had almost told Mark about it countless times, but always baulked at the last minute. He knew that if a flicker of scorn, or disbelief or even amusement were to flit across his friend's face before composing it into an expression of sympathy, he could not have borne it; especially not the sympathy. Mark would be embarrassed for him.

He also knew that the minute he told someone—anyone—he would have to do something about it. He sounded so weak when he rehearsed his tale to himself. He was incapable of explaining to Mark that Olivia was unpredictable and violent, and that he was too weak to stop her. How was he to tell him that he had allowed himself to get into such a situation? And worse, that he had failed to get out of it again? As for her 'little episodes', as he called her displays of violence, in the struggle to minimise their effects, he kept telling himself they would not happen again, that the set of circumstances that had set her off last time could be avoided. Olivia's unpredictability ruled out any forward planning in avoiding her ferocity.

* * *

He goes to check on Mel, to see if she is tucked up and safe from what is to follow. Although he has barely admitted to himself what has crept up on him so gradually, he has made moves to protect Mel from her mother's ferocity. He has moved her cot to the corner furthest from the door and put blankets round the bars to try to soundproof it. She's asleep with her thumb in her mouth. Rob loosens the blanket and kisses her forehead.

Looking in the bathroom mirror, he sees a stranger's white, almost gaunt face. It strikes him how ludicrous and futile his efforts are to protect his daughter. What if Olivia were ever to turn on Mel? What if she already has? He jolts himself out of his prolonged stupor. When the awakening comes, the plan to leave materialises so rapidly, that it must have clearly been forming for a while without his willing collaboration.

He goes back into the sitting room. Tonight, he will play her game—agree with everything she says, make her think he is keeping up with her drinking, laugh with her. He can stand it for one night.

She offers him a glass of wine, and then he knows how this is going to play out. If he refuses, she'll sneer at him. 'You're such a self-righteous hypocrite. Just because you don't drink like you used to, don't look at me like you're any better,' she said once when he refused a drink, angry he would not join in her sport. Oh yes, he used to. They drank and drank in the old days and snorted whatever was going. It was harmonious dissolution. If he accepts now, though, he'll have to engage with her. Whatever his response, she is going to be angry, because she already is. She is trying to catch his eye, piercing him with her furious stare, and he is working equally hard to avoid it.

Olivia falls into bed without assaulting him. He has pretended to drink and is, in fact, quite sober and clear-thinking. He is as furiously angry with her now as he was passionately in love.

* * *

The transition was very gradual. After the first slap, he was angry, but just thought he must have done something to annoy her; forgiving her; wanting to believe that she was sorry and unwilling to acknowledge that he was a victim. Who would believe him? He was clearly bigger than her, and stronger. Why could he not fight back? But he stopped being angry—till the next time. He did everything he could not to infuriate her. It was like walking around with tripwires everywhere, tripwires that changed their configuration frequently, rendering him into a constant state of anxiety. Over time, his anger began to remain with him longer after each incident and make-up sex was in the distant past.

She had threatened him more than once: that he would never get Mel, if he tried to leave; she would see to that; he would be sorry. He had not dared to ask her what she meant. He was drowning in a deep well of misery and anxiety, his natural state at the time.

He was surprised to hear raised voices in the apartment one evening just as he was about to go in. He hesitated.

'I don't care how you get it, I want it tomorrow,' a man shouted.

'I can't get it till next week. You'll just have to wait,' Olivia said, in an imperious tone.

The door opened, and Paulo came out and brushed past Rob without a word.

'What was that about?' Rob asked, fairly certain that he knew.

'Oh, nothing, it's nothing to do with you.' She picked up her phone in dismissal.

So it was money and not sex.

* * *

From the age of two, Olivia had spectacular tantrums. Since no one ever had the stamina to say no to her, the tantrums continued into her adult life. Her parents were unable and unwilling to cross her. The most dramatic of her frenzies took place when Charlie was introduced. She was three when her mother appeared with a new-born baby girl.

'Darling, this is your new sister. She's called Charlotte. Isn't she beautiful?'

With clenched fists, Olivia left no one in any doubt about her feelings on the subject.

'No, I hate her. Take her back!'

Her parents simpered ineffectually, commenting on Olivia's independent nature, and paid no more attention. Fortunately, there was always a nanny or au pair to protect Charlie from her elder sister's murderous intent, and Olivia was only infrequently given the chance to harm Charlie—physically at any rate. The minute any of them attempted to thwart Olivia's considerable will, she took against them and persuaded her parents to replace them.

Charlie was required to pander to her big sister's every whim. It was her good fortune to grow to be physically stronger than Olivia. Luckily, this took place before her sixth birthday when Olivia was nine and before her really murderous intent had taken hold. Only Charlie ever stood up to her. Her parents barely acknowledged that there might be a problem. They just caved before anything blew up into a full-scale war. Charlie was made of sterner stuff. Her sense of injustice became more and more finely tuned, and her capacity for holding a grudge increased on a daily basis.

Charlie showed quite spectacular instincts for self-preservation. At the tender age of eight, she asked her parents if she could go to judo classes. She did not tell them it was because her sister was a merciless bully, and she needed to be able to defend herself. She said it was because her friend Sasha was doing it. They agreed, so long as they did not have to get involved in any way. Sasha's parents had observed the lay of the land in the Atherton household and were willing to do all the ferrying, and even bought the outfits. They also provided the congratulations and treats every time Sasha and Charlie moved up a grade.

Olivia mocked her little sister relentlessly. When Charlie was around ten and Olivia thirteen, Olivia attacked her with a riding whip, due to some unspecified misdemeanour. She got in one vicious lash, leaving a reddened weal on each of Charlie's bare legs, and was poised for a second one, when her sister whirled around. Wrenching the whip from Olivia's hands, she threw her to the ground, winding her. Even when she could breathe again, she could not complain to anyone as Charlie had proof of the initial attack. From then on, Olivia employed subtler means.

* * *

Olivia learned early on that she could control people with her temper. She had the tenacity and will to scream until she got what she wanted. Her wealthy parents pandered to her every whim, and she grew to expect and, indeed, demand, that no sooner should she want something, whether it was a new pony or later a new car, she was bloody well going to have it. She preferred to be given things, but she liked to take things too. As for boyfriends, she could have her pick; and she mostly picked other people's boyfriends; then later, husbands. She swung her rich auburn hair to best advantage, like one of her horses' tails. It was the way she looked at a man, as though she could see into his soul which, of course, could not have been further from the truth. She was not interested in souls. And even if she could see into someone's soul, she would not have cared for what she saw. She found only desire, and that was all she wanted. So much the better if she was taking something that belonged to someone else, quickly discarding her conquests as soon as acquiring them.

When she stole Charlie's boyfriend, she did not give it a second thought. Charlie was deeply in love with 'poor James', as he was later known, and they were inseparable. Unfortunately, he was unschooled in the ways of Olivia, and when she told him that Charlie had asked her to dump him for her, she accompanied the claim with an invitation to fuck her, re-enforced with her putting her arms around him and showing him her wares, which 'poor James' was ill-equipped to resist. Olivia told Charlie. James was abject, but Charlie was unable to forget what had happened. The girls were still living at home at the time of this ultimate betrayal. Their parents remonstrated with Olivia in a half-hearted kind of way and bought her rationale: that it was better that Charlie found out how treacherous James was before getting in any deeper. Both parents knew exactly what had happened, but were not committed to anything much, least of all expecting good behaviour from their elder daughter. They admitted to no one, not even each other, they were somewhat afraid of their elder daughter. After a week or so, they told Charlie she needed to get over it. After all, Christmas was coming up, and she didn't want to spoil it for everyone, did she?

So she shut up—for the time being. The final straw came when James was mentioned in Olivia's company, and she had forgotten who he was. She was much too self-absorbed to notice her sister's face turning puce in an effort not to strangle her.

* * *

Rob is not quite so brave the next morning, but when Mel toddles into the bedroom first thing, Olivia roars at her. Mel goes white and climbs up to sob in his arms, and he finds his spine once more. He says nothing. He is nervous but hopeful. Olivia stays in bed. He drops Mel to crèche, saying he will pick her up himself today and that she will not be coming in for a while. He calls Patricia and then the office.

'Hey, listen Mark, I'm not coming in to work for a few weeks. I'll work remotely. Can I stay at yours for a couple of nights?'

Mark hesitates, puzzled. 'Sure, what's up?'

'With Mel,' Rob adds.

'What's going on? Are you OK?'

'Yeah, I'll tell you later on. I don't want Liv to know.' Mark is silent. 'I really mean it. I'll explain later.'

Now, he sits in the cafe across the road from his apartment building and waits for Olivia to leave for work. A cab pulls up, and he sees her jump in. She is gorgeous, he thinks, before pulling himself together. He has until 4 p.m. to pack as many of his and Mel's possessions that will fit in the car. Olivia will never give up Mel voluntarily. She resents every moment he spends with Mel, getting impatient after a few minutes. However, spite is a mighty weapon, and she knows Rob will never leave his daughter. She despises the way his face softens when he even mentions her, disgusted when Mel holds out her arms to her father.

'God almighty,' she roared one day when Mel turned away from her and toddled over to Rob. 'What a little daddy's girl!' Thus sealing Mel's distrust and fear of her mother, who was jealous of both of them. Olivia's malicious nature could not let them go. Rob knew it was the best thing for everyone, if only she knew it.

* * *

That night, kissing Mel goodnight in Mark's spare room, he breathed in and realised his shoulders were not pinched with tension. Mark was waiting for him with a large glass of red.

'Wrap yourself around that,' he said and, giving Rob the chance to take a good slug or two, continued, 'OK, let's have it then?'

Over the evening Rob told Mark all but the fact that Olivia had hit him, and Mark, at first, said very little, just the odd question or encouraging grunt.

'I'm going to Mum and Dad's for a couple of weeks to clear my head. Though, Christ knows what they'll make of it.'

'You're welcome to stay here; you can see I've got

enough room, and it's great having you, and Mel. And what about your parents, is that OK?' Mark grew up near Rob's family and knew the history.

'I told you they'd moved back in together. They've totally mellowed. One day, I went home, and they'd stopped fighting. Really unnerving. Mum stopped drinking, a few years ago now. None of us could believe it. Dad's cancer concentrated their minds. And he's OK. Frankie and Jess say they're fine, and that Mum goes to meetings all the time. I can't get over it. The only complaint is that she's always trying to get everyone else to stop drinking.'

'Wow, who'd have thought those two would end up together again? That's incredible.'

'I know. Anyway, I'm getting an apartment for Mel and me. Liv will kick up hell, and her bloody law firm will do their worst, but I have to try it. I've got a lawyer or two up my sleeve. I've had enough.' He looked down into his wine glass and his face tightened in an effort not to break down.

Eventually, Mark put down his glass and looked his friend straight in the eye.

'Look, Rob, I'm telling you, this is a bit of a relief. None of what you've said comes as a surprise, you know,' he said gently. 'We all know what a bloody nightmare she is.' Rob blushes. He thought he had hidden his injured self so thoroughly.

'I've watched you going downhill since Mel was born. You're doing the right thing.'

'I didn't realise you felt that way. Oh Christ! How come you didn't say anything?'

'Oh, come on, Rob, you know the answer to that. If any of us had said anything, you'd have stopped seeing us. You weren't listening to anyone. The only way to stay in contact was to keep quiet. I know one of her exes. Did you ever meet anyone she went out with?

'No, never.'

'Well, I'd say she made damned sure of that. I know this guy she was living with, and she started getting physical with him; punched him once, right in the face. He had a broken nose. You wouldn't believe it.' Rob did not look up. 'Or would you? She gets violent?'

Rob nodded, and then automatically began to defend Olivia, in spite of what he knew to be the truth. 'You know, it's not her fault really. She's really stressed about work, and she can't understand why they're being so terrible to her. I tried to help her. She's really sorr—'

Mark broke in with quiet ferocity,

'For fuck's sake, domestic abuse is a crime; it's not your fault. Don't fall into that trap.' He took a deep breath and continued less confrontationally,

'She'll want to avoid anything legal and, let's face it, she's not going to miss the two of you, so you could be all right.'

'No, I guess not, but she hates losing. She's made herself quite clear on that. I tried to talk to her more than once about it. I said she'd be better off without us, and she knows it's true. Thing is, she's started doing coke again, can you believe it?' Then he added, 'Remember the time I had the broken ribs?' Now that the forbidden subject of violence had been broached, Rob could not stop the flow.

'How could I forget? You were practically helpless. You're not going to tell me she did that? Holy shit! You told me you'd fallen.'

Rob nodded.

'I knew you were hiding something. You're a shit liar.'

'I'm shit at most things at the moment. I had to go to A&E.'

'I knew there was more to it. You're no good at deception.'

'Yeah, you said.' Rob told him about his trip to hospital. 'My side was killing me. She swung a cooking pot at me and got me in the ribs; broke two of them.'

'God almighty, Rob, that's outrageous!' Mark stood up and looked furiously at him. 'You should have said something. I hope you told them what had happened.' Mark sat down again but was clearly very upset.

'I did. They gave me a lecture and told me I didn't have to put up with it; that there were shelters and other help for people like me. I didn't think there were people like me, but apparently there are. I didn't tell them about Mel in case they legally had to do something to protect her.'

'Did they take photos?'

'Yes, they did. They also told me I could prosecute her if I wanted, and they had the evidence. Asked if I wanted the police to come then and there.'

'So what did you say?'

'I said no. There's no way I was going to press charges. I had to think about Mel.'

'Well, thank God you've left.' Mark was shaking his head. 'It's over.'

* * *

On the day he left for Edinburgh, Mark helped him put his belongings into the car.

'You know, Rob, you're all Mel has. Liv is never going to come round to being a mother. You look after yourself.' He grasped Rob's arm and looked him straight in the eye. 'Keep me posted.'

Rob stopped and hugged him. 'Thanks, man. You're the best.'

On the long journey north, singing 'Homeward Bound' with Mel, Rob thought about what Mark had said.

I'm all Mel has.

* * *

In the first few days in Edinburgh, he was on autopilot. He talked to his parents, his sisters, their children, without revealing why he had left, too humiliated, and afraid of what they might take it into their heads to do. His family swooped in on Mel, who was thrilled with being enveloped by all these new relatives.

Drinking coffee continuously and eating very little contributed to Rob's increasingly anxious state. There was no space in his head for anything other than 'what now?' It crowded his brain, leaving him unable to think straight or make any kind of coherent plan, and he was almost entirely sleepless. After the initial relief of escape, the fear and anger jostled once more for position in his mind. He got worse and worse over the following days, his mind never still enough to think, he sometimes forgot to breathe.

A future in which Olivia obstructed access to his daughter unfolded before him. If she were no longer around, how simple it would be. He was constantly trying to work out what to do, but it all came back to Olivia standing in his way. *I could kill her*, he repeated to himself, every time his thought processes brought him back to the impasse: what now? Certainly not a serious consideration at first, he slowly began to wonder if he might kill her. Could he? It would certainly solve everything. But it was a solution for other people, perhaps—impossible and wrong. However, the alternative was a lifelong battle with Olivia to have minimum access to his daughter, if any.

It kept resurfacing, this thought, and each time, more options occurred to him. He thought less and less about how wrong it was, and increasingly about how convenient. Soon, he began to think about it constantly. He finally began to consider possible methods, discarding them one by one: shooting, stabbing, strangling, pushing her down the stairs, poisoning, smothering (shouldn't be too hard, she was always almost unconscious with drink or coke); he could run her over or beat her with a cooking pot. Though thoroughly satisfying to contemplate, none of these seemed possible or desirable, and he was quite sure he would not get away with it. *I'd get caught*, he thought. *But is that the only reason not to do it, or am I fundamentally moral?* That thought flitted off as soon as it arrived.

Eventually, when he was not thinking about Olivia or how to do away with her, the image of her bent over the kitchen counter snorting a line drifted unbidden into his mind. Could he somehow manoeuvre her into taking an overdose, or cut the coke with something? He needed to work out how to administer it: now that he was not living with her, it would not be simple. But he had Paulo's number, and it would be easy to get the coke. Wracking his brains ceaselessly led him no closer to a solution. He would just have to turn up with the coke and see if he might make out it was a peace offering. Even as he had this thought, he knew it was ridiculous. Still, the idea of confronting her with his newly accessed fury was enough to spur him on.

* * *

Since his departure, Rob had received several vicious text messages from Olivia saying, in short, that she wanted Mel back, and that she would get her. Mark texted him as well:

Liv on warpath. Doesn't know where you are.

Olivia's latest text, received at 5.30 a.m., read:

Calling police.

It shook Rob from his labyrinthine dreams and into action. He packed a small bag, crept into his parents' room, and said, 'I have to leave Mel with you for a couple of days. Is that OK?'

Barely awake, his mother said, 'Sure, Rob, but where are you going?'

'There's a couple of things I have to do, Mum. I'll be in touch.'

'Don't do anything stupid,' she called after him.

He pulled himself to a stop in his rush to get out and whisper-shouted, 'Course not.'

* * *

Rob made his way back to London again, fuelled by yet more coffee. He pondered his plan—if he could even call it a plan, more like fantasy—and, even in his turmoil, he knew it was by no means foolproof. In a small town in the Borders, he found himself in a phone shop handing over cash for a prepaid mobile of the non-smart variety. He marvelled at his cunning plan before sinking back into indecision and misery.

The thought of Mel trying to negotiate her way through a life with Olivia gave him the impetus to finish what he had started. Continuing south out of the town towards the border, he had to pull into a lay-by, shaking. His fantasy might turn into a reality. It would have to. He had no choice. He copied Paulo's number into the new phone and texted him, asking him to meet him with the deal later, not far from the apartment. He signed himself: **Olivia**. He would sleep in the car and wait till early morning. He would let himself into the apartment and surprise Olivia.

Could he fool her into thinking he wanted her back? She won't doubt that for a second. To show how sincere he was, he had brought her some coke. *I can still back out*, he kept repeating every time his heart rate reached alarming levels. He stoked his resolve by rereading Olivia's threats. Courts were notorious for favouring the mother in custody battles, his lawyer had told him, mainly because old conservative men presided over them, and they all believed that mothers were automatically better equipped to look after children than their hapless fathers. No matter how good his lawyer, he could not risk a judge's prejudices.

Finally, he parked the car round the corner from the apartment, and texted: **Here**. Of course, Paulo would never report him when Olivia turned up dead. He would not care and would be implicated. He still did not know how he was going to get Olivia to take an overdose. He laughed at himself then. How did he ever think he was going to pull this off?

Though he waited only ten minutes, it could have been two days. He had reached hysteria, again, by the time Paulo turned up. He had no qualms about handing over the deal to Rob, though he asked him for the cash Olivia owed him. Rob said, 'Sure, I'll make certain you get it.' As long as he was paid now, Paulo asked no questions.

It was almost midnight by the time an exhausted Rob fell asleep in the back of the car, and managed to stay that way for about three hours, fitfully dreaming of chasing something that just kept disappearing over the horizon, tripping up, falling, and then waking in a blind panic. The remainder of the night he spent fiddling with the radio dial, not staying on any station for more than a second. It occurred to him that he might take the overdose himself, he felt so demented. How could Olivia do this to him?

Just as it began to turn light, he decided to get a coffee. He looked up from the radio to see someone—a woman—coming towards him along the empty street. Unschooled in the requirements of successful crime, he did not think to keep his head down. To his bewilderment, he spotted Charlie coming from the direction of the apartment. He ducked down now. What if she saw him? How would he explain himself? What the hell was she doing here? She was wearing a baseball hat, and black leggings with a grey hoody—most unlike her usual get up. Just as she was hurrying past, something made her look into the car. What was going on? He had spoken to her yesterday and assumed she was at home. In fact, she had said she was at home with her parents. So how was she here already? She stopped in her tracks, her face full of terror when she saw who it was. They stared at each other in horror, before she took off at a run. He began to race after her but thought better of it. What would it achieve? There was a conversation he did not want to have right now. He would just go straight up to the apartment. Better get it over with, whatever 'it' turned out to be. He was shuddering uncontrollably, but maybe Olivia would misinterpret that as desire.

He felt the usual stomach-churning as he turned the key. The atmosphere that greeted him was changed. The air was stale, musty, the blinds down. Turning back to the room after raising the blinds, he saw the line of coke on the table, unfinished and an empty wine glass, the rim stained with her lipstick. It was unlike her to leave it around. He walked slowly to the bedroom, with an increasing sense of dread. The smell became stronger here, and he almost gagged when he saw the vomit on the floor. In the gloom, a noise came from behind the bed that had not been slept in, a sort of gurgle. The blinds were down here too, but there was no time to raise them, because Olivia was lying on the floor—asleep, he thought first, but unconscious, he discovered when he knelt down to see.

She was alive, but her heart had almost stopped. He fumbled for his phone to call an ambulance, but just as he was about to dial, he hesitated. He could leave her. This would solve all his problems. If she didn't make it, what sweet freedom! No more fights, no lawyers, no custody battles. No Olivia. This was the perfect solution. He turned away and went back into the living room, and stood still, trying to breathe. For a second, he thought that he might have caused this, just by wanting it. The receding view of Charlie running away a few minutes ago might explain something. What had she done? If he just waited, Olivia might not make it. Or he could help her along. The deafening sound of his phone ringing roused him. It was Mark. Rob killed the call. Out of nowhere, an image of Mel learning to walk for the first time in this room came to him.

He had to save Olivia to save Mel, Charlie and himself.

He dialled 999 and told the operator he thought

Olivia had taken cocaine and wine, he did not know how much. The operator put him through to the ambulance service, told him how to put her in the recovery position. It was hard to concentrate on the instructions. He put a cold cloth on her boiling forehead. He could hardly bear to touch her but, after his initial hesitation, he was certain now that he could not just let her die. He rushed to clear up the mess on the glass table and knew he could never have carried this through, although she still might not survive.

He did not yet know if the police would have to be informed.

He told the paramedics he would follow them to the hospital, which he did not do. He headed straight to Mark's, stopping at a public bin on the way to dispose of the cocaine. He felt a little less hysterical when he had accomplished that.

Having miraculously avoided hitting any other cars on the way to Mark's, Rob could barely speak. Mark phoned the hospital for him and found that Olivia was still unconscious but stable.

He grabbed his keys. 'C'mon, I'll take you.' They did not speak on the way.

'I'll wait for you.' Mark parked while Rob went to the reception desk.

'Olivia Atherton, I'm here to see Olivia Atherton. I'm her husband.'

He took the stairs to intensive care, too impatient for the lift and met a nurse at the entrance. 'Olivia Atherton,' he repeated. 'I'm her husband.' *I'm going to have to stop saying that*, he thought as he was put into a mask and gown. The nurse guided him to Olivia's bed.

'She's just regained consciousness. Only a few minutes, now.'

It was deadly quiet in the room, apart from the whispering machines keeping people alive. Rob did not look around at any other patients. Masked and gowned medical staff swathed in blue were moving noiselessly around. There were about five people in beds. He saw Olivia the same moment she saw him. She was white and lying flat, hooked up to a drip. She looked so defenceless as she put out her hand to reach his, a look of entreaty on her face. Did she want him to hold it? He kept his hands where they were and said nothing. After a minute or two, he left, tearing off the gown and dropping it on the bench outside the ward. He ran down the corridor into the stairwell, taking the stairs two at a time to get out as quickly as he could. The enormity of what had happened and what might have happened hit him with such force that just as Mark spotted him, he bent over and vomited. Mark walked him to the car, gripping him firmly by the shoulders.

* * *

By the time he got back to Edinburgh, Rob was thinking straight for the first time since he could remember. He had eaten and slept. He was learning to breathe again. Mel had not missed him, he was relieved and wounded to hear. His parents had clearly upped their game for the grandchildren, who adored them.

* * *

Rob and Charlie met. Rob did not tell her that Olivia had tested positive for ketamine as well as cocaine. He had a feeling she might know that. She did not ask Rob what he was doing there that morning. Both were relieved to give that conversation a wide berth.

Charlie told him her parents had given Olivia a large parcel of land that was supposed to be shared between them. They mentioned it in off-hand tones, asking Charlie not to make a fuss. Olivia needed it now that she was going to be a mother.

'She laughed at me when I confronted her. "What do you want with the land, you'll never have kids?"' She mimicked Olivia perfectly. 'Amazing how she can accomplish such a kick in the teeth so casually and carelessly.'

'Well, I know how that feels. She's a master of the art of the deadly strike!'

They talked frequently after that. He told Charlie about his marriage to her sister, and she explained her childhood to him. Neither was the least surprised at the other's experience of Olivia Atherton.

* * *

Mark opened the door to Rob and Mel. Sitting at the table, clutching cups of coffee, Mel with building blocks on the floor, chatting away to herself, Mark just raised an eyebrow and said, 'Well?'

'Oh man, you have no idea.' Rob was shaking his head. 'You would not believe what's happened.'

'I've a feeling you're about to tell me. C'mon, I'm dying to hear.'

They were speaking softly; Rob glanced down to see if Mel was tuned in to their conversation, but she was busy on the other side of the room, singing 'Over the Sea to Skye'—with a Scottish accent already—and building a Lego tower. He never really knew how much she understood, or what she had witnessed, but she seemed thankfully unscathed, so far.

'You're looking great, by the way. That haunted look never suited you,' Mark said.

Rob shoved him and laughed. 'I feel great, thanks. I'm sorry again about work. Soon, honest. I got the apartment. Things are looking up. Honestly, when I look back, if it had been up to me, the only way I was going to kill her was by mistake.'

'You were desperate, Rob. You'd never have gone through with it. You rescued her, remember?'

'At least, she didn't plot to kill me.'

'Maybe not, but she might have killed you anyway. Don't start all that again, for Christ's sake.'

'I dumped the coke. I didn't know if the police had to be involved. That was up to the medics, apparently, and they must have decided it was self-inflicted. They're under no obligation to inform the police. They don't want people to be afraid to call in an overdose.' He did not mention Charlie.

'Anyway, after her discharge, her parents swooped down from the country pile and took her back with them. I haven't spoken to Liv. Charlie and I meet up from time to time. She's great. It's funny; her folks asked me nothing about what happened. They know their daughter, I guess. I don't think they'd known about the coke, because when I did speak to her mother, she was much less imperious with me than before. She'd never pass up the opportunity to let me know how well Olivia could have done for herself, if I hadn't stumbled along to corrupt her. Kept mentioning some ex-boyfriend, who was heartbroken when Liv dumped him to live with me. Hah, he's welcome! Anyway, now she's positively simpering. Quite nauseating, to be honest. Her father came on the phone to me and harrumphed away for a bit, clearing his throat, and I knew he was trying to say thanks for saving his daughter. Eventually, he came out with something like, "Hm, bit of a hero, eh?" The humility didn't suit him.'

Mark laughed.

'I haven't spoken to Liv, though. I blocked her on my phone.'

'I blocked her after that text. Even I could kill her for what she did to you.'

'When she was better physically, they packed her off to some celebrity rehab place claiming "huge successes". It's got to the stage that I don't know, and I don't care.'

'But are you OK now?'

'I am. I went to that woman you recommended. I've been a few times. She's pretty great. It was hell at first.

I could hardly bear to talk about it all. But every time now, I feel I've been on holiday.'

Mark laughed. 'About as expensive too, I'd say. And, now that I think about it, you found your true strength when you saved Liv. But listen, you got away.'

'It's true. I got away; I can't believe it.'

* * *

'I'm glad you are going to be all right,' Rob began as he walked into the apartment—now hers—and Olivia gave him a wan smile, gesturing towards a chair. He remained stony-faced and standing. 'But,' he said, 'I do not want to see you unless I have to. If you try to get custody, I have medical records, remember.' He was hissing now. She was silent. It was the first time he had ever thwarted her to her face, and it was liberating.

'Mel is better off without you, and you're better off without Mel; but, if and when, she asks to see you, you will see her. She sometimes asks about you and seems perfectly satisfied with my bland answers. They might not satisfy her in the future, and I'm not having her any more fucked-up than she is.' He was getting into his stride. He loved the power it gave him. To Rob's surprise, she still did not reply. It was as if she had lost something fundamental, more than just his devotion. The way she was sitting, her head slightly bent was unlike her. She seemed weakened, smaller somehow—diminished. Even her hair was slightly less red.

'I know what happened,' she said at last, not looking at him—a threat.

'I don't care. What you think you know is irrelevant. This is how it's going to be,' Rob fired back, not bothering to point out that she had no proof. There was no answer.

Then he turned away and, slamming the door, raced down the stairs, out into the clean, free air where Charlie and Mel were waiting for him.

Biographies

Adrian Taheny has appeared in many notable theatre productions, including Druid's *Threepenny Opera*. In 2017, he had two stories published in *Storytellers, New Writing from Ireland* and, in 2018, a further two stories were featured in *Sins, New Irish Crime Stories*. He is in the process of completing his first novel.

Alix Moore-O'Grady is a Londoner who followed her heart to Ireland in 2016. In 2017, her short story 'The Surprise' was published in *Storytellers, New Writing from Ireland* and, in 2018, she had a further two stories featured in *Sins, New Irish Crime Stories*. She is currently working on her first novel—a psychological thriller set in the world of music and medicine.

Caroline Bale writes crime fiction with a psychological twist, drawing upon her practice as a psychotherapist to create complex plots and engaging characters. In 2018, she was selected as a finalist in the Irish Writer's Centre Novel Fair for her novel *Remember Me*, and her short story 'Vainglorious Bastard' was published in *Sins, New Irish Crime Stories*. In 2019, her crime novel *I Will Make You Pay* was published by Joffe Books, becoming an immediate bestseller.

Jenny Wright was born in Edinburgh and lives in Dublin. Her short story 'Frankie' was included in *All Good Things Begin*, an anthology of new writing. Jenny's novel for children, *The Cinderella Project*, was published in 2018, and her short story 'A Casual Killing' was included in *Sins, New Irish Crime Stories*.

Mark Bastow's first two novels were fantasy adventure novels set in seventeenth century London. His third novel was a police procedural set in Yorkshire. His short stories, two of which were published in *Sins, New Irish Crime Stories*, include crime, supernatural, historical and children's fiction.

Martin Keating's stories have been prize-winners in the Dalkey Creates and the Maria Edgeworth Short Story competitions, and his story 'The Woodpusher' appears in the *Fish Anthology 2019*. His historical crime novel, *Moriarty*, was a winner in the Irish Writer's Centre 2108 Novel Fair. Two of his stories appear in *Sins, New Irish Crime Stories*.

Susan Rodgers worked as a freelance writer and editor for magazines in the United States before moving to Ireland in 2001. Her short story 'The Other Woman' was published in *Storytellers, New Writing from Ireland* in 2017 and her story 'Itch' featured in *Sins, New Irish Crime Stories* in 2018. She is in the process of completing a collection of short stories entitled *Body on the Beach*.

Also from **the3percenters**

NEW IRISH CRIME STORIES

PRIDE, ENVY, GLUTTONY, LUST, ANGER, GREED, SLOTH

Seven Deadly Sins. Eleven Killer Stories.

Nothing matches the Power of Seven. In this anthology, seven writers tempt you with a modern take on the Seven Deadly Sins, unleashing eleven riveting new crime stories, edited by **Ferdia Mac Anna.**

Take a walk on the dark side.

A woman seduces her boss and considers murdering his wife. A case of mistaken identity leads to disastrous consequences. An unexpected visitor arrives with a camera but takes more than photos. A bitter six-former at an English public school exacts the ultimate revenge.